OFFERING

ALSO BY
KIMBERLY DERTING

THE PLEDGE
THE ESSENCE

THE OFFERING

A PLEDGE NOVEL

KIMBERLY DERTING

MARGARET K. McELDERRY BOOKS
NEW YORK LONDON TORONTO SYDNEY NEW DELHI

MARGARET K. McELDERRY BOOKS
An imprint of Simon & Schuster Children's Publishing Division
1230 Avenue of the Americas, New York, New York 10020
This book is a work of fiction. Any references to historical events, real people,
or real places are used fictitiously. Other names, characters, places, and
events are products of the author's imagination, and any resemblance to
actual events or places or persons, living or dead, is entirely coincidental.
Text copyright © 2014 by Kimberly Derting
Jacket photograph copyright © 2014 by Ugla Hauksdóttir
All rights reserved, including the right of reproduction in whole or in part in any form.
MARGARET K. McELDERRY BOOKS is a trademark of Simon & Schuster, Inc.
For information about special discounts for bulk purchases, please contact Simon &
Schuster Special Sales at 1-866-506-1949 or business@simonandschuster.com.
The Simon & Schuster Speakers Bureau can bring authors to your live event.
For more information or to book an event, contact the Simon & Schuster Speakers Bureau
at 1-866-248-3049 or visit our website at www.simonspeakers.com.
The text for this book is set in Avenir.
Manufactured in the United States of America
2 4 6 8 10 9 7 5 3 1
CIP data is available from the Library of Congress.
ISBN 978-1-4424-4562-8 (hardcover)
ISBN 978-1-4424-4564-2 (eBook)

FIRST
EDITION

To Todd Kneer,
who had the most infectious laugh
and wasn't afraid to share it!

OFF
ER
ING

ACKNOWLEDGMENTS

Being the last book in the Pledge trilogy, it was hard for me to say good-bye to these characters that I'd grown so attached to. In the acknowledgments for the first book I discussed how I came up with the idea for *The Pledge*, but I just want to (again) thank Marie Lucas, the woman who told me her stories of growing up in World War II Germany that eventually sparked the idea for Charlie's world. She will always and forever be the original Angelina.

I've always said how much I love my U.S. covers for the Pledge trilogy, and I've had Michael McCartney to thank for those. But finding the right title for this final book was no easy feat. In fact, my editor and I had been going back and forth, when my brilliant cover designer, Michael McCartney, who happens to be a linguist as well, threw out the idea: *The Offering*. And just like his gorgeous covers, it fit this book perfectly . . . so thank you, Michael.

Also, because I love those covers so much, I have to give a shout-out to Anna Þóra Alfredsdóttir and her wonderful photographer Ugla Hauksdóttir, who have done all the covers for this trilogy. I only have one word for you both: *gorgeous!*

Thanks, too, to Ruta Rimas, who has been amazing and a genius and everything else I have ever wanted in an editor for these books. She's been fierce and tireless, and I cannot thank her enough! And for everyone at S&S/ McElderry Books, you guys are truly, truly, *truly* awesome! Thank you all for letting me tell Charlie's story.

To Taryn Fagerness, who has been a genius at putting my books in the hands of overseas publishers, and to my foreign publishers, who have been crazy supportive—I love you all! To Laura Rennert, who has been my champion from day one, never flinching even when I might have wanted to flinch—thanks for being the best agent in the business. And thank you to Alicia Gordon, Ashley Fox, and Erin Conroy at WME because, well, you know what you do.

And no writer can do this job without friends and family who learn, and hopefully tolerate, the strange patterns of a writer's life. So to all of you who've seen me in my pajamas in the middle of the day (you know who you are!), and have accepted that I may (or may not) call you back in a week because the voices in my head have taken over, and who don't mind that I stare off into space in the middle of a meal . . . thank you! *I really do love you most of all!*

PART I

PROLOGUE

Unflinching, the executioner stood on the bloodstained floor facing the prison cells as he wielded an axe with a razor-sharp blade.

"What's the matter, darling? You're not having second thoughts, are you?" a woman's voice crooned amidst the barbaric scene—the cavernous surroundings, with bars and cells, and echoing all around them the desperate pleas of prisoners begging for their lives.

Niko straightened, shifting his gaze away from the executioner. He tried to shake off any last-minute qualms the beautiful but treacherous queen might be able to sense coming from him. Her gossamer green gown was inappropriate for the occasion, as if she'd dressed for a ball rather than a slaughter. But that was typical, he'd come to learn. She was as frivolous as she was deadly.

"Of course not. How could I possibly have any doubts? If we don't do this, we'll never be able to convince Queen Charlaina that we're to be taken seriously." He matched her expression,

wicked smile for wicked smile, hoping she felt half the anticipation he did beating through his veins.

The sound of shackles and the rumble of an approaching
scuffle made it clear that Xander was nearing them. Niko was
a fool if he expected Xander to go down without a fight.

A part of Niko wanted to skulk back into the shadows. To
hide where Xander wouldn't be able to see him, so Xander
wouldn't know that it was he who'd betrayed him.

After all, Charlie had sent the two of them to make peace
with the Astonian queen. To find a way to come to agreeable
terms with Queen Elena so that no one—on either side of the
border—would come to harm.

Yet here he was, making his own bargains. Ones that would
keep him safe forever. Ones that would, hopefully, bring him
and Sabara back together again.

Even if it meant sacrificing those around him.

"Niko." Xander spat his name when he saw him standing
at Elena's side. Her hand was draped possessively over his.
"You . . . you *traitor*," he snarled, curling his lip. "And you." He
turned his silver eyes on Elena then. "How could you let this . . .
this coward convince you of anything? Are you so weak of will?
Don't you see he's only using you?"

Niko stiffened, wondering just how much Xander knew
about him. About his history—and how far back he and Sabara,
the old Ludanian queen, really went. About how long he'd
been alive.

But Xander continued as he thrashed against his chains and
the guards on either side of him. "I trusted you. You said if my
revolutionaries joined forces with you to overthrow Sabara,

Ludania would have peace with Astonia. Have you no conscience?" he shrieked at the queen with whom he'd come all
this way to negotiate. "I thought we were friends."

Her grip tightened, and with it her resolve. She drew Niko
along with her, forcing him out of the shadows, until they were
standing face-to-face with Xander, watching him resist, like an
animal caged. The guards shoved him to his knees and forced
him to kneel before her. "I suppose that was your first mistake,
then," she answered in a voice so devoid of emotion, it made
Niko shudder inwardly. "Because I most certainly do not have
friends." She gave a signal to the man in the executioner's
mask—a black leather covering that exposed only his mouth
and his unsympathetic eyes.

The two guards dragged Xander toward a small, round
opening in the stone floor, a hole through which blood could
easily drain away to the sewers. They, along with two others
who'd appeared, pinned him to the ground while he continued
to writhe and scream. They waited until he was too weary to
fight any longer, until he had no other option but to accept
this fate he'd been handed.

Then the executioner raised his blade.

Niko would have closed his eyes, if those of Elena hadn't
been observing him as keenly as they were watching the
scene unfolding before her. Unlike Niko, she had no interest in
turning away. She seemed to relish the moment.

When the axe fell and the sharp crack of metal struck stone
beneath, Niko felt the slightest jerk from beside him. But when
he turned his gaze on her, he saw that she was frowning at the
hem of her gown rather than at the grisly view at her feet.

"Will you look at that," she said, and clucked, craning her neck to get a better look, and ignoring everything else going on around her. "He got blood on my new dress."

She shook her head and turned her attention back to Niko. A smile replaced the frown. Her look spoke nothing of the horrors they'd witnessed or the defiling of her gown. Her entire demeanor shifted into something else as her hand slid from his wrist and moved up his arm to his chest, her fingertips finding their way along the ridges of his still tensed muscles. "Come, love. Let's go back to bed," she purred. "I need to get this *mess* off me. Besides, I have other things I'd like to show you."

He obeyed numbly, allowing the queen of Astonia to pull him along, back through the corridors and along the cobbled stones until they reached her opulent—if somewhat over-done—bedroom, where she dragged him back into her bed. He wondered if he'd ever be able to purge from his memory the image of what he'd just witnessed.

Or forget the sound of Xander's screams.

I

My lips stretched into a tight smile as I made my way to the front of the congregation of stone-faced officials who'd gathered in the crowded meeting room. Everyone stood when I entered, and I tried my best to appear calm, but my heart was racing as I looked out at all the intense expressions of the people watching me, judging me.

At any other time I might've explained my reaction away as nerves, but not today. Today I had something to prove.

I needed to show them that all the changes I'd been leading us toward, all we'd sacrificed, had been for the best. That today we would make progress.

That I hadn't made a colossal mistake in risking so much on one venture.

My gaze slid to the transmitter on the table in front of me, where it sat, still and silent. It was hard to imagine that something so bland-looking might possibly change everything.

I took my seat and waited apprehensively while everyone else in the room took theirs. Several moments ticked by, during which I could feel the weight of their misgivings searching me out, settling over me like a heavy blanket. I explored their faces, too, careful not to fix on any one for too long. I picked out certain features and tried to guess which region each council member might hail from, a game to kill time and distract my thoughts. A man with leathered skin might have been a farmer, or possibly a builder who'd spent many years laboring beneath a baking sun. I thought he might have been from the eastern region, where grains were plentiful. Another woman with perfectly coifed hair made me think of a large metropolitan area. From right here in the Capitol perhaps, or possibly from 3E, which had been recently renamed Charletown, now that cities were allowed to have names of their own. There was another man who had a distractingly bulbous nose, which had nothing at all to do with either region or occupation but caught my attention nonetheless. My cheeks heated when I realized he'd caught me staring for too long.

From outside, even through the closed windows, I could hear the people gathering on the streets below us, both allies and opponents, all awaiting word of the success, or failure, of our . . . experiment.

A thousand worries spun through my mind. A thousand reasons why everything could go wrong on the other end.

What if Aron hadn't made it to his destination? Or what if he had but work hadn't been completed on time?

Worse yet, what if those engineers and designers who'd said our project was impossible had been right after all? What if the lines were irreparable?

But if all that were true, if the lines were too faulty to fix, wouldn't we have learned as much before now? Wouldn't someone have told us so—at some point before I'd left the palace to stand facing a hundred administrators from different districts and boroughs around the country awaiting our very first message?

Suddenly the walls of Capitol Hall felt too close, and the ceiling far too low. I was suffocating.

"Give it time," Max assured from beside me.

I turned to Brooklynn, who stood near the entrance in her crisp black uniform, searching the room for the slightest sign of trouble. I hoped in vain that she might offer me the same sort of encouragement Max had. A smile or a nod. Even one of her hallmark winks. But she never even glanced my way.

Nothing much had changed between us over the past months, since we'd returned from the summit at Vannova. Not since that fateful moment when I'd killed her father.

She still couldn't forgive me for what I'd done.

So I'd spent my time since then focused on Ludania instead, and what I could do to improve my country's future.

Which meant going back in time, it seemed.

Funny, how things worked. Sabara hadn't just stunted our country; she'd turned back the hands of time for us. There was a time when Ludania had been considered progressive in the eyes of the world. A leader in both technology and strategy.

Yet Sabara had managed to strip us of those advances when she'd taken the throne. Where Ludania had been making strides in the fields of medicine, manufacturing, transportation, and trade, Sabara had halted all that. She'd stopped production in everything but the basics, putting an embargo on all trade into and out of Ludania, demanding that her citizens learn to be self-sufficient.

Then she'd cut all manner of modern communication, even within the borders of our own country. Because with communication came power. And Sabara would never risk allowing anyone to be more powerful than herself.

And despite her efforts to maintain her own power by moving forward, jumping from body to body, Sabara feared change. The real Sabara—whose name wasn't Sabara at all—yearned to go back to another time, another era, when it was just her and Niko.

When they were together.

I couldn't afford to look back. I'd decided that reestablishing those once-forbidden forms of communication was the key to our salvation. And that was where I'd decided to focus my first efforts toward reinstating Ludania as a world force.

There was a part of me, one I didn't dare give voice to, that clung to the desperate hope that maybe this resurrected form of communication might somehow restore peace between Ludania and Astonia. That Queen Elena might listen to reason, if only I could have the opportunity to reason with her, leader to leader.

I knew it was foolish, but I couldn't help myself. The idea of going to war, even on the heels of the assassination attempt the other queen had spearheaded, made my chest ache.

There would be too much loss. Too many lives on the line.

Always the fool, Sabara whispered within me. *Technology isn't the solution. Communication, in the wrong hands, is a weapon in its own right.*

I bit my lip, tasting blood as I struggled to keep Sabara's mounting objections at bay. Her caustic voice burned like acid in my own throat, her words trying to find their way to my lips.

She was wrong. Communication was the key.

My plan would be implemented in stages. We would start by reopening communication ports in the major cities first, starting with Charletown and 11South—a city that still struggled to find the right name for itself. Next the train depots would be outfitted, since it only made sense that word could spread most quickly from there. Eventually we'd have the entire country wired, in some form or another.

The venture would be expensive but, in my estimation, worth the cost.

Or so I hoped.

Even if it works, you'll only be giving those who plot against you the tools they need to destroy you.

Squeezing my eyes shut, I pounded my fist on the conference table. *Shut up!* I shouted back at her from inside my head.

But she wasn't the one staring at me when I opened my eyes once more. It was the delegates from regions all across Ludania. And it was Max and Brook and Zafir, too.

I frowned, pretending it was nerves as I turned my attention back to the small, black receiver sitting on the tabletop in front of me. I swallowed a lump of worry as we all waited for something to happen, and I wondered if possibly we weren't using the device correctly. If maybe we were meant to do something on our end to make it work.

Every eye in the country was watching me on this one. I'd

seen the articles in the periodicals. And even now I could hear the doubt trickling in from the streets outside.

I glanced at the woman seated beside me, the engineer in charge of the entire operation, asking her silently with my raised eyebrows the same question I'd asked her a hundred times already: *Are you sure this will work?*

The tightening of her painted red lips was all the response she offered me, the same terse answer she'd given me whenever I'd finally exceeded her capacity to be kind with my uncertainty. *I'm positive. Your Majesty.*

Still, I couldn't help myself, and my hand slipped from my lap and moved toward the device. I wasn't sure what I meant to do, since I wasn't certain how to work the thing myself. But my hand hovered there, my heart beating in my throat until it felt like I might choke. I could see my reflection staring back at me in the polished black surface, distorting my features and making me look the way I felt in that moment . . . like a carica-ture of a real queen.

Someone who had no idea what she was doing.

And for the millionth time I wondered if Sabara hadn't been right all along.

Inside me I could sense her satisfaction. Smug and filling me with self-doubt.

Stop it, I warned her, hating the ease with which the two of us could communicate. Hating that she could turn me against myself in that manner, make me question myself so easily. *It will work. It has to.*

I swallowed another wave of doubt, wondering if this doubt was real or if it was Sabara's doing, even as my mouth went bone dry. All around me the crowd grew restless. Chairs shifted and voices murmured, low and rumbling and skeptical.

My misgivings became tangible, like smoke, making it hard to breathe.

Then something happened that made all of us freeze, and caused a collective gasp.

Beneath my fingertips, which were still hovering expectantly, the receiver crackled to life.

I'd been told what to expect: the thing would make a buzzing noise. That's how we'd know if someone was trying to send a message.

But when the sound arose, it was more like a hum. And it was the sweetest, most glorious hum I'd heard in all my years. One quick significant vibration followed immediately by silence.

I turned to Carolina—the engineer beside me—once more.

Now she was the one raising her eyebrows, as if she were startled by the turn of events. As if she'd never really expected this to work at all. "I . . . guess . . . we . . . push it," she said, and then nodded, trying to appear decisive as she indicated my hand, which was still poised above a button on the transmitter.

The buzz-hum sounded again, reminding us all that whoever was on the other end was still awaiting our response.

I grinned out at the delegates who'd gathered for this occasion, absorbing the moment and taking in their dubious expressions as I let my finger drop firmly and satisfyingly onto the button.

I sat there for a moment, waiting for something more to

happen now that I'd done my part, but all I heard was the crackling of static. It was exactly like the static we used to hear when Sabara still ruled and the loudspeakers in the street would repeat daily recorded messages, reminding us to be diligent citizens, or to report our neighbors for suspected wrongdoings, or for immigrants to report to Capitol Hall to be registered.

I could feel the delegates' eyes fall upon me while I continued to stare at the box in front of me.

"IS ANYONE THERE?"

I jumped back. The voice that boomed through the speaker on the table was altogether too loud, and instinctively my hands flew up to my ears to muffle the sound. But just as quickly I lowered them, reveling in the fact that the voice had been so clear and vibrant from so far, *far* away.

Wonder and awe filled me all at once, and I heard a small giggle escape my lips. "Aron?" I asked through another bubble of laughter. "Is that you?"

But I knew it was him. He'd been gone for three weeks, and the only messages we'd received had been the ones he'd sent by courier, assuring us he'd be ready on time.

I'd been terrified to trust him . . . and now tears sprang to my eyes.

Within me Sabara withdrew, as her doubt was crushed by my hope.

"IS BROOK WITH YOU?" His voice was still painfully loud, but I hardly cared.

I looked out to where several of the delegates were standing now, unable to mask their amazement at the feat we'd accomplished—bringing dead technology back to life. I searched past them, trying to find Brooklynn among them, and saw that she was already shoving her way through the crowd. Anyone who'd been in her path parted without being asked to do so. One look at her in her black leather uniform, and it was clear she was formidable, even without knowing she was commander of the armed forces.

"I'm here," she called out to the box before she'd even reached the table. Static stretched between them as I stepped aside, making a place for her as she leaned forward, spreading her palms flat over the tabletop. "What do you want?" She was shades quieter than Aron was, and far more reserved, but I knew—I could hear it in her voice—that she'd missed him.

Brook hadn't confided in me, so I didn't know exactly what had transpired between her and Aron in the months since our return from Vannova. But even without Brook to tell me her secrets, I hadn't missed the private exchanges, the looks and discreet brushes of their hands that had passed between them whenever they'd believed no one was watching.

Aron's voice squawked over the line from halfway across the country: "I JUST WANT YOU TO KNOW THAT IF I DON'T MAKE IT BACK . . ." I could practically hear him grinning as he spoke, despite the distance that separated us. "THAT I LOVE YOU!"

Between any other couple it might have been a tender moment, that declaration of love. And maybe it was between them as well; it was impossible to know by trying to read Brooklynn's expression. Her face remained motionless. Impassive.

I lifted my hand to my mouth and pretended to cough to cover my smile.

"DID YOU HEAR ME? IS ANYONE THERE?" Aron's voice echoed when Brook—and everyone else in the room—stayed silent for too long.

The corner of Brooklynn's mouth quirked up. "You do realize this is a simple operation to establish communication, don't you? You're not a soldier who's gone off to war or anything?" Her smile grew then, becoming more mischievous than it had been before.

She caught my expression, recognized my feigned cough, and winked at me. I hated that I so badly craved her forgiveness, that I'd missed her so much, for so long, that her simple gesture made my heart soar.

"In fact," she added, "I'd venture to say you're more like a child with a new play toy, wouldn't you?"

There was a momentary silence from the other end, and then Aron's voice returned. "OUCH, BROOK. THAT REALLY STINGS."

"You'll be fine. Trust me," she answered, just as her finger moved toward the button.

"WAIT FOR ME—" Aron started to tell her. . . .

Right before she disconnected him . . . in front of the entire room full of witnesses.

And then the applause started.

I couldn't stop grinning.

It had been years since a message had been able to travel

from one end of our country to the other in an instant. And today we'd done just that. I'd spoken to Aron from inside the halls of the Capitol, while he'd stood in one of our southernmost cities. It seemed like something out of a far-imagined dream.

But it wasn't, and now I couldn't keep the excitement from my face.

We hit a bump in the road and I bounced unsteadily, my head colliding with Max's shoulder. His musky scent filled my nostrils as I leaned against him, sighing dreamily.

"Can you believe it?" I asked, turning to gaze up at him, and wishing I could say something more, but coming up empty every time I tried.

"You know why I can believe it, Charlie?" He pushed a wisp of hair from my cheek. "Because you're the most amazing person I've ever known. Because you're clever and iron-willed and selfless. You can do anything you set your mind to," he whispered. "You're going to take this country and turn it on its head."

"Maybe when Xander and Niko return, we can open a line of communication with Astonia," I said, exhaling.

Just saying Niko's name made Sabara stir within me. And as always, I had to concentrate to quell her. To stop her from surfacing all the way.

"Charlie . . ."

I frowned at the caution I heard in Max's tone, my eyes searching his.

Max scrutinized me, and I watched as his expression changed from warning to worry to something softer. "I just don't want you to get your hopes up. It's already been too long since we've heard from Xander, or any of them, for that matter. We've no idea if he's even made progress. It was a long shot to begin with. Elena's not to be trusted, not after the stunt she pulled with Sebastian."

Max was right. I should never have let Xander convince me to send him in the first place. I should've denied his request and come up with another plan. There was no excuse for putting him in harm's way. But hearing my former stable master's name made me bristle all over again. Sebastian had turned out to be both a spy and a murderer, enlisted by the queen of Astonia, who we'd later discovered had been working in tandem with Brooklynn's traitorous father to assassinate me.

I'd never so much as suspected the stable master in my employ, someone who'd taught me everything I knew about horses. Who'd taught me to appreciate them, even if he hadn't broken me of my discomfort around them.

"I know," I said, shrugging and trying not to let my disappointment show. I knew I was being fanciful, entertaining such notions, but I couldn't help myself. I wanted to start anew. For Ludania to live in amity with our neighbors.

I let my palm drift over the exquisite fabric of Max's suit. I wondered if I'd ever tire of the feel of fine fabrics, if I'd ever grow accustomed to that aspect of my new life. Wools woven so tightly, they could feel like silk; silks so delicate, they were sometimes transparent; and velvets, creamy fleeces, and luxurious cottons that were weightless against my skin.

His fingers, however, ignored my clothing altogether. They slipped beneath the hem of my skirt and traced a path to the back of my knee, making my pulse quicken and my breath catch. His hand moved higher, finding its way up the back of my thigh as the rhythm of our hearts beat dissonantly. He leaned in close, until our lips nearly touched and our breath fused.

Fire flared in the pit of my belly as my fingers clamped into a ball and I clutched his jacket, clinging to him for balance. My head swam in dazzling confusion. He didn't kiss me right away. He just stared at me, his eyes devouring me, and the hunger in his eyes was nearly enough to undo me completely. He willed me, with that steel gaze as firm as the fingers that stroked the flesh beneath my skirt, cupping my skin, making me quiver and ache, to close that minute distance between us.

"I . . . I . . ." Breathlessly I held on, not sure what more I could say.

And then, from the front seat, Zafir cleared his throat, and even though I knew he couldn't see us, facing forward the way he was, I was sure he'd sensed our restlessness. Our impropriety. Zafir always seemed to know what we were up to.

"We're arriving at the palace," he said, his voice insinuating none of the censure that his simple throat-clearing had.

I glanced at Max, and hoped he could tell from my expression that this wasn't finished.

He didn't release me right away. His hand stayed where it was, hidden beneath the folds of my skirt, and he gave me one more distinct squeeze, letting me know, in no uncertain terms, that it most definitely was not.

MAX

Max had grown accustomed to watching Charlie sleep. It was his favorite pastime.

Well, one of them, anyway, he thought as he grinned at her still form in the shadows of her bedchamber.

She had no idea the way her skin sparked in her sleep. The way her dreams made it glimmer and glow and sometimes blaze, like a torch that set the room aflame.

She also had no way of knowing the way those illuminations affected him.

Even now, seeing the barest of sparks swirling far beneath the surface, almost invisible as she delved into the deepest recesses of sleep, he wanted to climb back into bed beside her. To feel that warmth. To curl against her and guard that fire so it would never go out.

That was his greatest fear. That Charlie would burn out. That this was all too much, this responsibility—the pressure put on her by those around her and the pressure she put on herself. She expected perfection. She expected to make grand, sweeping changes.

And she expected them to be immediate.

She didn't understand that change—the kind of change she intended—wasn't just about intention and resources. They would take time.

But Charlie was impatient.

She wanted to see her country in a better place, and Max admired her for that. But it was taking a toll on her. She was putting too much of herself into it, working too hard. She couldn't keep up this pace indefinitely.

Already she'd managed to abolish the work camps—abhorrent places where unwanted and neglected children had once been carted, only to then be victimized by wardens who'd tortured and abused them. She'd begun efforts to get those from the Scablands who'd served their time and no longer belonged there—and those who'd never belonged there in the first place, like Avonlea—integrated back into society. Those who still remained in the Scablands were being trained to work the resources in the wasteland regions—mining for ore and ranching.

She believed that everyone could be useful. Everyone had a place in Ludanian society, even those who'd committed crimes.

Max believed she was amazing. And fiery. And beautiful.

Yet he knew she'd been damaged by the attempts on her life—and by the fact that she'd had to kill to save herself and Angelina—despite her best efforts to hide her pain.

He crept closer, kneeling on the carpet beside her bed and sweeping a curtain of her hair from her face. He watched as her eyelids fluttered.

"I love you, Charlaina di Heyse," he whispered, saying the words as silently as his voice would allow. "I'd follow you to the ends of the world and back if you'd let me." And he meant it. From the moment he'd met her, he'd belonged to her.

Silently he got to his feet, not wanting to disturb her, and not wanting to give anyone reason to gossip about his being there in the morning.

Just as he was turning to go, her hand shot out to stop him. "You don't have to follow me anywhere." Her voice was rough with sleep. "You just have to stay." And when he hesitated, her fingers tugged at him. "I insist. You can't deny a queen, you know."

Max grinned when he saw she was already pulling the blankets back for him. And then he bowed low. "Yes, Your Majesty."

II

"Your Majesty! Your Majes—"

I almost hadn't heard the boy's voice above the clash of steel, but when I finally heard his shouts, I whirled in time to see him come crashing through the trees.

His sudden presence in the clearing startled me. We were normally alone, Zafir and I. We'd never been caught training before. No one but the two of us knew that I'd given up learning to ride horses altogether and had focused solely on learning the ins and outs of battle. I was determined to learn to fight.

More so since I'd first discovered that my country—and I, in particular—had come under threat from Queen Elena.

The boy's round face was red and blotchy, and sweat beaded along the edges of his hairline. I could see that he was panting, and his eyes widened as he caught sight of me standing there, dressed in full battle armor, wielding my sword against my own guard.

I dropped my blade, ignoring the moisture that trickled down my spine. "What is it, Gabriel?"

He glanced at me, uncertain, and then he looked to Zafir, mutely assessing the unusual situation. "It's just that . . . well, I was sent to tell you . . . there's someone coming." He clutched and unclutched his stubby fingers in front of him as he spoke.

I turned to Zafir. "Xander?" I breathed. And then to the boy. "Are they back? Are Xander and Niko here?"

This time I couldn't subdue her, and Sabara's hopes became my own. *Niko,* she whispered, his name filling every part of me.

I squeezed my eyes shut, trying to block her out.

"I—I don't know, Your Majesty." My question made Gabriel shift even more, made him fidget and stammer. "I—I was only told to fetch you."

I barely heard his last words as I was already running toward the palace. I'd dropped my sword—a cardinal sin, I knew—and left it lying in the grassy field, unsheathed, and I'd left myself unarmed. Something no real warrior would ever do.

For now at least I was not a real warrior. I was a queen, awaiting word of one of my chief advisers.

Waiting for my friend to come home.

I saw horses tied up in the courtyard and knew immediately by the banners that flapped in the breeze that they were from Astonia. I'd have recognized Queen Elena's red flag, with its crimson laurel border, anywhere. Sebastian had used that same emblem to wipe his brow one too many times, all while pretending to serve me. All while reporting back to his true queen and preparing to slit my throat.

Traitors sometimes presented themselves in the most

trustworthy forms, and Sebastian had seemed about as honest and loyal as they came. Which was why I'd never suspected him. Why I'd let him get so close to me and my family.

And why I'd never trust anyone in that way again.

"They must be inside already," I called to Zafir, not waiting for a response as I raced past the horses, practically stumbling over my own feet in an effort to reach the entrance.

For two months we'd been waiting for word from Xander. It had been two months since he and Niko had taken a small party of soldiers and gone to try to reason with Elena, to try to get to the bottom of her betrayal and see if there was any way to forge a tentative peace between our two nations.

From where I stood, it seemed an impossible task, but I'd let him go because he'd been certain there had been some sort of mistake. That the Queen Elena who'd helped him when he'd fought against his grandmother would never betray him— would never betray *us*—in this manner. He'd been convinced she couldn't possibly have been behind the plot to have me assassinated.

Despite all the evidence to the contrary.

I slowed when I entered the main hall, the sound of my heavy boots still echoing off the walls around me. I stopped short when I realized that everyone in the room had turned to watch me.

On my way back to the palace, I'd managed to strip out of my heaviest outerwear, leaving not just my sword unattended but also my breastplate and the bulk of my armor. But I hadn't been able to wiggle out of everything, and now I stood before an audience of gaping stares, not just from the travelers who'd already been awaiting me, but also from those who knew me best, including Max and Claude, and Brook, Eden, and Avonlea. Even my parents were there, anxious for word of Xander and Niko.

I was suddenly aware of how I must have looked wearing a carapace of chain mail, even one so delicate that it was practically feather light. From their vantage point it looked as if I were wearing nothing more than long underwear and military-grade boots, the kind Brook's soldiers wore.

I avoided making eye contact with any one of them, knowing I'd have to answer for my appearance—and my actions—eventually. But for now I leveled my stare on the visitors, noting that neither Xander nor Niko was among them.

My heart sank, even as my voice found purchase. "You've come from Astonia?" I inquired as firmly as I could manage after running all that way. "You have news from your queen?"

There were four of them—messengers, one and all. My only real thought was that it was an odd number, because messengers didn't typically travel in packs.

"Yes, Your Majesty," one of the men answered, stepping forward. He bowed, as was customary in Ludania. The other three followed suit, but they were tense, bending stiffly at their waists. Then the man in front reached behind him, and one of the others carefully handed him a box the size of one of my father's bread loaves. I vaguely wondered what kind of gift Elena thought might assuage me at this point. I had no intention of being bought into submission.

He held the package out to me in both hands, his eyes never leaving it, and never truly meeting mine.

My gaze slid over it. There was nothing remarkable about it, the box. A carton like any other. But there was something about the way the messenger held it that made my stomach tighten ever so slightly. Or maybe it was Eden, my sister's guard, that I sensed, her curiosity charging the air around us.

I reached for the box, but I hesitated, my fingertips running over the coarse papery surface as I considered what might be inside. I tried to gain the messenger's attention, to find his eyes, but they remained where they were, fixed on the package. The other three remained where they were too, still entirely too rigid, positioned behind him.

I scanned the room now, looking to Max, whose intense gaze was directed to Zafir, and I could practically hear Max willing the guard to move closer to me, even though I could already feel Zafir's breath at the back of my neck. Brook's scowl was equally severe, although she refused to meet my eyes for too long.

Deep within me Sabara's voice whispered up from the chasm of darkness where she preferred to dwell. *Don't trust them*, she warned. *Be cautious, Charlaina.*

I wasn't sure how much more cautious I could be, but the box beneath my fingertips beckoned me, and a roomful of people waited to see what was inside.

Taking the box from his grasp, I held my breath as I lifted the lid.

From inside, crisp purple flowers tumbled free, spilling onto the toes of my boots. Their fruity scent was so overpowering that I was startled by it.

I glanced questioningly at the messenger, but his face remained impassive.

When I looked into the box full of brittle blossoms once more, I noticed there was something hidden there, just beneath the layer of withered blooms. Something that made my throat squeeze and my stomach lurch, despite the fact that I couldn't quite see past the layers of crumpled petals.

Zafir had noticed it too, and he snatched the box from my hands without asking my permission. He dropped to his knees as he reached inside, thrusting the flowers aside, until I heard his breath catch. I didn't wait for him to give me the go-ahead. I peered over his shoulder to see what it was that he was looking at.

I wished I hadn't.

I gasped and stumbled, falling backward and blinking too hard. I wished I'd never seen what I had, because I couldn't take it back. I couldn't undo what my eyes had just witnessed. I wasn't sure whether it was tears or fury that clouded my vision. My throat felt like it was closing, and all I could see, even when I closed my eyes, was what was in the box. All I could imagine— maybe forever all I would ever imagine—was that hand . . . the severed hand that Queen Elena had sent to me.

It wasn't until Max was there, pulling me back to my feet, that I recalled I wasn't alone. And then I looked up into his face and remembered something else. It wasn't just me who would be damaged by the dismembered limb.

If Max saw it . . . then he'd know who it belonged to. . . .

It was the scars that had given it away. Even as decayed as the hand was, I had glimpsed the intricate lacework of pale scars tracing the withered skin that outlined the knuckles. Scars I would've recognized anywhere.

Scars belonging to Xander.

I clung to Max, searching his eyes and trying to make my lips move. I struggled to find a way to tell him that his brother was likely dead at the hands of the queen he'd gone to make peace with, when I heard the sound—the bellow, like the piercing yowl of a wounded animal—at my back.

I knew it was Eden even before I found my next breath—her outrage and pain filtered through every part of me.

She'd seen it too. Xander's hand.

Her sword had been drawn, and before anyone could stop her or even had the chance to blink, she impaled the first messenger. The body hadn't even crumpled to the ground when she withdrew her weapon and repositioned herself, her blade readying to stab once more, a scream erupting from her as if it were being ripped from her gullet.

Zafir reacted first, and thrust himself in front of the wide-eyed, unarmed messenger who stood to be skewered next. The look in Eden's eyes didn't register recognition of the other royal guard. The only thing in her expression was misery. And ferocious determination.

But Zafir was determined too, and unlike me, he hadn't thrown his weapon down in the field. He drew his sword too—a sword named Danii—just in the nick of time, his blade clashing against Eden's and throwing hers off course less than a moment before it would've met the soft belly of the cowering messenger. The remaining two couriers had scattered, fleeing somewhere into the palace while their companion had been under siege by the heartbroken guard. I thought I should shout for someone to go after them, but I heard footsteps in their wake, and I was too focused on Eden to summon the order.

I thought she would stab, or swing, again—she was too far past reason to stop herself. Behind both Eden and Zafir, I saw Brook, who was also armed but not with a blade. Her gun was readied and aimed at Eden's head. I knew she wouldn't hesitate to shoot if Eden attacked Zafir, and inside my chest my heart pounded wildly. I tried to give Brook a silent signal to wait, but she wasn't looking at me. Her attention was trained solely on Eden now.

Time seemed to slow as I watched Zafir, standing stoically, patiently, in front of Eden. He never moved, and I wondered if he even breathed.

Ultimately something must have registered with her: the earsplitting crash of their swords or the reverberation she'd surely felt moving up her arm. Or perhaps seeing her own comrade staring her down as he stood in front of her. And instead of striking him, she wilted to the ground. No longer a sentinel of the palace but a broken woman. A woman who may have just lost the man she loved.

Dropping her sword at last, she fell forward, her palms splayed as she clawed at the polished floor, her wail resonating, deep and hollow and pain-filled.

I ached for her, as I imagined we all did.

I ached for her and for Xander.

And for what this message from Queen Elena meant for our nation.

🐉   🐉   🐉

It took nearly half an hour—and an entire squadron of palace soldiers—to drag Eden away from the great hall. And away from the box containing Xander's hand. Yet it took only Angelina's presence to soothe Eden's mournful cries and settle her into an uneasy sort of peace. The fitful kind that comes with fevers or nightmares, but a peace nonetheless.

Angelina hadn't lost her capacity to heal, and there was no reason for her not to use it. Our abilities were no longer dangerous secrets that had to be hidden.

Once we were in Eden's small, no-frills room, Angelina laid her hands on her royal guard, and the energy in the air changed immediately . . . from the gut-wrenching anguish that had caused bile to rise in the back of my throat, to an apprehensive sort of acceptance. A sense that this was the way things were now. There was no going back.

Whatever had happened to Xander was already done.

Eden, who'd been thrashing beneath the hands of the three large men who had accompanied us to her chamber, stilled on her bed, which seemed more like a cot with a cushion too thin to be deemed a true mattress, and I couldn't help wonder why, in a palace filled with such sumptuous furnishings, Eden would choose to deny herself such a simple creature comfort as a decent bed. For a moment I thought Angelina had somehow damaged the woman rather than calmed her. Eden seemed comatose, she was so motionless. But then I realized I could still sense her, could still see her eyes, watching Angelina . . . and only Angelina now.

The two of them seemed to have their own language.

One I wasn't privy to.

I suppressed the jealousy that twisted in my gut at seeing the two of them together, wishing Angelina would look at me like that. Wishing she would look at me at all. For now, I supposed it was enough that Eden had settled down.

I watched Eden then, studying her hair, which had once been spiky and blue but was now glossy and black. It had grown just long enough so that it skimmed the sharp bone of her chin when she marched—which was what she did rather than walk, wherever she went.

Now that same hair was plastered, like an oily second skin, to her scalp, still damp with sweat. Her skin, normally pale—not luminous like mine but opaque like polished ivory, chiseled and unbreakable—appeared ashen. Bloodless.

Her awareness became tangible. I could sense her reluctant acknowledgment that what she'd seen was real, and that she couldn't remain in that state of anguish indefinitely.

Angelina had told her so. With her eyes . . . and her touch.

There's nothing more for me to do here, I told myself, and Sabara concurred silently. The fact that I understood her wordless support worried me. We were too close, too enmeshed with each other.

We were two queens trapped in the same body, a complicated situation. One I wished I could remedy.

And I heard her response. *Me too*, she thought. *More than you can possibly know.*

I went back to the main hall, relieved that it was deserted now. Zafir had gone with Max and Claude to round up the two messengers from Astonia who had run off when Eden had executed their companion.

"Stay here," I told the young guard who'd been charged with shadowing me in Zafir's absence.

He frowned at being left near the door, but since the room was empty, and easily discernible from where he stood, he allowed me go inside. I knew exactly what I was after, the box from Queen Elena.

It was still there, right where I'd dropped it.

Xander's hand had been removed, but the flower petals were still strewn like purple confections all around the marble floor. Their fragrance masked their bitter purpose—to conceal their gruesome offering.

I approached the box warily, apprehension turning my blood to ice. I couldn't imagine the kind of woman, queen or no, who could do something so reprehensible. When I knelt down, I let my fingers trace the outside edge of the cardboard, assuring myself it was only paper. Merely the means for delivery.

Convinced the box was harmless, I set it on my lap and peered inside, still considering Elena's motivations.

Why Xander? Why now?

To what end had she sent his hand?

Did she expect me to retaliate? Was I to declare war and risk the lives of millions over the loss of one?

I couldn't say I wouldn't. Xander meant enough to me that I might. But I couldn't make the decision that easily.

I blew away several of the withered flowers that were still inside the box, spilling them onto the floor, where the rest were spread. Only then did I see that one was lodged in the bottom edge. Lodged between one wall and the floor of the container.

A floor that looked to be . . . detachable.

I plucked the blossom free, examining the box. I ran my finger along the inside of it, slipping my fingernail barely into the bottom edge.

It moved. Shifted just enough that I was able to get the rest of my finger beneath it.

I glanced around, searching to see if anyone else had seen what I'd done. It was only me and the guard watching from the door, and he was oblivious to my discovery.

Turning back to my task, I shimmied and wiggled the false bottom until I'd managed to free it from the box. Beneath it a flash of red caught my eye.

Red, the color of Queen Elena's flag.

I knew exactly what I was looking at.

A message, sealed with red wax.

My throat tightened as I reached for it. Like the box, the letter was made only from paper, but my reaction was visceral.

Even Queen Elena knows you don't need great technology to deliver a powerful message, Sabara jeered.

I ignored her barbs, concentrating on the letter instead. Its red wax seal, stamped with the unmistakable crest of Astonia, was unbroken. I thought about reading the message later in the privacy of my own bedchamber, but curiosity got the best of me.

Sliding my finger beneath the edge of the envelope, I felt the seal break, and my pulse quickened.

I scanned the missive, and then closed it again.

"Is she okay?" Max's voice found me, and my hand shot down to my side. I tucked the letter into my hip pocket before he could see it.

"What? Wh-who?" I stammered, jumping to my feet as the box tumbled to the floor. My pulse felt thick in my throat.

Max frowned at me. "Eden? Didn't you just come from her room?"

I sagged beneath the weight of his words. "She will be. Angelina's with her now." I searched his flint-colored eyes. I'd been so consumed with Eden, and now the discovery of this message, that I hadn't taken the time to consider Max, and the fact that Xander was his brother. "Max. I'm so sorry."

He winced at my words, and his jaw flexed ever so slightly when my hand reached across the distance to his. I knew what he was going to say even before he said it. "I'm fine," he answered in a voice that was too brusque and dismissive to ring true.

I tried not to be offended when he pulled his hand away from my touch. It was a lot for him to take in, the fact that his brother's severed hand had just been delivered to us. "What do you think it means, the . . ." I almost said "the message" but I stopped myself, thinking of the letter buried in my pocket, and instead said, "The box?" I hated asking the question, but Max wasn't just the man I loved. He was my adviser, and I counted on him.

Still, I couldn't bring myself to ask the other question that lodged in my throat. About what he thought it might mean for Xander.

He shook his head, and I could see him trying to wall off his emotions behind duty. "I don't know, but we'll figure it out. We rounded up the two messengers who ran off, and the three of them are being questioned now. If they know anything at all about Xander, we'll find out. Until then . . ."

He looked past me as his words trailed away and he lost his train of thought. My heart broke as I saw the fracture in his resolve. He wasn't as impervious as he pretended to be.

"Are you going to be okay?" I asked, this time shifting so he was forced to meet my eyes directly. I took his hands and gripped them, not letting him shake me off this time. "It's all right if you're not. I know the two of you are . . . *complicated*, but this is your brother we're talking about." I squeezed his fingers to emphasize my point, frowning tenaciously.

Max sighed as he reached for me, his arms dragging me against him. He settled his chin against the top of my head as he let out his breath. After a long, thoughtful moment his hands tugged at the lightweight body armor I was still wearing. "What are you up to, Charlie?"

I tipped my head back and glanced up at him, hoping he couldn't feel the sudden flutter of my heartbeat against his chest. "I—I just want answers. Same as everyone else."

He shook his head, telling me that wasn't what he was asking, and I knew he was onto me, that he'd recognized my attempt to be oblique. "You know what I mean. I'm talking about your chain mail, and you know it." He drew back and regarded my attire with a suspicious eye. "Explain, please."

I tried to think of a million ways to shrug it off—the strange garb, my ruffled hair, and the dirt I'd already tried to rub from my face. But Max wouldn't be put off by anything and would demand the truth.

If only I could find a way to soften it . . .

"Zafir is teaching me to fight," I blurted, my heart stuttering as the words burst from my lips, surprising even me when I heard them aloud.

Max regarded me, his dark eyes clouding. "To . . . fight . . ." He repeated the words slowly, as if they were foreign and he couldn't seem to absorb them. As if he understood each of them individually but not all together in their context. "You?" he asked, giving me the strangest look, and again I got the distinct feeling that my explanation hadn't quite registered yet.

A pair of guards entered the main hall, and suddenly the enormous space felt overcrowded, and my patience grew thin. I smiled weakly as the men passed us, and I no longer cared about how I looked or about things like manners or etiquette.

I reached for Max and half-dragged him from the hall, until we were deeper down the passageway, to the part of the palace where my family was housed. Once we were away from every possible prying ear, I straightened my shoulders and lifted my chin.

"Yes, *me*, Max." My voice was firm now. "Zafir has been teaching me how to fight for months. And not just how to defend myself should I be attacked," I explained stubbornly, wanting it all out in the open now. "But how to wield weapons too . . . swords, knives, even guns. I can shoot at both short and long range." I cocked my head. "I can also break a man's wrist." I remembered how I'd taken Zafir out of commission for a few days when he'd underestimated my grasp of this technique. I might not have actually broken his wrist, but he'd certainly had to lay low. He would have had a hard time explaining that I'd been the reason he'd had to bandage it to keep it immobile.

Max's frown deepened, but at least he seemed to be grasping the words as a whole now. "But . . . why? You have guards for that. You don't need to know how to fight."

I crossed my arms. "You can fight. I've seen you. And *you* grew up with guards," I challenged.

"That's different," he countered. "I joined the military. What kind of soldier would I have been if I hadn't been able to fight?" He shook his head, still scrutinizing me as if the idea were preposterous. "You're not thinking of joining the military, are you, Charlie?"

I considered his question, and my reasons for persuading Zafir to teach me in the first place. I'd had dreams about being tougher, stronger than I ever thought I was. And I'd proven that I could be—I'd very nearly broken my own guard's wrist.

So, I could fight. What did I really plan to do with that skill now that I had it?

I shrugged, biting my lip and stuffing down the desire to tell him yes, that I would like nothing more in the entire world than to fight, to prove my mettle in battle. "Of course not," I said quietly instead, my words feeling like a betrayal of my own heart. "What good would a queen be on the battlefield?"

III

When winter had first settled over our region, and the palace grounds—the gardens and the calm, canopied woodlands surrounding the estates—had become too cold and inhospitable as an escape from the duties that sometimes overwhelmed me, I'd gone in search of a new place where I could be alone with my thoughts. I'd scoured the castle, spending hour after hour, long after the others had retired for the night, combing hallways and searching chambers and passageways—even those that were hidden behind the walls and beneath the floors—until I'd finally found a space. One where I felt safe, and free to be myself.

Now, alone in one of many dank underground storage chambers that were brimming with crates and paintings and musty furniture from dynasties long forgotten, I curled myself tightly into the corner of a settee that I'd rescued from the treasures that had been carelessly packed in on top of one another. To me, these vaults were wondrous. Treasure troves that I'd spent days on end exploring, as I'd unearthed relics and art and—yes—junk, too. But incredibly fascinating and thought-provoking junk.

Once, I'd uncovered an intricate glass sculpture of a colorful bird with plumes as varied as a sunrise, while in yet another crate, I'd discovered a gorgeous drawing of the sea, with sandy knolls and great, frothy waves—a place that seemed mythical, despite the knowledge that it existed. More often than not, however, the crates were simply filled with garbage, rotting mounds of molded papers that might have been something once but now just stank as they decomposed.

It had taken me several of these expeditions to choose this particular room to make my own, and many hours more to rescue the settee from the wreckage once I'd realized it smelled the least like mildew and still had most of its cushions intact. I'd positioned it just so in front of a carved wooden table—another rescued treasure—with feet like lion's claws. I'd arranged candles in holders of varying sizes and materials—ornate irons, heavy carved woods, and golden gilts from indefinable eras—all over the table's surface to stave off the blackness that seemed to engulf everything belowground.

I stared at the portraits I'd gathered, my own private gallery. I had no idea who these women were, but there was something haunting about their images, especially in the candlelight that flickered and danced over the brush-stroked surfaces. As always when I studied their faces, I was keenly aware that these were likely rulers who had come before me, presiding over Ludania in succession, only to be swallowed up by Sabara.

Sabara, of course, heard my musings. *And not one was*

half as fortunate as you, Charlaina. You, it seems, have swallowed me.

I grimaced at her words. I could've been happy with my lot in life, as a vendor's daughter, but I was a different person now, and I was still getting to know the new me. I wasn't just a queen, or a vessel to carry Sabara from one place to another, or even someone's daughter. I was unsure, exactly, who I was, or who I would turn out to be. I was still growing and changing. Evolving.

"There you are." The low timbre of Max's voice interrupted my thoughts and made me forget Sabara altogether. His words were muffled by the damp stone that encircled us, and they sent a shiver along my spine that had nothing at all to do with the chill of the room. "Zafir said you'd slipped away again. He said you needed to be alone. I hope it wasn't because of me."

I knew Zafir's confidence in letting me stray had nothing to do with my newly developed fighting skills but more to do with the fact that he knew exactly where I was, even when he pretended to turn a blind eye. Knowing I was simply seeking a few moments' respite within the palace walls made it easier for him to give me the space I so desperately craved.

Frowning, I picked at a stray thread of the ancient fabric on the arm of the settee. "Why would you think it had anything to do with you?" I didn't want him to see how close he was to the truth. It bothered me that he'd questioned my need to train in the art of battle. I'd felt mocked for my desire to be something other than a girl wearing a crown.

The candles shivered as Max approached, casting new and different shadows over the worn woven rug I'd positioned on the slab of stone beneath our feet. He knelt on the floor before me, putting his finger just beneath my chin but not forcing it up. "Charlie, please. It's me. You don't have to pretend." His eyes, when I finally dared meet them, were liquid gunmetal that brimmed with so much reassurance, they were hard to ignore. "I'm a horse's ass, of course." He smiled then, and I did too. Partly because he was right, partly because he was so damned beautiful.

"You sort of are," I agreed, nodding, and that scant motion brought me just the slightest degree closer to him. My pulse fluttered as he leaned closer to me as well.

"I should never have questioned your motives." I could taste his breath, warm against my lips. His scent made it hard to concentrate, as suddenly all these words seemed pointless, and all I could think about was how badly I wanted him to close the gap and kiss me already. "You can do anything you want to do. You've proven it time and time again." When he paused, he reached into his pocket and pulled something out, then presented it to me. "Charlie, I want you to have this."

Curious, I watched as he uncurled his fingers, revealing a brilliant sapphire pendant set in beautiful bronze that had darkened with age. Around the large, glittering stone the metal had been sculpted with a fine latticework of designs and symbols that were now archaic but had once held great importance to the royal line.

More than one of the queens in my portrait gallery wore necklaces identical to the one he offered me.

"It was my mother's," Max said, and I raised my eyes to his.

I'd already guessed as much, but still I shook my head,

my heart squeezing at the gesture. "Max, I can't. Not yet." The last thing I wanted was to deny him, to hurt him, but the timing . . .

"Take it," he insisted, his eyes glancing uncertainly to mine. He pushed it into my hand.

I let him drop it into my palm, even though the feel of the chain against my skin felt like exactly that—chains. I couldn't be bound to him, not in this way. Not until I was certain I was ready. "I'm not asking you to commit to marriage until you're sure. It's just a gift. Something that once belonged in my family but now belongs in yours. It belongs on a queen," he said, and I knew he was at least partly right.

"Right," I agreed, a slow smile finding my lips. "But it's also an engagement necklace."

The candidness of the smile he returned to me made me question my hesitation. "Consider it a gift, Charlie. Wear it or don't. But I want you to have it. Every time I look at it, I think of you."

I blinked, determined not to cry, and reprimanding myself for being so sentimental even as I studied the intricate necklace in my hand. I wasn't sure I deserved either the gesture or his patience, but I was grateful for both.

"It's beautiful," I told him, letting my thumb trace the filigree design around the edges. I could make out tiny birds and a crescent moon, and a small flower design, all crafted from a single strand of bronze. There were other symbols as well, all interlocking and never-ending. Eternal.

His voice dropped. "*You're* beautiful."

My breath caught as I lifted my eyes to his. "Do you ever

miss her?" I asked. "Your mother? Do you ever think about her? Wonder what happened to her?"

I'd never asked him before, but if he was bothered by my curiosity, it didn't show in his expression. I'd heard the story, about how Sabara had paid Max's mother to leave after her husband—Max and Xander's father—had died, and I couldn't imagine what kind of mother would be so willingly bought off that way. How she could have agreed to take Sabara's money and leave her two small sons under their grandmother's roof.

But Max just shrugged, as if the matter were inconsequential. "There's not much to think about," he answered. "What kind of mother abandons her children?"

It wasn't an answer, at least not to the questions I'd asked, and to be honest, I didn't care about her. I cared about him. About the little boy he'd been—who'd lost first his father and then his mother, and had then been raised by a cold, heartless grandmother who'd cared about no one but herself.

Within me Sabara didn't bother to deny my allegations.

I looked back to the necklace in my hand. A woman like Max's mother hadn't deserved a necklace like this, any more than she'd deserved to have sons like Max and Xander.

"Fine," I told him, a grin sneaking over my lips. "I accept your gift. I'll even wear it now and then. As long as you realize that until *I* say it's an engagement necklace, it's only a trinket." My grin grew. "A really nice trinket," I finished as I passed it back to him and swept my hair aside so he could fasten it around my neck.

I raised my eyebrows expectantly, waiting for his reaction. "Well?"

"It's perfect." His voice was rough, almost a growl. "You're perfect."

Color sprang to my cheeks, and my own voice felt thick when it reached my lips. "You think so, do you?"

The change in Max was instantaneous. I could see it in the way his eyes glazed and his beautiful, full lips parted. I never tired of those lips. Lips that could coax sighs from me. Lips that could make mine tingle in sheer anticipation.

He was still on his knees before me, and this time when his hand curved around the back of my neck, it had nothing to do with the necklace. He drew me forward, and I followed his lead, my knees parting to make a space just for him. He studied my face, the way he always did, as if he couldn't get enough of it, and I felt restless beneath the intensity of his stare as everything inside me went fluttery and molten all at once.

When those perfect lips finally touched mine, so gentle and persuasive, my head whirled. I was both shocked and amazed that, even after all this time, he still had the same effect on me.

My fists clutched the soft folds of his shirt as I tugged him up from the floor until he was buried between my knees. I wrapped my legs around him. I needed him to be closer, and I drew him back with me, shifting to make room for him on the settee. But there was hardly enough space for the two of us, and we became entangled together on the too-small sofa.

I told myself I was doing this for Max, that this was a good distraction to keep his mind off what had happened today— the box, and worrying about Xander. But it wasn't long before all I was thinking about was me and Max, and how I could get closer to him.

I groped his buttons, my grasp clumsy, and I felt the fabric tear. Still, I didn't stop until I'd stripped his shirt away and it was lying in a rumpled heap on the floor. I needed to touch him, and my fingertips outlined each sinewy muscle of his shoulders and arms, running the length of his back. I'd changed out of my training armor, and now there was just the thinnest of cotton blouses keeping us apart. It was a poor barrier.

I pressed myself against him as close as I could get, basking in the feel of his skin so close to mine. My fingers sought his, and when I found them, I clung to him. And still we kissed, our tongues testing each other . . . delighting in the sensation, the movements, the longing.

I arched my back, my entire body aching to be one with him. Max groaned into my mouth as his teeth bit into the tender flesh of my lower lip. "Charlie, stop," he gasped. "Just . . . stop for a minute. There's no door on the chamber. Anyone could walk in at any moment. Zafir . . . he knows exactly where you are. . . ." His words trailed away when I lifted my hips again, intentionally trying to distract him from his train of thought.

I didn't want to be rational, not when every part of me was begging for more. To be impulsive and reckless, and wild and imprudent. Right here, right now, door or no.

Max wanted it too. I knew he did.

And then I heard him howl. He shoved me away from him, his face a mixture of anguish and confusion.

My breath coming in sharp gasps, I blinked several times. "What's the matter?"

"What do you mean *what's the matter*?" he accused. "Why would you do that?" He rotated so I could see what he was talking about, showing me the angry red marks on his shoulder.

Scratches.

I glanced down at my fingers and saw his blood on my nails.

"But I . . ." *I didn't do that*, I wanted to finish, but I couldn't bring myself to say the words, because obviously I had.

I closed my eyes as a sensation overwhelmed me, something close to satisfaction.

No. I fought against myself. *This can't be happening. She can't have this kind of control over me.*

But I knew I was lying to myself, that the line between her and me was blurring. That she was just showing she could still manipulate me if I let my defenses down.

And that's what I'd done. I'd let myself be distracted.

"Max . . . I'm so sorry," I offered, hoping it was enough, that he wouldn't make me elaborate. "I guess I . . . got carried away."

He grimaced. "Carried away? Is that what you call it?" He inhaled deeply, and then his shoulders relaxed and he grinned. "I suppose I should take that as a compliment. Is that what you're telling me?"

I groaned at his conceit, but I was glad he was so easily letting me off the hook. Glad he was so willing to believe it had been his *skills* and not something darker and more sinister that had caused me to react so savagely.

He leaned forward and gently pressed his lips to mine, reigniting that spark that had been so jarringly extinguished, and just like that I was under his spell once more. I knew with that kiss that all had been forgiven.

He eased away from me then, ever so slightly. I followed,

moving with him, meaning to settle myself on his lap. I still wanted to be close to him. I still craved his touch, the feel of his skin . . . the beat of his heart.

He grinned down at me as he firmly gripped my hips, setting me away from him and making his intentions clear. "I don't think you should sit there. Not a very good idea at the moment."

I couldn't help the small swell of arrogance I felt at the fact that I could affect him so tangibly, especially since I could never hide the way he affected me. My skin glowed, from head to toe, awash in the fever Max had stirred in me. I leaned my head against his arm.

When I finally dared a sidelong glance his way, my chest tightened. Max's features were strained as he closed his eyes and exhaled audibly.

My thoughts flashed back to earlier, to what had happened today with the messengers from Astonia. Shame flushed my cheeks as I shook my head. "I'm sorry, Max. You're right. This isn't the time or place. There are far more important matters than . . ." I glanced at him again, a different kind of flush spreading over me, and I grimaced. "Kissing."

Max grinned over at me, his arm dropping heavily around my shoulder. The gesture was chaste, and I realized he was still struggling with his control. "Damn, Charlie. There's nothing wrong with kissing," he muttered, pressing his lips to the top of my head and sighing. "But we do need to figure some things out. Brook's ready to fire the first shot. She's tired of diplomacy. In her mind the war's inevitable. In fact, to hear her tell it, it's already begun."

I already knew as much. Despite our differences—or rather, despite the fact that Brook was still keeping me at arm's length—I knew her feelings on the matter. She believed I'd been too lenient when we'd discovered that Queen Elena had infiltrated our country with her spies. The fact that one of them had turned out to be Brook's own father had only galled her more, spurring her desire for vengeance against the Astonian queen.

Now this with Xander . . .

"What do *you* think, Max? Xander was—" I stopped mid-sentence and corrected myself. We had no way of knowing whether Xander was dead or not. "*Is* your brother. What do you think we should do?"

Max didn't hesitate. He'd already considered this matter. "It's not about whether he's my brother or not. It's not about Xander at all. It's about whether peace can be reached. Xander believed it was possible—"

"But look where that got him." It was Brook who'd interrupted him, startling me, and I shot upright. I guess my "private place" wasn't as private as I'd assumed it was.

I glanced at Max, who didn't seem to notice that he was still shirtless. He stretched his arms casually across the back of the settee, leaning back as if he didn't have a care in the world, even though we all knew we were discussing whether or not to go to war. "Xander knew the risks when he went," Max retorted. "Besides, we can't be certain it was really Elena who sent us that message. What if it's a ploy to incite a war between our nations? What if some outside force is behind this?"

Brook strode forward, her boots kicking up dirt as she stomped across the chamber. She plopped down on a stack of crates, settled on the edge of them and leaned forward, her eyes filled with fervor. "We both know this was her doing, and Xander was a fool to believe that Elena has any integrity. You know it too, don't you, Charlie?" Her eyes met mine, and something about the way she said my name and not "Your Majesty" made me hesitate. I wanted to open up to her, right then and there, about the message, but I stopped myself.

Because I still didn't know where she and I stood.

I longed for us to go back to the way we used to be, to when we were friends and I could trust her to keep me safe.

That wasn't entirely fair, though. We might not be friends anymore, but I could still trust Brook. I knew as much as I stared into her bottomless brown eyes. She was still loyal. To me. And to Ludania.

"Who else could it have been? They were her messengers." I didn't mention the letter I'd found, the one with her unmistakable red seal.

She gave me a quick nod, and I realized it was a start. Not a smile, but an acknowledgment that she was still with me.

Brook stood abruptly. "That's it, then. My forces have been ready for weeks. I can send word and have units deploying by dawn. We can have our first troops at her border within a day."

I stood too, already shaking my head, unwilling to accept that this was the only option. I couldn't let others risk their lives when there was still a solution remaining, even if I couldn't share with them what that solution was. "Not yet. Let me have some more time to think." I looked at each of them, first at her and then at Max. "And I guess I need to start looking for a new place to be alone."

Max bent forward to retrieve his shirt. "What if we just go back to pretending we don't know about *this* place?" He winked at Brooklynn over my shoulder.

I sighed. "You might as well tell me, then. How long have you known about this one?" I asked, feeling suddenly foolish for ever considering it private in the first place.

It was Brook who chimed in first. "There are no secrets around here, Charlie. You should know that by now."

I spun to face her, trying to decide which bothered me more, that everyone knew about my underground hiding spot, or that she might be right. That nothing could stay hidden inside the walls of the palace.

My tongue was dry and I swallowed hard. I hoped neither of them knew what I'd found hidden in the bottom of the box. Hoped neither of them knew about the letter from Queen Elena . . .

And the proposal she'd made me.

"Charlie." Max's voice emerged from the darkness, and I halted, my heart crashing hard against my ribs.

When he reached me, the pale light coming from my skin made it easier to make out his outline. The way his feet were planted and his arms were crossed. His already dark eyes were made darker by the murkiness of the subterranean passage-ways.

"You scared me," I accused. "I thought you and Brook had gone. What are you still doing here?"

"You shouldn't be wandering around down here alone, even

if Zafir does know where you are. I figured I'd wait for you, walk you back. It'll give us a chance to talk about Brook, and what she's suggesting. She's just upset, you know. We all are after . . . after that message Elena sent." He frowned, but suddenly the letter from Elena felt incriminating and I worried that Max knew I was keeping it from him.

I glanced away. "You didn't have to wait. I'm fine. Really."

But Max crossed the space between us. "Don't bother, Charlie. Today's been anything but fine." He slipped his fingers through mine. "So what was it? Something happened. Something you're not telling me."

I had to remind myself he had no way of knowing how fast my pulse was racing, and I hoped my palms weren't a sweaty mess against his. But I knew that the sparks beneath my skin could just as easily betray me. "It was nothing—" I tried, but Max interrupted me.

"Charlie, I can't make you tell me anything." He chuckled and tugged my hand, bumping my shoulder against his arm. "I've never been able to make you do anything, but I feel like you're keeping something from me. I wish you'd trust me."

"Trust." Right now I hated that word. I didn't want to lie, but I couldn't tell him the truth. The fact that it was Max only made the situation worse. I hated lying to him, especially after everything we'd been through and all the secrets I'd already kept from him. Just when he'd finally started believing in me again, I was about to stand here and shatter that trust. "Nothing. I'm just worried, is all. The idea of going to war, of putting Ludania at risk like that, it . . . well, it makes me ill."

Max's eyes narrowed as he studied me, his brow furrowing. "Is that all?"

I sighed and leaned against him, burying my face in his chest. He probably thought I needed his strength, but really, I couldn't stand to face him any longer. "Isn't that enough? You know I'd do anything"—I choked on the word, because that, at least, was the truth—"*anything* to keep Ludania out of war."

"I know," he said, his hand finding my back. And he stood there stroking me like that, unaware that he was comforting me because I was a complete and utter fraud. That he was making *me* feel better for lying to *him*.

It was hard to stay still in the quiet of my bedroom as the hours dragged by. I still felt guilt over lying to Max, but it had been the right thing to do. I couldn't afford to let him stop me. Besides, it was better to keep him out of what I was about to do.

My guilt was compounded by the fact that I had only Sabara to keep me company. She was an abysmal conversationalist, trying to convince me over and over that the plan I'd come up with was absurd. That I would get myself killed.

What she really meant was that I would get *her* killed.

Her selfishness knew no bounds.

But I understood her concerns. I had them too. My idea *was* reckless, albeit necessary if I intended to keep Ludania out of war. And I did, no matter the cost.

You're an idiot, Charlaina. You think Elena intends to honor her word? She'd sooner slice your throat than negotiate a treaty. Sabara's voice left no doubt as to what she thought of my plans, and I wished, again, that I could somehow shield my thoughts from her.

But no matter how loudly she protested, I refused to be swayed in this matter.

Because Elena had offered me something I wanted even more than just a treaty. And no matter how much I tried to convince myself that my reasons were selfless, the truth was, I desperately missed the sound of silence.

Clenching the edges of my vanity, I stared at myself in the mirror, willing Sabara to show herself, although I knew she wouldn't. I summoned her all the same.

"Show yourself, Sabara. Face me. I dare you."

I waited, watching my own image. My face remained impassive, my eyes as cold as ice chips as they stared back at me, unblinking and frosty. My skin, although dimmed with time, now shone with determination, tiny detonations erupting just below the surface, the only movements I could see.

I could almost believe I was a force to be reckoned with, almost imagine I wasn't terrified by the mission on which I was about to embark.

"Coward," I whispered when she didn't emerge, but a part of me wondered if I was really talking to her at all.

When the palace had fallen silent for the night, I slipped soundlessly from my room and crept down the deserted hallway to another bedchamber, one I'd been in just hours earlier.

The guards who'd been standing outside were gone now, abandoning this post for another, more pressing matter. Their absence bolstered my confidence, and I reached for the door handle, and let myself inside without knocking first.

I knew she was awake even before I entered her tiny room. I could sense her awareness of me immediately, although I was certain she wasn't alarmed to find me creeping into her bedroom in the dead of night.

"Eden?" I called just to be sure I hadn't misread the feeling in the air. I'd have hated to have the royal guard thrust her sword through my gut by mistake. She didn't answer, but I closed the door behind me all the same. I couldn't risk making anyone else aware of where I was.

Now that I was here, ensconced within the cramped space of her private quarters, I was no longer certain where to start my explanation. I shifted from one foot to the other, silently replaying Sabara's arguments in my head and allowing them to fracture my earlier resolve. Inside my chest my heart hammered painfully, and my breathing grew erratic.

"What do you want?" Eden asked from the darkest corner of her bedchamber. I studied her motionless outline, still lying outstretched on her back as she stared up at the ceiling. From the sound of her voice, which wasn't groggy at all, I could tell I wasn't the only one who'd been awake throughout the night.

"I want to talk to you . . . ," I began. "I have an idea. A proposition, really."

I heard the sound of rustling and the creak of bedsprings. I watched as her outline shifted until her back was facing me. "Go away," she stated flatly. And then, "What I meant, of course, was, 'Go away, *Your Majesty.*'"

I smiled at that; I couldn't help it. Something in her tone, the caustic sting that laced the edges of her words, told me I'd chosen correctly. She was the perfect person to turn to.

"Eden, I need your help," I insisted, but this time I didn't wait for her to tell me to piss off, which she was most certainly leading up to. Eden had learned to show me a degree of loyalty as her queen, but only because Xander had demanded it. And Eden respected Xander above all else.

Which was exactly what I was counting on.

I crossed the room and knelt down beside her, my heart racing as I did so. I'd seen what she'd done to that messenger, how swiftly she'd disemboweled him. I knew how deadly she could be.

Dropping my voice to the quietest whisper I could manage, I breathed into the darkness where she lay. "We're getting out of here."

At first there was nothing from her, no response at all, save that electric crackle of energy of hers that fed the air. She'd heard me, all right. She was considering my words.

Then she rolled over abruptly, and I found myself staring directly into her unblinking black eyes. They were unnerving, and I had to force myself not to flinch beneath their scrutiny.

"What exactly are you trying to say?"

"Just you and me. No one else can know about this. I need you to take me to Astonia." I swallowed, willing my throat not to fail me. Not wanting to stop until I'd said everything I'd come to say. "It's the only way," I implored. "I need you to help me sneak out of the palace and cross the border. If I can get to Queen Elena, I might be able to stop her from attacking Ludania. I can prevent thousands of soldiers from having to give their lives over a senseless vendetta." My eyes were wide now, and my words tumbled over one another. "Please, Eden. You're the only person I can trust with this. You're the only one who has as much reason to get to Astonia as I do."

Eden sat up as she considered my pleas. "What about the princess?" she asked of Angelina, the only person other than Xander whom Eden truly loved.

I nodded. Of course I'd considered this. "I'm putting Zafir in charge of her. He'll protect her as valiantly as you would."

Eden snorted, scoffing at the notion that someone—anyone—could replace her.

"Fine," I conceded. "But he's at least the second best in the queendom. He won't let anyone near her. You know I'd never let anything happen to my sister."

Her eyes narrowed. "Not intentionally. But you kept Sabara a secret, didn't you?"

I stood then, my shoulders erect and my chin high as I scowled down at her shadowed form. "You're walking a dangerous line, Eden. I came here because I trust you, and because I believe we can help each other, but that doesn't give you the right to insult me."

She held my gaze a moment, and then sighed, rubbing her hands through her greasy black hair. "No, you're right . . . Your Majesty. It was uncalled for." She eased herself up from her bunk until she was standing upright, and then it was she who looked down upon me as she stood at her full height.

"And what if I don't want to help you? What if I turn you in to Zafir or Max or your parents? Tell them your plan to . . . to do whatever it is you plan to do once you get to Astonia? Then what?"

I'd considered this too. I didn't have a plan B. Eden was my only option, but I couldn't let her know that. If I'd thought I could get to Astonia on my own, I would have tried. But I'd never been anywhere on my own before. I wasn't even sure which direction to travel, or how to keep myself from getting mauled by animals or slaughtered by thieves. I was useless.

Eden, on the other hand, was competent and experienced and could lead me right to Astonia.

And with the right timing, with just a moment alone with Queen Elena, we both might get what we wanted from her.

Keeping my face blank, I shrugged as dispassionately as I could manage. "You could do that, I suppose. But then we'll never know for certain what happened to Xander." As I said the words, I wished the knot in my stomach would loosen. "It's a risk I have to take," I finished, hoping I didn't throw up right there in her chamber before she could give me her answer.

Eden paced toward the door, and my stomach acids churned, the back of my throat burning in their wake. I felt suddenly dizzy, and the urge to bolt ahead of her and run away almost overwhelmed me.

Maybe if I got a head start . . . Maybe I stood a chance of escaping into the forest.

Maybe I could somehow reach the border on my own.

And then Eden stopped pacing and turned to face me. Her expression was hard to read, but her mood wasn't. "I don't want to be a guard any longer," she stated with impervious resolve, and I remembered her the way I'd first seen her, when she'd been part of Xander's underground resistance. When all I had been able to think was that this woman, with her muscular arms and her piercing black eyes, was a weapon in her own right. "I'm done with all that nonsense. All I want is to get Xander back."

I didn't know if I could give her that, because I didn't know if Xander was alive or not. She surely knew as much too.

I nodded, agreeing to every unspoken term being forged between us. "Good," I told her, my blood hot and my skin starting to glow beneath the heat of our new alliance. "Because I don't want you to be my guard. I want a partner. And if you help me get to Astonia, I'll do whatever I can to help you get revenge."

IV

I lifted my finger to my lips, warning Angelina's temporary guard not to give me away. I slipped behind a massive tree trunk and watched as Angelina climbed the rope ladder that led into the fortress built high above the ground. The guard, who probably wasn't thrilled to be taking Eden's place while she was supposed to be resting, simply nodded while Zafir remained hidden with me.

Despite its less than stable appearance, and its precarious position among the thick, twisting branches, I was certain the tree fort was more than sufficiently secure. I knew no one—Eden specifically—would have allowed Angelina to play up there unless its architecture had been deemed sound.

From my spot below the structure, I listened to Angelina whispering something, and wondered if I'd somehow missed the presence of another child while I'd been observing her. I'd been almost certain she was alone.

Before I could question my sister's escort, I heard Angelina again, her voice louder now as she answered her own question, and I realized that she was carrying on both sides of her own conversation. Chatting, and then responding in kind.

Something about that hit a little too close to home for me. It was much too close to the way Sabara and I communicated, save that Sabara's voice remained silent to everyone but me.

I was glad Angelina had her own place of refuge, like I did. But my heart ached for the fact that my little sister was just as isolated out here at the palace as she had been when we'd been in the city, when she'd been unable to speak at all, and I wondered if she longed to play with other children. If she wished for friends her own age so she wouldn't have to carry on imagined conversations with herself.

I stood indecisively for only a moment before making up my mind to follow her up the steps to the tree house. With my plan now in place, Eden had given me less than twenty-four hours to make my final preparations before we would vanish.

Mostly, she had warned me to squeeze in a few hours' sleep before our first overnight journey, and I'd tried to follow her instructions, but I was too keyed up to rest. We'd be departing just after midnight, and all I really wanted to do was say goodbye. I didn't know when, or if, I'd ever see my family again.

As Sabara insisted on reminding me, I was about to embark on a suicide mission.

I gave Zafir the signal to wait for me, preferring to be alone with my sister, if only for a few moments.

The ladder was harder to climb than I'd expected, especially considering I'd just watched Angelina scale it deftly, like a small and agile little monkey. I glared through the rungs at Zafir, who was watching my progress with increasing amusement. I didn't have the heart to tell him that soon he'd be climbing this very same ladder. That he'd be entertaining my sister with tea parties and pony rides and other games she saw fit to include him in.

Eden would never admit as much, but I knew she'd enjoyed the childish endeavors. Zafir almost certainly would not. But he'd tolerate them all the same, because it was his duty to do so.

When I reached the top, my head poked through an opening in the rough-hewn floor, and I saw Angelina sitting cross-legged, staring at me. Her direct gaze made me aware of the fact that I hadn't snuck up on her at all, but rather that she'd been expecting me. Perhaps she'd known I'd been watching her all along.

It had always been hard to fool Angelina.

Her eyes never left me as I clambered the rest of the way inside, but she didn't flinch or try to move away from me, which I took as a good sign. We'd come to a truce, she and I, ever since I'd admitted to Sabara's existence inside me.

Angelina had already known, or suspected at least. She'd sensed the old queen's presence—her Essence still clinging to life within me—long before anyone else had realized it.

Maybe too she was aware that Sabara would be just as willing to take her as a host as me. Angelina's blood was just as royal as mine was.

She'd only have to say the words, Sabara had uttered in my head time and time again, making it sound like mere sport— moving her Essence from body to body.

The words, I thought. Those three simple words that would end Sabara's control over me once and for all. That would give me back my body.

"Take me instead."

I'd already traded my life for Angelina's. And forcing anyone else to say the words was a potential death sentence, whoever she was. I was the first person to ever coexist with Sabara. The first royal to survive the transfer and to share a body with Sabara. Every other girl had simply . . . vanished, surrendering her body completely to Sabara's dark soul.

I couldn't do that to someone else.

I wouldn't do it.

"It's okay if I come up, isn't it?"

Angelina didn't answer, just blinked at me with those achingly beautiful blue eyes. But still she remained where she sat.

I came in anyway and settled down across from her, crossing my legs like she did. Looking around, I could see she spent a good deal of her time up here, and that it was roomier than it appeared from below.

The walls and the floors were unfinished mostly, but there was a small table, just about Angelina's size, and I couldn't help wondering how Eden had managed to sit at it. I imagined the tall woman scrunched up in one of the undersize chairs, with her legs bent and her back hunched over as Angelina chatted and clucked over her.

There were more ladders inside the fortress as well—boards, really—hammered into the enormous tree trunk in its center that led to another level, creating a small loft above us. Surrounded by more small chairs, there was a rug made from some sort of furry pelt. There were plates and cups, and drawings stuck to the walls, and the outline of a checkerboard that I recognized as a miniaturized court for playing Princes and

Pawns. This last item had been carved into the floorboards.

"Wow," I breathed, more impressed than I should have been. I was suddenly envious of her hideaway and couldn't help wishing that *my* place were like this—hidden among the trees. Away from the palace walls.

Glancing her way again, I saw that her eyes were shining, and I saw her reach for something that was hidden behind her back. When her hand emerged, she was clutching Muffin, and she placed the threadbare rag doll tentatively on her lap. I felt a lump stick in my throat.

The last time I'd seen Muffin, the doll had been covered in blood that I'd thought surely had belonged to Angelina. Muffin looked no less tattered today than she had when I'd first given her to my sister, a hand-me-down from my own childhood.

I grinned at the both of them, wondering how in the world I was ever going to leave them. "I wasn't sure you even had her anymore," I whispered.

Angelina eyed me doubtfully. "I'm never getting rid of her," she stated matter-of-factly. "She's my best friend."

Again I was so sorry for my sister. I wanted her to have *real* friends. Ones she could run and jump and laugh with, not just a beat-up rag doll she had to do all of the talking for.

"Angelina—" I started, but she interrupted me.

"You're leaving, aren't you?" Her blue eyes cut through me like no one else's, and not for the first time I had to ask myself just how far her powers of observation extended. Angelina had always had the ability to know who could and could not be trusted. It was how she'd known that Sabara had remained inside me, that it was no longer just me anymore.

But this . . .

How could she know what I'd planned?

"Why would you say that?" I tried not to fidget, but her words made it difficult. Suddenly the floor felt too hard beneath me, the walls too close for comfort.

She cocked her head—it was such an Angelina thing to do, that simple gesture. So familiar that the lump in my throat grew larger. I'd missed her so much over the past months. I'd longed so many times to grab her up and squeeze her in my arms. To hold her and never let her go.

Yet here I was, trying to tell her farewell without revealing my plans.

"You . . ." She hesitated, pinching her tiny lips into a puckered flower as she concentrated, searching for the exact right words. "You just have that look. A good-bye look." She frowned, her lower lip jutting out now. "I . . . don't like it, Charlie."

A tiny gasp escaped my lips when I heard her utter my name. The last thing I wanted was to hurt my little sister. Not again. Not ever, *ever* again.

But here I was, preparing to lie to her too. To tell her that I had no intention of abandoning her.

I opened my mouth to do that very thing, to insist she was wrong, that I would never, ever leave her, but nothing came out. Instead I nodded.

"You can't tell," I told her. "Not anyone." I reached across and my hands closed over hers, my heart soaring when she didn't try to stop me. "But I have to go. I can't explain why, but it's important, and it's a secret. Do you understand?"

She knew I was telling her the truth, and she nodded, tears brimming in her eyes. "Am I going to have to be queen?"

I blinked once, and then more furiously, understanding full well the implication of her question. She was asking if I was coming back. She wanted to know if she'd be taking my place on the throne.

If she would ever see her sister again.

I tightened my hold on her hand, frowning as I bit my lip to keep from falling apart completely. "I don't know, Angelina. I'm going to try my very best to make it home. I'm taking Eden with me, and Eden's tough. She'll protect me. You know she will." I wished I could promise her more, that I could guarantee the outcome. "But I promise you this, I will do whatever I have to do. No matter what. I'm going to do everything in my power to make it back to you." I flinched at my own use of the word "power," worrying that it would serve as a reminder to Angelina of what—*who*—I was. That Sabara still resided within me.

Instead she considered my vow, and then nodded again, looking so much younger and so much more vulnerable than she had when I'd first climbed inside her tree house hideaway just a few minutes earlier. She crossed the space between us, and she and Muffin settled onto my lap. After a moment I felt her shudder, and then she asked, "Will you take care of her?"

The question took me by surprise. "Who? Eden?"

Angelina nodded, and I wondered if she was the one fighting tears now. I knew how close the two of them had grown over the past few months, and I knew Angelina would miss her guardian.

I sighed and settled my chin on the top of her head, flyaway hairs tickling my lips and nose. "Of course I will. I'll do my very, *very* best to keep her safe." But even as I said the words, I felt silly. Eden didn't need my protection. *I* was the one who needed *her*.

Angelina nodded again, accepting my word, and we sat there like that, in total silence for so long that the sky began to darken around us. I had just hours remaining before Eden and I would be gone. I inhaled the childhood scent of grass and dirt that seemed to cling to Angelina, and relished the feel of her warm body cocooned within the circle of mine. And even when my arms and legs cramped, I didn't move.

It wasn't until Zafir attempted to ascend the swaying rope ladder that either of us stirred.

Angelina glanced up at me from her spot in my lap. "Is he gonna be nice to me?"

A shiver ran down the length of my spine at the fact that she already knew he'd be taking Eden's place as her guard. But I smiled at the idea of Zafir trying to carry on a conversation with a five-year-old.

His head appeared through the opening and he glared at me. "Are you about finished, Your Majesty?"

Angelina untangled herself from me and crawled over to him, her gaze level with his. "Are you getting cranky, Zafir? Maybe you're hungry?"

His eyes widened as he stared back at Angelina, his expression changing from shock to confusion to . . . something else.

Something I almost swore was wry amusement. "No, Your Highness. I'm not hungry," he intoned, more quietly for her benefit. "Just . . . impatient."

Angelina turned back to me, her childlike concern taking over—as if she were fawning over a puppy or an injured bird. Her nose wrinkled as she tried to explain the situation to me. "We should get him a snack. He prob'ly needs a snack."

I raised my brows at Zafir, trying not to giggle at the thought of this massive giant of a guard watching over my waif of a sister. Or rather, of her watching and fussing over him.

"Yes, Zafir. I think Angelina's right. I think a snack might do you good."

"Charlie." The sound of Brook saying my name sent prickles of foreboding over my skin. My emotions, after seeing Angelina, were far too close to the surface, and I worried that I might somehow give myself and my plans with Eden away if I had to face Brook now.

I stopped but didn't turn to her immediately. Instead I gave the new guard, a man who just hours earlier had been temporarily in charge of my sister, the signal to give us some privacy. He didn't leave us, but he pivoted away, affording us some confidentiality at least.

If it had been Zafir, I might not have even gotten that much. I had Angelina to thank for that, since she'd insisted on dragging Zafir to the kitchens to find him a biscuit or some sliced fruit, believing it was his empty stomach that made his scowl so ferocious.

I'd merely winked at him when he'd tried to protest, and had allowed him to be taken hostage by the five-year-old. They'd be fine together, the two of them, and I felt certain I'd made the right decision to entrust her to him.

"Look," Brook breathed impatiently behind my back. "I get why you're mad at me," she said, misreading my reason for not turning toward her. "And I—I probably deserve it. I've been . . ." She hesitated again, and I was taken off guard. It was unlike Brook to be so unsure of herself. The Brook I knew was confident and brazen, definitely not prone to stammering.

I craned my neck to see what had her all twisted up.

Her dark eyes were clouded, her delicate black brows furrowed into a tight bunch. "I've been confused. Ever since . . . well, since my father *died.*" She frowned even harder when she said the word "died," as if he'd keeled over from natural causes. As if he hadn't been murdered by my hand. "It's not that I loved him, or even that I miss him, exactly. But . . ." Biting her lip, she paused, and I could read every bit of the confusion she'd just professed to.

I knew all this, of course. Brook's dad had been the reason she'd had no qualms about taking up with the resistance. He hadn't made her feel welcome at home, and Xander and his followers had given her a place to fit in. Taking up weapons had given her the opportunity to take out some of her aggression.

She scowled at me, and I waited for her to say something else. She opened her mouth, more than once, and closed it time and again, as if she were at a loss, as if she wanted to keep going but didn't know how.

After a few minutes Brook sighed, straightening her shoulders and clearing her throat, and I realized our brief respite was over. "I have a message ready to go with word for the troops I have positioned near the border of Astonia. I can have them deployed and on their way to Queen Elena's palace within hours of receiving my command." She didn't have to explain the geography again. She'd already spent hours with me and Max and countless ambassadors and generals pouring over the maps, and outlining where her forces were amassed and awaiting her order. I'd been so busy on the communications project that I hadn't realized how serious she'd been about preparing for war. The very idea that we were so close to setting things into motion terrified me. "All you have to do is give me the go-ahead." Her dark eyes studied me closely, and I felt myself withering beneath the scrutiny.

"I—I just need more time. To figure things out," I stammered.

"What *things*? There's nothing to think about. Queen Elena has made her intentions clear. We saw what she did to Xander, and you said it yourself—she has no interest in negotiating." She cocked her head. "Unless there's something else, something you're not telling me."

"I'm still your queen!" I shouted the words, drawing the guard's attention and Brook's as well.

Her eyes went wide as her gaze moved nervously to the guard, who took a hesitant step toward us.

I shook my head at him, my heart tripping over itself inside my chest. He fell back, and I turned to Brook, taking a breath and softening my tone, finding *my own* voice again. "I'm sorry," I said, hating how many times I'd had to say that recently, all because of Sabara. "But what more could there be?"

Brook exhaled as she considered my words, and my apology. She pursed her lips, trying to decide whether or not to believe me. My heart was trying to beat its way out of my chest, and my mouth went dry. After several long moments she finally nodded. "Don't take too long. I don't imagine Queen Elena will waver, and it would be better for the war to start on Astonian soil than on ours."

I tried to imagine how either was acceptable, but simply dipped my head in return. Brook took the gesture as my promise to get back to her about whether I would consent to starting a war with Astonia.

She spun on her heel, and I watched longingly as she paced away from me, and I wished we could start this whole conversation over. Wished we could go back to talking about her father so I could tell her, again, how sorry I was. Wished I could tell her everything about the message from Elena, and how I felt myself getting lost in Sabara. But I was unwilling to let Brook get caught up in my plan to save myself.

I pressed my hand to the wood, feeling for something, although I wasn't sure what that something was. The guard in the hallway ignored me; they were accustomed to my nighttime escapades. I was a restless sleeper, with Sabara waking me, and keeping me up, far too often. I'd become an unofficial member of the night watch.

Straining, I tried to sense Max somewhere on the other side of the door, to hear him maybe. But I was certain he was already sleeping, as was most everyone at this hour. I leaned my cheek against the cool barrier that separated us, wishing I could say a proper good-bye—the way I had with Angelina.

But Max was different. Max would try to stop me.

A part of me wanted him to; stopping was the logical course of action, because what I was doing—me and Eden— it was crazy. Even I knew as much. But that other part of me, the part that could no longer bear sharing myself with Sabara . . .

It was worth the risk.

But this was huge, the chance I was taking. It wasn't just my life, or Eden's or Sabara's lives on the line here. I was about to abandon my throne. I was leaving my country at a time when everything was topsy-turvy. That's how it would seem at least, to those who didn't understand that I was doing this not just for me but for them as well. Those who didn't understand that my actions might be able to save everyone.

If I stayed, I feared I'd become so enmeshed with Sabara that soon there'd be no distinction as to where one of us started and the other ended.

Still, if I didn't trust those I was leaving behind, I might never take the risk. But I did trust them. Max could handle things here, as could Brooklynn, and Zafir and Claude and my parents. Even Aron, when he returned, had learned a lot, and could manage the engineers and the communications' installations on his own.

I could count on them to make the right choices for Ludania.

I only hoped Max would forgive me when I returned. Or, more to the point, *if* I returned. And if I didn't, I prayed that Max would be okay, and that he wouldn't seek retribution against the other queen, the one who'd summoned me with promises I hoped she could keep.

Things might have been different if I could have changed the past. If I could have gone back in time and commanded Xander to stay in Ludania in the first place, rather than travel with Niko to Astonia to try to forge peace with Elena. I should've known not to trust her, and now here I was, leaving Max all alone.

My fingers curled into a fist, and I ran it over the door, exercising all my restraint to keep from going inside and climbing into his bed and staying there until morning. Eden and the whole plan be damned.

But I wouldn't do that, because of the message Elena had delivered.

The message that implied there was a way out of my predicament.

V

I jumped when my door opened, and even though I'd been expecting her, seeing her standing there left me speechless.

Sensing her mood was even more amazing.

Eden was electric.

It was like I was standing in the middle of a lightning field, and the best I could hope was that I wouldn't be struck by a stray bolt coming off her.

She no longer looked like the same Eden I'd gone to see just one night ago, the same woman who before that had been shivering and screaming and dripping with sweat when I'd watched my little sister creep into her cramped, utilitarian room to calm her.

She'd shorn her hair, and now half of it, on one side of her head, was cut all the way to her scalp, nearly shaved off. It was only somewhat longer, and spikier, around the top, the way it had been when I'd first encountered her, and then it fell to her chin on the other side. It was a lopsided style, but it was severe and made her look fierce. Like a soldier. Like the old Eden.

And it was purple now too.

Not exactly what I'd call inconspicuous, I couldn't help thinking. But I trusted Eden, so I didn't give voice to those doubts. She knew what she was doing. It was why I'd gone to her in the first place.

"It's time," she thundered, not bothering to ask if I was ready or if we were still doing this, simply stating that we were leaving.

"What about the guard? The one outside the door?" I whispered, my voice shades lower than her own had been.

"Already taken care of."

I wasn't sure what that meant, "Taken care of." But again I put my faith in her. I grabbed the small bag I'd packed, a worn knapsack I'd brought with me when I'd first come to the palace, one that had belonged to me long before I'd been queen, when I'd been just another student in the Vendor's school. I'd packed only a few items, clothing meant to keep me warm, things I could travel in. I reached for the cloak Eden had insisted I wear, to cover my incessant glow.

It wasn't until we were leaving my room, and I practically fell over a man's prone legs, that I understood what Eden had meant about the guard.

I stared at the poor man, my eyes wide. "What? Is this what you meant?" I searched Eden. Her expression was stern and impassive, as she seemed to be oblivious to the man lying, unconscious, at our feet. She frowned as she waited for me to gather my wits and put together a complete sentence. "What did you do to him?" I finally managed.

She made a face at me, not one that said she was concerned

for the guard's well-being or remorseful for what she'd done, but one that made it clear that she took umbrage at my daring to question her methods. "What did you think? That I'd tell him our plans and he'd just step aside and let us get away scot-free? Surely you knew there'd be casualties in this little operation of yours, Your Majesty."

"I—of course I knew there'd be casualties," I sputtered, not really sure I'd considered the implications at all, but now that I was saying it, I knew she was right. "I just didn't expect it to happen so soon."

"He's fine. He'll have a headache," she told me, doing a poor job of concealing her eye roll about my distaste for her tactics. "But he'll be fine." I tried to remember the last time someone had dared to roll their eyes at me, and I realized the gesture didn't offend me as much as it probably should have. It was refreshing, in a way, to be back on even ground with someone again.

Well, not on even ground, I thought as I stared down at the guard Eden had managed to level, and wondered what else she was capable of doing. I realized that once we left the palace and I abandoned my position as queen, I'd be infinitely more dependent on Eden than she would ever be on me.

"We can't just leave him here," I insisted. "Come on. Help me drag him inside." I opened the door to my room, making enough space to pull him through.

Eden didn't wait for my help. She just hoisted his entire dead weight by herself and tossed him through the doorway like he was nothing more substantial than a sack of feathers. He landed on the floor without even stirring, and I worried about just how much damage she'd done to him.

I felt sick leaving him behind like that, but we had no alternative. We couldn't afford to waste any more time. I tried to be more like Eden—tough, and heartless even, and I followed her lead, staying as close to her as I could manage without actually touching her.

Eden seemed to have mapped out our route in advance and knew exactly where we could navigate within the labyrinth of hallways without being discovered. The cloak did its job, and I gave off almost no light at all from beneath the heavy fabric. We became invisible, blending into the very walls themselves. Like shadows.

When we reached the final stretch, the corridor that would lead us to the exit we'd use to make our escape, Eden raised her finger to her lips.

As if she had to warn me to be quiet. I was like a mute already, too afraid to speak. Nearly afraid to breathe for fear the sound of my too-shallow breaths might give us away.

And then I realized it wasn't me she was worried about.

I could tell by the stiffening of her spine and the odd cock of her head that she'd sensed we were no longer alone. She held up her hand in a signal, warning me to stay put. I did as I was told, fear that we'd be discovered making me incapable of being anything but obedient.

I told you that you'd be discovered, Charlaina. I knew your plans would be short-lived. Sabara's virulent words tried to infiltrate what little composure I had left, and I had to remind myself that she was impotent now. She couldn't harm me.

I watched as Eden faded farther into the shadows until she'd been swallowed up by them completely. Whatever calm

Sabara hadn't managed to crack vanished the moment Eden was out of my sight and I was standing all alone in the darkness with only the insipid flickers coming off my own skin. To call it a glow was laughable. It was feeble at best.

My chest constricted until my breath, which had already been thin and hard to catch, felt like the sheerest of wheezes as it finally found its way to my lips. It grew more labored the longer I stood there, as if the darkness itself were suffocating me.

Just as I was about to strip out of my cloak, to try to at least create more light for myself, I saw Eden emerging once more.

"Oh, thank goodness," I gasped, lunging toward her inelegantly. But there was something in her expression that stopped me cold in my tracks. "What is it? What's the matter, Eden?"

And then I saw what had her face contorted, why she looked like an animal snared in a trap.

Brooklynn was behind her, matching her stride step for step. There was nothing casual in their pace. From where I stood, I could see the grip Brook had on Eden's wrist, and the way Eden's arm was wrenched low behind her back.

As they came closer, however, everything snapped into place. Eden's elbow was straight, but her arm was twisted at her shoulder, so that if Eden so much as dared to resist Brook's hold, if she tried to break away from Brook, Brook had only to elevate the arm, to torque it the slightest bit. It would send Eden into immediate and extreme agony.

I recognized the move from my own training with Zafir.

I wondered what exactly had transpired in those few

moments when Eden had been out of my sight. I wondered not just why Brook was gripping Eden in that manner, but how she'd managed to get the drop on Eden—who was taller and more muscular—in the first place.

I was reminded again of Zafir's tutoring. Size isn't always the most important thing in battle. Skill—and sometimes surprise—will carry you further than sheer bulk.

"Going somewhere?" Brook questioned, her eyes drilling into me. "Something you forgot to tell me? Some *plan*"—she paused over the word—"you forgot to mention?"

Eden tried to straighten, but Brook rewarded her with a sharp jerk of her arm. Eden's face distorted in a mixture of fury and agony that made every muscle in my body tense in reply. Nausea rolled through me as I waited to see what Eden might do next. I imagined she wanted to rip Brook limb from limb. Instead Eden said, from between gritted teeth, "You weren't invited."

Brook leaned closer, standing on her tiptoes so she could reach Eden's ear, her own face a study in unwavering resolve. "Well, here's your chance. Invite me now. Because you two aren't leaving these walls without me."

"Brook, no," I gasped, not sure whether I was reacting to her request or to her treatment of Eden, or both. "You can't go," I insisted, finally breaking free from the stupor I seemed to have fallen under as I'd stood watching the two of them. "How did you know anyway? You should be in bed at this hour."

Her mouth twisted into a wry grin. "I already told you. There are no secrets around here."

With that, my stomach lurched. I wondered how much she

knew, and worse, if anyone else had figured out what I was up to. "Who did you tell? Does Max know?"

Brook scoffed at the notion. "Are you kidding? He thinks you're sleeping like a baby at this very moment. You have him as hoodwinked as everyone else around here. No one suspects you're sneaking around under the cover of darkness, planning to go who knows where, with . . ." She glanced at Eden, her smile growing. "Me and Eden here."

Eden's eyes narrowed, but she remained silent. A smart move, considering her precarious position.

"Brook, I'm serious. You can't come. What you're suggesting . . . well, you'd be defecting from your position as commander of the armed forces. You can't do that."

Brook laughed, almost a snicker, as she countered, "But you can defect as queen? To do what? To go where?"

She didn't know everything, I realized, but her words pricked my conscience. I brushed aside my own guilt as I glanced at Eden. "I'm not *defecting* as queen, Brook. Let Eden go and I'll explain."

Eden's black eyes snapped up to mine, and I saw a flicker of something there. Something very close to triumph.

It didn't take Brooklynn but a moment to weigh my request before she shoved Eden away from her. Eden rolled her shoulder, lifting her arm as if loosening the stiff muscles. The gesture appeared casual, a natural response to the angle she'd just been pinned in. But it was a deception, and before she'd finished a single rotation of the joint, she'd spun around, her fists at the ready and her shoulders squared. She moved so fast that if I had blinked, I would have missed it.

Fortunately for me, I hadn't.

Her attack stance was thwarted, though, when Brook reacted just as rapidly, and I heard an unmistakable click. Even in the shadows, I could make out the silhouette of Brook's weapon—a handgun that was now directed at Eden.

"Nice try," she said with a note of genuine sincerity. "I'd have expected nothing less."

Eden looked blandly at the firearm. "And I expected a lot less." She shrugged halfheartedly. "I suppose I'm somewhat impressed. You're better than I realized."

Brooklynn raised a perfect dark eyebrow. "I was trained by the best."

The reminder that they shared a bond, these two women with very little else in common except that they'd both been revolutionaries in Xander's army, eased the tension, if only somewhat, and Eden nodded.

Brook lowered her weapon as well, even though she didn't holster it. "So I'm guessing this has something to do with Xander. Am I right?" She didn't wait for either of us to answer, and it was easy enough to let her think she'd guessed correctly. "So let me repeat myself: Neither of you is leaving here without me. Have I made myself clear?"

PART II

MAX

"This can't be happening!" Max exclaimed, shoving his hands impatiently through his hair as he waited for Joseph di Heyse—Charlie's father—to read the letter he'd thrown down in front of him. "What was she thinking? Your daughter's a madwoman. You know that, don't you?"

When Charlie's father was finished, he set the paper down beside the ornate place setting—hand-painted china trimmed in gold leaf—and even that casual gesture set Max's teeth on edge.

How could he just sit there at a time like this? How was he not climbing out of his skin with worry?

Instead her father treated the letter as if it were yet another trivial matter in a day like any other, even though they both knew it wasn't.

He was too calm by half. Certainly calmer than Max had been when he'd discovered the note propped against Charlie's pillows that morning, on a bed that had been unrumpled. She hadn't even bothered to make it look as if she'd slept there. He might not have even found the letter, had it not been for a night guard with a very large bump on his head and an outlandish story about being attacked by a purple-haired assassin.

No doubt who the purple-haired assailant had been.

Max had had to read the letter several times before the words had started to make sense to him, until he'd finally realized what Charlie had been trying to tell him in her abrupt handwritten scrawl—that she'd taken Eden and gone on a rescue mission to save Xander.

Xander! Xander whose hand had been delivered to them in a box.

Charlie had also left the letter that she'd discovered in that same box, the one addressed to her from Queen Elena. Although, whether Charlie had left it as justification for her actions or to explain them, Max wasn't certain. Not that it mattered, really. There was no excuse for what she'd done. What she was risking by her actions.

And the letter was quite clear:

> *Charlaina,*
> *I know your secret. I know how to cure you of it.*
> *Surrender yourself to Astonia, and I'll give you*
> *peace. I'll give you everything you want. The*
> *choice is yours.*
>
> *—Elena*

Her secret? Only those closest to Charlie, including Max, knew that the secret was Sabara, of course. But they'd gone to great lengths to hide Sabara's existence from the outside world. How could Elena possibly know about Sabara's Essence being fused with Charlie?

He thought of Xander's hand, and wondered if the other queen had tortured the information out of his brother, searching for weaknesses with which to lure Charlie to Astonia. If so, she'd succeeded. She'd found the one thing Charlie would be unable to resist—the chance to purge Sabara from within her.

The offering of peace for Ludania only sweetened the deal.

But why couldn't Charlie have come to him for help? Why hadn't she confided in him?

He raked his hand through his hair again, frustrated because he already knew the answer. Because he'd have stopped her. He'd have rounded up an army and insisted they go to war instead, which was exactly what Charlie wanted to avoid, so instead she'd turned to the one person who had as much to gain as she did from sneaking off to Astonia.

The fact that she'd decided to take someone as unpredictable and revenge-minded as the former revolutionary only made her situation all the more precarious. Who knew what would happen to the two of them?

"She's loyal to a fault. I'll admit that much, at least," Joseph said, as if that somehow excused Charlie's midnight escapade. As if that made it all okay.

"Loyal? Loyal! That's all you have to say about this? She'll get herself killed, and then what? Is Angelina prepared to take the throne?" Max saw the muscles in the older man's jaw twitch, and he knew he'd gone too far, but he couldn't stop himself. This was Charlie they were talking about.

Joseph struck the heavy wooden table in front of him with both fists, his chair scraping across the floor. He stood facing Max now, and there was nothing calm in his demeanor. His body trembled with ill-concealed fury. "Don't you dare for a second think that I don't care, Maxmillian," he barked. "That's my daughter you're talking about, but what do you want of me? I'm an old man. I can't very well go myself. We'll send an army after her if necessary."

Max looked more closely at the older man, assessing the strain that made the lines that etched his face grow deeper, furrowing in places Max hadn't noticed before. The man's eyes tightened ever so slightly at the corners, and his pupils were constricted as he glowered at Max. It was there, the worry, but it was hidden, veiled just beneath the surface.

"I'll go myself," Max stated, leaving no room for argument. "Claude's getting Brooklynn now, and as soon as we can, we're heading out to find Charlie."

The older man nodded, settling back down once more.

"I'm sorry." Max put his hand on Joseph's shoulder. He'd been out of line to accuse Charlie's father—overtly or not—of not caring enough for his errant daughter, not after all he'd done, all the secrets he'd kept to keep her safe her entire life.

Joseph shook his head, looking wearier than he had just moments before. "Don't be, Max. Just bring her home."

The doors opened then, and both men's heads snapped around to see who it was.

Claude came in, alone, a scowl on his face. "The commander's gone," he announced, not waiting to be asked. "Brooklynn," he amended as if they didn't know who he meant. "She's gone too."

Max shook his head and muttered beneath his breath as he paced toward the door. Then he stopped to face Claude. "Get word to Aron. Let him know what's happening here, and gather some of Brook's soldiers. We're going after them."

BROOKLYNN

By the end of the first day, the only one talking was Charlie, and Brook contemplated shooting her just to shut her up.

Brook wasn't sure it would be considered treason at this point, since Charlie was no longer sitting on the throne, only on a horse they'd stolen from the palace stables. She didn't even think Eden would try to stop her. Charlie was driving the both of them crazy.

"Don't you think Aron will worry when he finds out?" Charlie asked for the millionth time.

Brook glanced over her shoulder to where Charlie was at least seven horse lengths behind both her and Eden. It was hard enough to wait for Eden, who was a decent enough rider, but waiting for Charlie to keep up was downright painful.

Hell, if Brook shot her now, no one would ever be able to catch her anyway, not even Eden. Brook was a better rider than she was a markswoman, and that was saying something.

When she'd actually realized just what a drawback Charlie's riding was, Brooklynn had doubled back and left a trail of broken branches and hoofprints in the mud to make it look as if the three of them had taken an entirely different route, hoping to send any search parties off on a wild goose chase. She might not have stopped them from discovering their direction entirely, but she hoped she'd bought them some time.

"He's probably already been notified," Charlie went on. "I wonder who it was who told him." Brook watched her as she kept talking, the way her eyes never left the ground in front of her, as if somehow by watching the terrain, she was helping the horse keep its footing. Her grip on the reins was so firm that her knuckles would be stiff for days. "Do you think it was Max? Do you think he used the new communication device to send word?" Charlie looked up then, her eyes straying from the path to catch Brook's gaze, but only for a moment before returning to the ground again. Brook wondered what Charlie thought was going to happen if she looked away. That the horse was going to trip on a twig or a pebble? Or maybe a fallen tree that no one but her might notice?

Brooklynn turned and righted herself in her saddle, spurring her horse forward. She increased the distance between her and her . . . *What am I supposed to consider Charlie at this point, anyway?* she wondered. Charlie had insisted she was no longer to be referred to as "Your Majesty," so what was she, then? Neither Eden nor Charlie had clued Brook in to exactly what their mission was or where they were headed, so she still didn't understand what their plan was.

My queen, Brook reminded herself. *Charlie is still my queen, as annoying as she might be*, Brook thought as she listened to

Charlie prattle on about Max and Zafir, and even her parents now.

Brook eased up to where she'd let Eden take the lead. "How much longer? I think Her Majesty needs some sleep. Or food. Or more likely a gag." She winked at Eden, grinning deviously.

Eden, who'd said barely two words since they'd left during the night, just squinted at Brooklynn, giving her a look that reminded Brook she was a stowaway on this mission and that her input wasn't at all appreciated. "We'll be there just after nightfall. And stop calling her that. You never know who might be listening."

"Oh, come on. We're in the middle of nowhere."

Eden's gaze moved upward, shifting toward the evergreens that filtered out the late-winter sun. The only sounds were the horses' hooves and the branches rustling over their heads, and even the branches barely shifted.

At first Brooklynn thought Eden might be calculating the time, the way she concentrated on the cold, barren sky through the occasional openings in the thick canopy, trying to guess how much more daylight they had, but then her black eyes fell back on Brook, unflinching. "You never know who's listening." She made a clicking sound then and flicked her wrist so that her reins slapped the horse's neck. The animal responded, increasing its pace and pulling away from Brook once more just as Eden called over her shoulder, "We're getting closer. Mind every word now. The trees have ears."

An eerie sensation settled over Brook, prickling her skin and causing her scalp to pucker as every hair stood on end.

She looked up too, her eyes tracking over the same places Eden's had, finding the same hollows in the trees, the same forks in the branches, tracing the same twists and gnarls and bends until she realized there was nothing there. That she'd been spooked by words, and words alone.

Spirit stories, like the ones she and Charlie and Aron had told when they were younger, as each had tried to convince the others of hauntings and apparitions and ghoulish occurrences.

The same way Eden had tried to convinced Brook with her tale of eavesdropping forests.

Nonsense, Brook told herself. But she slowed her horse anyway, deciding to keep closer to Charlie now despite her doubt.

Because regardless of all else, and no matter what Eden and Charlie insisted, Charlie was still her queen. And Brooklynn was there to defend her.

VI

Sometimes nightmares were real.

That was my first thought when the imposing razor-wire fences came into view. Even in the glow of the colossal torches that had been placed at uneven intervals along the perimeter of the settlement, the enclosures themselves were intimidating. The metal was oxidized from weather and time but still appeared rugged and sturdy. The barbed spikes protruding from the fence were so long and so sharp that I was sure they could impale an entire human torso. And they likely had, from everything I'd heard about these places.

From what I could see, the buildings behind the fence line were no less daunting. No more inviting. I shuddered for their inhabitants, wondering what it must have been like . . . before.

I wondered too what it was like now. Now that the work camps had been dismantled. Now that the unwanted children who lived here were no longer wards of a barbaric system in which they were worked to the brink of collapse, and then tortured as a punishment for their lassitude.

Still, it wasn't exactly what I'd imagined—the settlement— nestled deep in the forest and hidden away from the rest of the world. I supposed I'd imagined a place more barren and desert- like. More like the vast regions of the Scablands, although I knew there were camps there as well. This was only one of many.

As far as I was concerned, there were too many of these camps in Ludania. Camps where children who'd lost their parents, or whose parents could no longer provide for them, or children who'd been forced to leave home because their parents were the more dangerous option, had been sent to live under Sabara's rule. Here they had labored and toiled until they'd reached the age of legal consent, at which point they'd been reassigned to society, where they'd been required to labor and toil under a different kind of regime.

I'd already outlawed the work camps, but like all my deci- sions, it had caused a scandal of sorts. There were always those who were opposed to change, even when it benefited the greater whole of society. Even when it benefited those without voices of their own.

My plan was to reorganize the camps into something more humane, a place where children would be fed and cared for and educated. A safe haven. Many of those who'd been in charge of the camps had been detained and arrested for their crimes against the children they'd been in charge of.

Those who were found liable would be grateful that they lived under my rule, where the worst I would do was exile them to the Scablands. Sabara's gallows were unforgivable.

"Are you sure it's safe to be here?" I asked, following Eden's lead and tethering my horse to a branch.

Eden glanced up once more, just as she'd done when we'd been riding earlier, when she and Brooklynn had been discussing me as if I couldn't overhear them, when I'd been nervous and talking too much. I'd ignored them then, but now I followed her gaze, wondering what she was searching for.

The sky had shifted from pale and cold to a frigid field of black. There were hints of a bright moon and pinprick stars that made intermittent appearances from between the trees that had grown denser and made it harder to navigate.

And then I saw something, in the branches high above me. At first just the barest shift. A quiver so minor that I nearly missed it against the dark canvas of night. But as I waited, it came again. Stronger this time.

No, not stronger. Louder. It came like a sound, a crackling whisper. A rustling.

I tried to pinpoint it, to track it with my eyes, but it was as fast as it was slight, and the darkness seemed to swallow it up before I could reconcile it.

"There," Eden said, pointing to the place I hadn't been able to find.

"Where?" Brook was standing behind us now, trying to see what Eden had.

I held my breath, waiting, my heart pounding too hard. And then it came again . . . shifting, rustling . . . and a leap. "I see it," I exclaimed. But as quickly as I'd made the announcement, whatever it was vanished amid the backdrop of black foliage and tree limbs.

"He's there," Eden explained, her voice whisper soft, and I

tried to read her mood, which was as dark and ambiguous as the night itself.

I frowned. "He? It's a *he*?"

"What's he doing up there? He standing guard or something?" Brook asked, her voice matching Eden's, quiet and low.

But Eden ignored us both and instead cupped her hands around her mouth. She didn't call out to him, not in words, anyway. What she did was make a sound—a whistling sound like none I'd ever heard before. It wasn't that of a bird or a train or the kind of whistle a person makes when they purse their lips and blow. It was more like that of an instrument, the kind carved from old, hand-rubbed wood. It was deep and mournful, and beautiful.

And it was nothing I could decipher.

After she finished, there was a moment of silence . . . a long, still moment during which my pulse beat just a little too fast as I waited.

Then came the response. An equally resonant and melancholy whistle from above us. From the exact spot Eden had just been pointing to.

"You can come down now," she called up to the trees. "You've had your fun."

There was nothing subtle about the way the leaves rustled after that. It was as if the very ground were trembling. As if the earth beneath our feet were trying to spit the soaring trees right out of it. And it wasn't just the one tree, the one Eden had pointed to. It was all of them, as every leaf and every branch and every offshoot of every branch shook at once.

When the boy landed in front of us, I jumped back, bumping into Brooklynn, who instinctively thrust me behind her. I didn't have time to be offended, or to worry that she looked too protective and might give us away by her actions, because I was too shocked by the boy's sudden appearance to think of any of those things. Eden didn't so much as flinch, however.

The boy was gangly and thin, but not small, exactly, making it hard to pinpoint his age. But it was also the smeared grease or mud that coated his face and arms—everywhere his skin was exposed—that made it difficult. I couldn't see the ridges of his brow or his jaw, couldn't tell if he'd passed that divide between child- and manhood. His clothing, rags of varying fabrics that seemed to be patched together, was as grimy as everything else about him, and I couldn't help thinking it was meant to be some sort of camouflage. That all this filth was meant to keep him hidden among the forest foliage.

But before I could imagine why he would need to blend into the trees, another pair of feet hit the ground with a definitive thud. Another mud-covered body faced us. Followed by yet another . . . and another . . . and another. Until it seemed as if we were faced with an army of soldiers, each staring at us from behind a screen of grime and grit.

The boy who'd landed first was also the first to step forward.

Eden met him halfway.

Neither spoke for an instant, as if silently appraising the other. Sizing each other up. And then Eden said to him, "You weren't fooling anyone. I saw you about a thousand paces back." Her voice was flat, but there was something charged about her, an anticipation or an expectation that hadn't been there before. Almost like she were on the abyss, hovering on the verge of delight.

But why? I couldn't help wondering. What was it about this place, about this meeting, that could cause her to feel such joy?

"And I saw you two thousand paces ago. You're losing your touch," the boy answered. His voice was lower than I'd expected, and it made me aware that he was older than I'd first imagined, despite his narrow build.

Eden's reaction wasn't at all what I'd anticipated, as she threw her head back and laughed. The boy's face cracked then, literally, as mud crumbled from around his eyes when he smiled at her, his lips parting to reveal the pink skin.

That was when I noticed it, the odd coloring of his eyes—those peculiar eyes. Coloring I'd seen before. Coloring I'd always found unnerving, most especially when they were focused on me.

Black, like a bird's. Black as night.

Black . . . like Eden's.

She reached out and grabbed the boy then, not caring that he was caked from head to toe in dirt so thick, it probably reached to his bones, and she dragged him against her as she wrapped her arms around him and kept laughing. She laughed into the top of his crusty hair, and she may have even kissed him too. It was hard to tell, since the boy began to wriggle within her grasp. But Eden was unyielding in her affection, unwilling to release him just yet, and she clutched him and buried her face in his head and neck, still laughing.

"Stop!" the boy insisted, and when she didn't at first, his

muffled shouts climbed into his throat, making him sound more childlike than he had just moments earlier. "Eden, stop! Stop!"

She relented, but only reluctantly. She loosened her grip but didn't release him quite yet. "Fine, fine," she muttered, but there was nothing but humor in her voice, and I couldn't remember ever hearing Eden sound so . . . so jovial before. Not even with Angelina. "You don't have to be such a baby."

"I'm not a baby," the boy grumbled, but it came out so quietly, I almost didn't hear him. "Just lemme go." He motioned behind him with his head, his voice dropping even further. "They're watching us."

Eden's grin grew, and even without sensing her, I could tell she was enjoying herself more than she should have been. She shoved him away from her, causing him to stumble. He nearly tripped over his own feet before catching himself and coming to stand before his scruffy legion of followers.

The boy straightened his shoulders and then addressed those gathered in front of him, some of them having grown restless, shifting and scratching and whispering among themselves. His voice sounded more grown-up now than it had when he'd been caught in Eden's arms. "We have guests," he announced, and I could feel all those too-bright, unblemished eyes that blinked at the three of us from beneath the mud-laden faces. I wondered who they thought we were. And then he continued, and suddenly his relationship to Eden became strikingly clear as he turned to face her, his hands landing on his skinny hips. "Some of you might remember my sister . . . Eden."

Eden had assured Brooklynn and me that we'd be perfectly safe for the night. Right before she'd deposited us in a bunker no bigger than a shed and left us alone with a group of ragged-looking kids who watched us as if they'd sooner strangle us in our sleep than share one of their beds with us.

Fortunately, they were more accommodating than they appeared, and they willingly parted with two of the bunks that were scattered around the planked floor, giving us each a place to sleep.

I wasn't sure if we were taking bunks of kids who'd been displaced to accommodate us, or if the bunks had already been empty, but when I asked, all the girl told us was, "You sleep here." It was the same answer she'd given when I'd tried rewording the question, and when I'd finally given up and thanked her, and again when Brook had asked her for an extra blanket. Just "You sleep here" in her strange, tired lisp that made her *S* sound like "th."

I couldn't help thinking the girl didn't know any other phrases.

"S'not her fault, you know." The voice came from several bunks down, after Brook and I had finally settled in.

I made sure that my cloak and blankets were sufficiently covering me, diffusing any light that might try to escape while I slept. I couldn't take the chance that news of the glowing queen had traveled all the way to this forsaken work camp.

Brook had insisted on pushing our bunks together, despite the fact that none of the others were. She said we needed to sleep back to back, to stay on guard, even though Eden had assured us we could trust these people, and even though, as far as I could tell, they were nothing more than children. We hadn't seen anyone who looked older than Eden's brother, whose name we'd learned was Caspar.

"What's not her fault?" Brook asked before I had the chance.

"Selena. Not her fault she can't tell you nothin' else. She's a Repeater. It's all she can do, what with all the beatings and the messin' around the docs did on her head." The girl speaking was younger than Caspar. I'd seen her in the forest when they'd all still been covered in mud, before Caspar had sent them down to the river in the dark to rinse off before turning in for the night. It was her hair that gave her away; even caked with mud, the brilliant fiery strands had been impossible to hide.

The way Caspar had given the order, it was clear he was the one in charge around here. "Where are the adults?" I asked. "Shouldn't there be someone here to make sure you're all okay?"

Moonlight poured in through the dirt-caked windows, and I could see the girl's outline as she sat cross-legged on her bunk, the way Angelina so often sat. Her hair was still damp and hung in drooping waves around her face. She stiffened at my words, and I felt as if I'd somehow insulted their leader without meaning to do so. "Caspar's doin' a fine job. Better'n the rest. The doc was arrested and taken away," she explained indignantly. "And so was the chief—that's what he made us call him, the warden who used to be in charge. Never knew his real name, just 'the chief.' He liked hurtin' us.

"At first when those people came around askin' us questions, we were all too scared to answer, too afraida the chief. But then Caspar said we had to. Said if we didn't tell 'em what they wanted to know, the chief'd keep hurtin' kids forever. So we did." She shifted, so she was sitting sideways on her bunk. She kicked her legs, swinging them back and forth and back and forth as she spoke. "The day they took the chief away was the best day ever." She glanced up, and her eyes sparkled in the pale moonlight. "Best day ever," she repeated, a dreamy, faraway smile on her lips.

I couldn't imagine what the chief must have done to these kids, and my skin flushed as I remembered the other girl and the way she'd simply repeated the same words, "You sleep here," over and over again.

Gritting my teeth, I fought to contain my reaction. I couldn't risk my skin blazing to life if I didn't keep my emotions under control. I clutched the fabric closer to my face so I could peer through a narrow opening.

"There's no way they'd just allow Caspar to run the place. How did that end up happening?" Brook shot back.

The girl's feet stopped swaying, and she looked around, nodding smugly, and I realized that the others must have been listening too. A roomful of children all lying in their cots and listening to our conversation like it was a bedtime story. "We chased 'em off."

Brook sat up, more than a little interested now. "What do you mean, 'chased them off'? Who? How many of them?"

The girl's face screwed up as she concentrated. "Three," she answered. "They sent three more to run the place, after the chief."

"Four!" piped up another voice from somewhere down the row—a little boy's voice.

The girl paused and counted on her fingers, then nodded once more. "Yep, that's right. Four," she corrected with a quick jerk of her head. "Four that we had to *persuade* to leave."

"Why?" I wondered aloud, hating that I might somehow be responsible for putting others like the chief in positions of authority over these children. "Were they all so terrible, like the chief?"

She waved the idea away. "Nope. They was fine. We just didn't need 'em, did we?" She wasn't asking me now. She was asking the other children, and the response was resounding.

They were all in agreement as "no" echoed through the bunkhouse. They most definitely did not need adult supervision. Caspar was their leader. He'd take care of them.

"So." I was almost afraid to ask my next question. "Where did they all go exactly? The adults, I mean."

The fiery-haired girl shrugged. "Don't know, don't care. Long as they don't come back." She started swinging her legs again. "I'm Ku," she announced, grinning widely at me, and I could make out a wide gap between her two front teeth.

"I'm Cassia," said another girl.

"Santiago," said the little boy who'd corrected Ku.

And then they were all saying their names. All of them at once, a snarl of voices that twisted together, making them sound like one jumbled mess.

These were the children who'd been sent to the work camps. Abandoned by parents and relatives—by society—and now they'd banded together to form a new family. Taking care of one another.

And now taking care of us.

"I'm Cha—" I stared to say, but Brook elbowed me so hard in the ribs, I gasped, reminding me that even my real name was too dangerous. I faltered, trying to think of something else to say, struggling for a lie—a name I could offer in place of my own.

And then I heard Sabara, offering me a name that no one else would recognize, one that hadn't been used in decades . . . centuries. Maybe eons.

When it hit my tongue, it tasted bitter, but there was no going back. "Layla," I said instead of my own name. "My name is Layla. And this is Brook." I wanted the attention off me, and off the fact that I'd just given an entire room of people— children or not—permission to call me by the name Sabara had confessed was her original name. The name she'd been born with all those many, many years ago.

Before she'd taken possession of the first body that hadn't been her own—her sister's body.

Before she'd killed to stay alive time and time again.

I hate you, I silently told her, hoping my message was clear. Hoping she understood how badly I wished I could just be myself again. Alone inside my own head.

When there was no response, I thought maybe our connection wasn't as strong as I'd thought it was, that maybe she couldn't hear me as clearly as I could her. But then her response came, as slick as oil as it slithered up my spine.

I know you do . . . Layla. Hearing her call me by that name was as inciting as knowing what the chief had done to these poor kids in his work camp, and I could feel myself responding, my skin growing hotter.

I hoped Sabara wasn't right, that I wasn't walking into a trap.

I couldn't stop thinking about Queen Elena and wondering what exactly she'd meant when she'd written, *I'll give you everything you want*. Because I wanted too many things.

I wanted Xander to still be alive. I wanted peace for Ludania, once and for all.

And more important, and more selfishly, I wanted to believe she really did have a cure for me. That she really did know a way to banish Sabara's Essence. Forever.

I considered that long after the children had settled down in their bunks, and long after Brook had given up keeping watch and had drifted to sleep, her back pressed against mine.

And long after I'd stopped worrying about Xander and Ludania, and whether Max would ever forgive me for keeping yet another secret from him.

SAGE

Bare feet were best for this kind of work, the kind of work for which she needed to be furtive. As quiet as a sigh.

No one could know what she was doing. If she were caught, even her title wouldn't be able to save her head.

But it wasn't unusual for her to be skulking about under the cover of darkness with no shoes. The calluses on her feet proved as much. She prided herself on her ability to become one with her surroundings—day *or* night. To blend and go unnoticed. To find things that others considered unfindable.

And to kill without a second thought.

Yet she'd need none of those skills this night. Tonight she knew exactly where her quarry was, and she had no intention of killing him. At least not yet.

"You," he barely managed to croak out, a strangled sound caught somewhere between a moan and a whimper when he caught sight of her. He didn't even bother to lift his head from the cold ground he was lying upon. *A bad sign*, she thought as she studied his motionless form.

She glanced all around, noting the fact that no one had heard his feeble attempt to voice his contempt for her. She couldn't have cared less that he despised her. She had every intention of being his salvation, whether he wanted her help or not.

Noiselessly she removed the key from her front pocket and slipped it into the lock. Without a single creak or scrape, she slid open the door to his cell. Had he been stronger, he would have stormed her, mounting an attack to try to regain his freedom. She knew because she'd seen him fight before. But he'd been a different person then. As it was, he stayed down, unable to even lick his own swollen and bleeding lips.

"Here," she said, ignoring the stink of his unwashed skin and the smell of human waste and rotting flesh that emanated from him as she twisted the cap from the water-filled flask that hung from her waist. She held the flask to his lips and let the water trickle into his mouth. She was careful not to choke him, since he barely seemed able to swallow. "We'll try again later," she finally told him, when she realized most of it was dribbling down his chin.

"Wh . . . ," he tried, but the pathetic attempt to question her died on his cracked lips as if the effort were too much.

Why had she come? What did she want? Why him? It could've been any or all of those questions, and she half-wondered herself what the answers were. If her sister discovered what she'd done . . .

Well, she would discover it eventually, all right. The trick was not getting caught for it.

"I need you to get up," she told him. "Just long enough

so I can get you out of here. There's a vehicle waiting for us. We'll be safe until we reach the border, and then we'll have to travel through forests. You'll have to ride on horseback then." She didn't know why she was explaining all of this to him; she doubted he understood. She wasn't even sure he'd heard her.

She slipped his arm around her shoulder, again trying to shut out the stench coming off him, but failing miserably. He cringed against the movement but didn't resist her. Despite the pain he was in, and his weak physical state, she was surprised to see that he actually managed to help haul himself from the ground. He wobbled, and leaned heavily against her, but he allowed her to lead him toward the cell door.

"It'll be okay," she assured him in a voice so quiet, it was almost nonexistent. She didn't want to risk being discovered.

They slipped through the passageways more noisily than she had on her way in, but because she'd timed it so perfectly, they managed to go unnoticed. As they emerged, with the vehicle still there, waiting for her, she let out a breath of gratitude.

She eased him inside and watched the way he clutched his arm, keeping it close to his chest. His skin was greasy and pale, and she noted the way the bandages surrounding his hand were saturated with a mixture of blood and pus. She wondered what kind of infection she'd find when she uncovered them. She wondered too if she'd have to take the entire arm.

With the last of his strength, he lifted his head. "Why . . . are . . . you . . . doing . . . this?" he rasped, right before he passed out again.

Because you're being used, she answered silently as she slammed the door, checking once more to make sure no one had spotted them, before she climbed into the front. *And if I don't get you out of here now, I run the risk that Niko will make good on his promise to keep my sister alive forever.*

VII

Eden pulled us out of bed while it was still dark outside, but I knew it was close to dawn when we crept from the bunkhouse onto grass that was damp the way it was in the early morning hours just before daybreak. As we followed her, staying quiet and keeping close, I briefly wondered if she'd even managed to doze, since she didn't appear to have changed out of the clothes she'd been wearing the night before, and she didn't look nearly as rumpled as I felt after sleeping in mine.

Brook grumbled about the hour, about needing more sleep, about the cold, and about wanting food. What she got instead was coffee when we arrived at yet another cabin. It was a poor substitute for all that she wanted but was a substitute nonetheless.

I curled my fingers around the warm mug and sniffed the bitter contents as I sat down across from Eden and her brother, still marveling at the resemblance between the two of them. It was stronger now that Caspar, like all the children he was in charge of, had rinsed the muddied grime from his face. His strong brow and sharp jawline and black eyes were so similar to hers that if they'd been closer in age, I might have mistaken the two of them for twins. It was his size that gave him away as younger, but it was his hair that truly set him apart from his sister. It was almost too light to be called blond. A sharp contrast to Eden's natural crow-black hair.

I lifted the coffee in front of me, which smelled nothing like the savory blends we'd become accustomed to at the palace, and I realized how spoiled I'd grown over the past months. There was a time when I wouldn't have dared turn my nose up at such an indulgence, despite the fact that I wasn't a coffee drinker by nature. A hot drink was a hot drink, and hospitality—no matter its manifestation—was always hospitality.

"Thank you," I told Caspar, keeping my face as straight as I could while I sipped the pungent beverage. It didn't matter how it tasted, though. It went down hot and thawed my belly.

Eden didn't have to pretend, nor did Brook, both of whom swigged the scalding liquid as if it were the sweetest elixir they'd ever tasted. Clearly they'd been accustomed to worse.

"So what's the plan? How long are we staying here?" Brook asked. She shoved her empty mug toward our host, her way of requesting a refill, but she looked to Eden as she spoke, not Caspar. "I'm thinking we need to move on by daybreak or we're begging for trouble. These kids are all alone here now, but they won't be for long. Eventually someone'll come to check on 'em, and we can't be here when they do." Caspar filled her mug and passed it back to her. She offered him a quick nod of appreciation in return.

He, like so many before him, grinned back at her, not invulnerable to Brook's smoldering looks, even when her hair was matted from a night of restless sleep. She barely seemed aware he was watching her with such eager intensity.

But Eden noticed. She glared sideways at her younger brother, and I wondered how it was that he'd come to be here in a place like this without his sister. She kept her eyes trained on him the entire time she spoke to Brook. "We'll stay for the day, gathering the food and supplies we'll need. Then we'll leave at dusk."

Brook slammed her mug onto the table, barely aware she was spilling her coffee as she did so. "No! We can't risk another nighttime ride. The first one was too treacherous. It's difficult enough for the horses—every step they take is like walking through a minefield." And then she shot a disapproving look in my direction, making it clear that *my* riding skills were in question as well.

She was right about riding in the dark, of course. It *was* dangerous, although less so with me along, shedding light wherever I went.

Once we'd gotten far enough from the palace that there was no chance we'd be seen, Eden had allowed me to shed my cloak, and we'd used the glow from my skin as a lantern of sorts, illuminating the trails and making it at least a little easier for the horses to see where they were stepping. It wasn't until we'd entered the forests surrounding the work camp that she'd clamped down on us once more, warning us to remain quiet and keep close.

But it wasn't just the darkness that put us in harm's way.

There were also nighttime predators, both animal and human, waiting for their chance to pounce on us.

Eden shook her head. "We're not taking the horses," she told Brook, and now I was the one who set my mug down.

"Then, what? How will we travel?"

Caspar grinned, not just at Brooklynn this time but at me as well. "Come on. I'll show you."

He pulled on his coat, which was patched and threadbare, with sleeves that were too short, as he led us back outdoors. The sun was just coming up on the horizon, bursting into the gunmetal sky with fingers of orange and pink and the oddest blooms of gold. It was spectacular, and I breathed deeply, trying to inhale its glory.

Keeping his head low, Caspar led us along an overgrown path that was so encroached upon on both sides by weeds and grasses that only the narrowest space of path was even visible at all. We followed him between and around more of the small cabinlike buildings, similar to the one where Brook and I had slept, and it soon became clear that the compound was massive and mazelike, and as unkempt as the pathways we walked on. It could have easily been regarded as abandoned by anyone looking at it from the outside.

It was no place for children. Especially those who were all alone in the world.

As we rounded a corner, a girl joined us. She didn't say anything, just nodded to Caspar, and then to Eden. She was younger than Brook and me, and I put her somewhere around her thirteenth or fourteenth year. Her skin was darker than mine—as was everyone's, it seemed—but not from spending time outdoors. Hers was naturally browner, as if she'd inherited it from her parentage, the way Brook had. Her hair, too, was dark, almost black, and was long except around her face, where it looked as if it had been hacked and chopped with a dull-edged knife, likely to keep it away from her eyes. But that wasn't what was most notable about her, nor was it the fact that her eyes themselves were the most unusual shade of blue. Not like Angelina's or mine, pale and crystalline, but rather piercing . . . electric. Much like the sapphire I wore pressed against my heart.

No, the most startling thing was her bird. A stark black crow sat, unmoving, on her shoulder, like an inanimate prop. It wasn't until the bird blinked that I realized it was truly alive.

I waited for someone to introduce the girl as she fell into step beside us, but no one did, as if her presence were just accepted, like an unexpected gust of wind.

We approached a crumbling circle of stacked stones that I recognized as a well. Around it there were several rusted buckets, most of which had succumbed to various forms of plant life that grew in and around them. It was a good indicator of just how long ago they'd been discarded.

As we neared the well, I wrinkled my nose at the odor coming up from the ground. "You don't . . . drink from that, do you?" I probed, eyeing the corroded bucket that hung from a pulley above the well.

Caspar and the nameless girl exchanged a look as we passed the disintegrating stone structure. "Well went bad years ago. We get our water from upstream. Near the mouth of the river."

I thought about the children I'd met the night before. Most of them were small, and I tried to imagine them toting heavy buckets of water to and from camp. "Is that far?"

Caspar grinned at me, clearly understanding my concern. "Never mind 'bout us. We'll be just fine. From what Eden here tells me, you got enough on your minds without worryin' about a buncha kids."

I shot Eden a glance, wondering how much she'd told him. But she shook her head discreetly, her silent reassurance that my identity was still safe. I turned my attention back to Caspar. "How come you're here? I mean, why aren't you with your sister instead of being here, in the work camp?"

I could feel Eden's irritation as surely as I saw her lips purse and her eyes narrow. Her glower made my toes curl, but I had no intention of letting her intimidate me. I had a little sister, and the idea of her in a place like this . . .

Well, it would never happen.

Caspar either didn't notice Eden's scowl or was accustomed to his sister's irritation, and he laughed at my curiosity. "When Eden left, I was just a boy. I wasn't old enough to go with her."

Brook skidded to a halt. "Wait! Are you saying Eden was here too?" She nudged her way to the front of our group so she could be heard. She surveyed Eden, as if seeing her in a new light altogether. "You *lived* here? In the work camp? I never knew that."

Eden kept walking. "There's a lot of things you don't know about me" was all she told Brook, and then she turned her attention to Caspar. "I told you I'd come back for you, and I did. You were the one who didn't want to leave." She didn't sound disappointed, the way a sister might if she hadn't been able to persuade her brother to come with her. She sounded bitter, as if this were a sore spot and Brook had just jabbed a stick into it.

"You can come with me now," she maintained. Her eyes narrowed on him, and Brook and I stopped too.

Caspar sighed. "Look around, Eden," he said, his voice and his face softening. Eden didn't look, but I did.

We were standing on a hillside now, overlooking the encampment as it stretched in front of us—larger and more widespread than I'd first realized. Than I'd ever imagined. I tried to guess how many children it housed, how many orphans Caspar was responsible for. It was baffling that they'd done so well for so long on their own.

"I can't leave here," he went on. "You have your cause and I have mine."

They stared at each other, neither blinking. Neither looking as if they had any intention of backing down. They shared that same determination, that same inflexibility.

It made me squirm to witness.

Just when I started to consider sneaking away, creeping back down the path to hide in the cramped barrack where Eden had deposited us last night, Eden reached out and punched Caspar playfully in the arm. "You've gone soft. I always knew you'd be the motherly type," she taunted.

Caspar, refusing to let Eden see that her blow—or her words—had stung, did his best to hide his cringe. "And you're about as lovable as a thorny shrew." He scowled at her. "Only not half as cuddly."

Eden grinned, and I couldn't help thinking she'd taken his insult as a compliment. Caspar just shook his head and started walking again. We followed until he finally came to a halt in front of a large building that reminded me of one of the oversize storehouses in the warehouse district of the Capitol. Unlike the rest of the compound, this building wasn't dilapidated at all. The outside was made from concrete and steel, with paint that wasn't chipped or peeling. It was as tall as it was wide, and likely as deep. Even the ground we stood on here was smoothly laid asphalt, new and even and black.

"How is this possible?" I asked, staring at the building, which seemed so out of place here.

Eden chuckled, and I suddenly felt like I was the butt of the joke. "What? That the work camps were given resources for the commodities they were expected to manufacture, but not for the children they housed? Did you think Sabara would have expended anything more than she had to for the care of orphans?"

I closed my eyes and tried to remind myself that this was why Ludania needed me. That these were the kinds of changes I'd been working so hard to make.

"So what was it you were manufacturing here?" I asked Caspar.

"We were a munitions camp."

My eyes strayed to the dark-haired girl with the bird perched on her shoulder, and I felt sick that children like her, and like the others from the bunkhouse last night, had been exploited so freely under Sabara's reign. It was hard to imagine children making weapons.

I had never considered where Ludania's weapons had come from, or where they were coming from now.

You did this, I accused Sabara. *They're only children, and you turned them into slaves.*

They were nothing, she hissed back. *They had no homes, and I housed them. No food, and I fed them. I gave them a purpose.*

She ignored the part where they'd been overworked and tortured and experimented on, but there was no way she hadn't known. She just didn't care.

You cannot maintain an empire without an army, and that army must be invincible, Sabara justified, as if there were any excuse for her actions.

I shook my head, trying to purge Sabara from my mind. Not wanting her corrupt logic to poison me.

Casting me a curious grin, Caspar continued, unlocking the massive warehouse door. "But this . . ." He tugged the handle, and the door started to open. "This is what we're most proud of," he announced smugly.

"This? This what?" Brooklynn asked, sounding skeptical. I felt my thoughts clearing. What could a bunch of kids possibly have inside that warehouse that could be useful to us right now?

Slivers of sunlight streamed into the dark interior from windows high above, shining at odd angles and casting squares on the concrete floor like checkerboards. Above us we heard the frantic beating of wings as a flock of birds from within the building took flight into the rafters. The girl's bird, however, remained as still as ever.

But all that faded into the background the moment we spotted the machinery taking up the center of the floor. I wasn't entirely certain what it was, but it was most definitely a vehicle. Some sort of massive, strangely shaped, motorized vehicle.

"What the . . ." Brook's question trailed off as she approached the beast of a machine, her fingers outstretched toward it. "Can I?" She turned her wide brown eyes on Caspar, beseeching him to say yes.

He was powerless against her, and he nodded mutely.

When her hands fell against the steel, Brooklynn let out a sigh. A sound that was equal parts ecstasy and relief. "What is it?"

"We call it a Vehicular Assault Navigator. Or VAN," Caspar said with a chuckle. "It's like a portable armory. We got it outfitted for travel too, though. You can hole up in there for weeks on end. Trust me, we know. We had to do it more than once when we been out hunting."

I hadn't thought about how they'd gathered food, but it made sense that they'd have to hunt, I supposed. I had to admit they were a resourceful lot, and I respected Caspar for taking care of his charges without help.

I hated that I'd have to turn him in once we returned home, but I couldn't just leave them out here to fend for themselves.

"So, what? You're just letting us take it?"

"Yes," Eden told Brook. "It'll make it easier to travel at night. Safer to keep . . . her . . ." She looked at me and frowned, as if she hadn't considered what she was supposed to call me in front of anyone else.

"Layla," Brook offered, with a roll of her eyes as she glanced meaningfully at Eden, waiting for her to continue with her explanation.

Eden frowned at me. "To keep *Layla* here hidden."

I ignored the looks they exchanged and hoped Caspar hadn't noticed, as I turned my attention back to the VAN.

The vehicle was long—as long as three of any other vehicle I'd ever been in before, and it was painted no singular color but rather a mishmash of blues and reds and greens and browns, all smattered together like a slapdash collage. The tires were enormous as well, almost as tall as I was, and they seemed almost too large for the VAN itself.

It was hideous, but magnificent all the same.

As I rounded the VAN, I noted there were windows that ran all along both sides. Most of them still had glass, although some had been painted over and some were crusted with age-old dirt and grime. But there were other openings in the sides as well, small rectangles below the windows that had been cut all the way through the metal and were soldered around the edges.

I ran my finger around one of the welded gaps.

"For weapons. So you can fire without opening a window," Caspar explained from behind me.

I nodded. "Can we go inside?" I didn't even have to ask the question. Caspar was already opening the door to lead us in.

I wasn't sure what my trepidation was all about. I wasn't afraid, but I was most definitely awed. It was very much the way I'd felt when I'd first held Zafir's sword in my hand, like it was too powerful for me. Too much to handle.

The interior of the VAN was dark, and the oily scent of petroleum mixed with the smells of mold and stale dirt. Even without much light I could make out five rows of bench seats, paired two by two across a short aisle from each other. Each seat could hold two people—and perhaps three, if they squeezed together. After those five rows, there were metal shelves that were battened down to the floors and walls with large metal rivets. They were likely sturdier than they appeared. Beyond those there were three large steel barrels and some floor mats and blankets.

The inside was as colorful, and as daunting, as the outside.

Brook sat in a bucketlike chair at the very front of the VAN and ran her hand around the steering wheel. "Who'll drive it?"

Caspar clapped Eden on the shoulder. "Eden here can drive just about anything. She can fix about anything too." His chest puffed up with obvious pride. "Taught me everything she knows. Isn't that right, Sis?"

Eden glared at her little brother but didn't argue.

Brook eyed the control panel, all of the gauges and dials, her fingers hovering just above—but not touching—them. "Do you think I could learn to drive too?" she asked, sounding far more hopeful and childlike than she'd probably meant to.

I thought Eden would bark at her, tell her not to mess with anything and ridicule her for thinking she'd ever allow an amateur like Brook behind the wheel of such a formidable vehicle. Her mood was definitely impatient.

But something stopped her, and her answer wasn't at all what I'd anticipated. "We'll see," she answered instead, surprising both me and—from the way Brook's eyes widened eagerly—Brooklynn, too. "Not sure I want to risk my life. Let's just see how things work out."

Brooklynn practically squealed, a giddy sound that made me grin, and if it had been anyone but Eden—and if I hadn't been afraid she might push me or punch me or abandon me altogether—I might've hugged Eden for giving Brook that moment of glee.

Instead I turned to Caspar; I had more pressing matters on my mind. "How will we fuel it?"

Caspar marched to the rear of the transport and knocked on one of the disfigured steel drums. "There's enough fuel in here to get you across the country and back. Twice."

"Where'd you get it all?" I asked, impressed and a little uneasy that anyone had provisions like this. I wondered if my own army had this much fuel at its disposal.

"That was one of the perks of being a munitions camp. We were never short of fuel around here," he replied, winking at me.

He turned back to the drums again and pounded on the third one—one that looked identical to the other two. "This one's water. You'd be smart not to mix 'em up," he told us, then winked at me again.

The idea of drinking anything that came from one of those barrels made my stomach turn.

"We better get moving," Eden interrupted. "We have a lot to do before we go."

NIKO

"That bitch," Elena cursed, pacing once more to stand in front of the mantel. She stared into the empty fireplace, a space she'd been contemplating for the past hour, ever since hearing news of her sister's betrayal. "What could she hope to gain by freeing Xander? What good could she possibly expect to come from this . . . this escapade of hers?" Her fists clenched at her sides and she threw back her head, writhing as she struggled to maintain her composure, her fury getting the best of her. "I needed him. I *needed* him!" Her shrieks echoed into the yawning black space of the hearth.

Recoiling from her words, Niko tried to ignore the way they knotted around his gut. She was right, of course. Sage had derailed his plans by stealing away with Xander, and now they'd lost some of their leverage. Even if Charlaina came now, they might not be able to coerce her into making the transfer. They'd planned to use Xander as a bargaining chip if she balked.

And after all the time he'd spent convincing Elena how

simple it was, that all she had to do was say the words, and she could take Sabara—*Layla*—from Charlie.

But Charlie had to be willing to release the Essence, and there was no guarantee she would be.

There were still so many things that none of them knew about this process, since no girl had ever survived alongside Layla before. And now Layla and Charlie were so intertwined, so enmeshed in each other's psyches, he wondered if they even knew where one of them ended and the other began. Niko wasn't convinced Charlie would live when Layla was removed from her. Surely Charlie had considered this as well.

Not that it mattered, really. He had no intention of letting Charlie escape Astonia alive.

If only Charlie hadn't been so difficult, so headstrong. If only she'd been more willing to share that part of her that was still Layla with him, then he wouldn't have been here now. Plotting her demise.

"It'll be okay," Niko promised, joining Elena, running his hands over the cool skin of her arms in an effort to soothe her. He needed her cooperation. Losing her now would put an end to all of his carefully laid plans. He could feel her quiver beneath his fingertips, and he hoped that meant he hadn't lost her support. "Xander wasn't our only option. You know that as well as I. There are other ways to take down a queen. Ways that can be even more beneficial to your people. The peaceful way is less messy, but brute force can be more . . . persuasive. And just imagine it, my love; you'll be more powerful with two countries under your rule than one. You'll have more land, more resources. And when at last we capture

Charlaina, you'll be immortal, too." He pulled her around so they stood face-to-face, and he cupped her chin in his palm. He knew the effect his golden eyes had on her, the same effect they had on most women, and he watched as she succumbed to his molten stare. He settled his mouth over hers, claiming her in no uncertain terms. This body would be Layla's next host, he told himself, allowing himself to get lost in the taste of Elena.

And when he was sure he'd convinced her, both with his words and with his kisses, he pulled back.

She shuddered, collapsing forward against his chest, and he smiled, knowing he had her exactly where he wanted her. "So, it's time then," she affirmed—not a question, just a declaration of fact.

Niko nodded, and expertly untangled her fingers from his—like a master puppeteer. He raised them to his lips in a calculated kiss, reassuring her she was doing the right thing. "What choice do we have? It's time to stop playing around. Sometimes war is the only answer."

VIII

Even with all of us working together on separate tasks, Eden was right, it took us the rest of the day to get the bus prepared for our departure.

Eden stayed with Caspar and a group of kids he called "the mechanics" to work on getting the vehicle "shipshape," whatever that meant. There were a few minor repairs and one major one—something he called a transmission—that would require several parts to be salvaged from other vehicles they had lying around. Eden assured me it was a simple task, and that she'd have it completed by day's end.

Brook and I had been split up to gather food, much of which still had to be scavenged, or caught and prepared. Brook had gone to collect canned goods and to inventory supplies, while I'd asked to be assigned to a hunting party.

At first I'd thought the idea of hunting sounded like another new challenge—like fighting or riding. But I quickly learned that the animals we were up against, forest creatures that were agile and adept in their own environments, were evasive, and trying to capture them was like trying to capture smoke with your bare fingers.

It was an exhaustive game, and one I soon realized I failed at miserably.

The others, however—children much younger and smaller than me—seemed to understand things that I didn't, and watching them was as fascinating as watching an intricate dance with complicated steps I had yet to master. It was as if they'd been born with spears in their hands.

One of the girls who called herself Havana warned me to remain silent by pressing a dirt-caked finger to her mouth. She left me then, in the branches of one of the ancient trees that we'd climbed, as she whooped and hollered, creating a ruckus of her own. She threw herself downward, crashing loudly through the leaves and whipping them into a frenzy.

In the process she sent a family of ground rats scurrying across the forest floor and then set after them on bare feet that seemed to skim across the top of the ground without actually touching it.

I wasn't sure I'd ever seen such grace as she captured one after another, first with a snare she'd pulled from her ropelike belt, then another with a hand-carved spear, and yet another with a knife she chucked from at least twenty paces away.

She felled each one with the precision of a seasoned soldier.

I'd never realized hunting could be so exhilarating.

That is, until she signaled me to come down from my perch in the tree and taught me how to kill and skin the tiny beasts. That was when my breakfast of soft cheese and crusty bread started to come back up.

It wasn't the blood. Somehow she knew how to minimize the bloodshed. It was the smell as she peeled the pelt away from the stringy layers of muscle and fatty tissue beneath. I had to cover my mouth and nose to keep from retching.

I caught her giggling in my direction more than once. It was humiliating but enlightening. And at least I now knew how to hunt and kill, even if I might never be capable of putting that particular skill into practice.

By the time we'd had a chance to bundle our catch and clean up, Brook was just loading the last of the supplies onto the VAN.

Eden gave her brother one last reproachful glare. "You can still change your mind," she told him in what I could only assume was her idea of an invitation to join us.

Caspar didn't answer her. Instead he wiped the grease from his hands on the front of his pants and then threw his arms around his older sister. "Take care," he said in a voice that sounded like it might crack at any second. "And just so you know, I fully expect you to bring that beast back here in one piece."

Eden hugged him back, and grinned when she responded, "I assume you mean the VAN and not Brooklynn." And then she used the back of his shirt to wipe her own hands.

"Aw," he complained, shoving Eden—and her greasy hands—away from him. Then he considered her words and winked in Brook's direction. "Now that you mention it, I'll take either."

With that, we climbed inside and started the engine, filling the entire building with fat clouds of black smoke.

ARON

Aron threw the last of his belongings into his satchel and zipped it shut. He'd be glad to leave this place. Not that it didn't have its charms, what with its lack of running hot water and the shortage of privacy and all. But despite the lack of creature comforts, he'd been prepared to do his job and stay for the duration of the install, until the last of the communication equipment was up and running.

As it was, he'd be leaving with the job incomplete. All because of the message he'd received from Max.

Brook, Charlie, and Eden were missing.

No, not missing. They'd taken it upon themselves to go to Astonia to try to stop the war.

Brooklynn. How many nights had Aron lain awake thinking about her? How many times had he imagined going home to her?

Sure, she was rude and unpredictable, but damn the girl could kiss. And he'd never known anyone nearly as passionate. She loved and hated with equal intensity.

He just hoped he fell on the right side of that line.

The last thing he'd ever expected was that he'd have to abandon his duties to go in search of her. Not Brook. She was too tough and independent to need his help. Yet here he was, packing his bags and preparing to run after her.

The message that had come in over the communication device had been specific. He was to meet Max just outside the Left Harbor no later than nightfall tomorrow.

That didn't give him much time, especially in light of the fact that there were no trains running along the coast, and that he'd be traveling alone—another explicit message from Max. He was to tell no one of their plans, or what Charlie and the others had done.

They couldn't risk letting anyone know that the queen of Ludania had gone AWOL.

"Aron." He spun around to see one of the communication engineers he'd been assigned to share quarters with. His roommate wasn't much older than he was but had attended university with the other former counsel kids, and he had a way of making Aron feel inadequate because of his education and his upbringing. No one ever said so out loud, but Aron got the feeling they considered him the queen's lapdog.

"Yeah," Aron answered absently, tugging his satchel up and adjusting the straps.

"We got another message. Just a few moments ago."

Aron stopped what he was doing and raised his head. His roommate was watching him, and the graveness of his expression made Aron set his bag back down on his bed. "For me?"

"For everyone." That somberness permeated his voice. "It's bad. You should come to the communication depot."

Aron shook his head, his stomach plummeting. "Just tell me."

There was a moment before his roommate spoke, and in that moment Aron held his breath, imagining the worst—about Charlie, or Brooklynn. His heart ceased to beat as too many possibilities raced through his head.

But what he heard was worse. Much, much worse.

"Queen Elena's troops have been spotted nearing the border and will be crossing in a matter of hours." He paused, but only long enough to swallow. "She's declared war on Ludania."

Aron reached for his bag and ran for the door, more desperate than ever to reach the Left Harbor and Max. He'd be damned if he'd leave Brooklynn and Charlie out there on their own.

He had to find them before they ran right into an army of soldiers who'd like nothing more than to put Charlie's head on a spike and present it to their queen.

IX

"Look how far the lights extend." I pointed past Brook's shoulder as she and I hovered in the front of the VAN while it lurched over the uneven land. The light from the headlamps of the vehicle stretched into and past trees and boulders, penetrating every space it came in contact with, and even bounced back at us. The headlights turned the night into day, revealing a hostile landscape that looked like it could chew our VAN up and spit it out.

It had been years—more than I knew, really—since vehicles like this had been commonplace in Ludania. Paved roads, real ones, the kind with flat surfaces that were unmarred by pits and rocks, were rare. There were some, though, and a few were even maintained to keep them passable, mostly by cart, but also by the occasional, albeit rare, motorized vehicle.

Most roads, however, were broken and cracked. Weeds, shrubs, even groves of trees had overrun them. Many had been smashed into unrecognizable fragments of their former selves, and were often impassible even on horseback. But even those that hadn't been preserved were still used as trade routes, to demark the way from city to city, village to village. Along many of these forgotten thoroughfares, we could see the abandoned hulls of what had once been vehicles, long-since stripped of anything valuable. Time had corroded what had remained.

We stayed close to these trade routes, using the map Caspar had marked for us to show which roads were safe, and which were most treacherous.

I tried to imagine what it had been like centuries ago, before Sabara—with Ludania in its prime—when vehicles like these had been plentiful, and all of the roads running in every direction had been teeming with them, day and night. When technology had been on our side, and fuel had been plentiful.

For decades now trains had been our most dependable source of transportation, and now many of the rail lines were under repair after Xander's revolutionaries had destroyed them in his efforts to overthrow his grandmother.

Ludania was in sad shape.

"You know, it's hard to concentrate with the two of you breathing down my neck," Eden grumbled. Her point was emphasized when we hit yet another hole in the pocked ground and the VAN pitched, throwing both Brook and me backward into a pile on the gritty floor.

"Oomph," I gasped when Brook landed on top of me. She floundered, like she was having a hard time getting up, and I half-believed she was doing it on purpose, trying to get a rise out of me as she became an uncoordinated mass of elbows and knees—everything Brook wasn't.

I shoved her off me when she wasn't making enough progress on her own.

She laughed at my attempts to free myself. "You, Layla," she accused between giggles, "make a terrible cushion. It's like you were *trying* to be lumpy."

"Well, *you*," I shot back, deciding to play along with this more jovial Brooklynn, and grabbing a handrail to pull myself up, "are an even worse guard. Shouldn't you have tried to catch me or something?" I brushed the sand from my backside decisively.

Brook's eyebrow lifted as she started to say something more, but then Eden called out, "HOLE!" in warning.

Brook and I both reached for the rail just as one of the giant tires dropped into another of the craters in the ground and the VAN listed heavily to the side.

We both giggled now and clung to the bar. We refused to let go as Eden continued to shout out warnings. It became a game to us, seeing which of us could stay on our feet the longest.

Brook won, like she always did in feats of strength or agility, and eventually I had to call a truce when both my arm and my head were aching. I released the bar and wandered down the short aisle, then sank onto one of the thinly padded benches. I stared out ahead, still marveling at the panoramic view spread before us. From behind me Brooklynn began rummaging through crates that had been crammed together on the shelving to keep them from shifting.

The rocking motion of the VAN, which had at first been jarring, began to take on a rhythmic motion, lulling me as exhaustion took its toll. Sure, I'd slept, but not soundly, with Brook's bunk right at my back, and not nearly long enough, since Eden had woken us before the sun had risen.

My eyes had just started to drift close when I heard Brooklynn's voice, low and filled with awe. "Man, these kids have some serious firepower. Check out this Stinger, Charlie."

"Layla," Eden corrected from the front of the VAN, and I wondered how she'd even heard us above the rumble of the engine, which sounded like successive bomb detonations.

"Yeah, right . . . Layla. Check out this Stinger, *Layla*," Brook drawled, and I turned to see what had her so enthralled.

The Brook I'd grown up with had always enjoyed the finer points of femininity: wearing pretty dresses, impractical shoes with tall heels, dancing with boys, kissing.

The Brook I stared at now would most surely have preferred a switchblade to a high heel, or a grenade launcher to a party gown. I could tell as much when I saw her stroking the shiny carbon crossbow she held, with its sleek scope and fine-tipped arrow. It looked like it was fresh from the manufacturer, which it likely was, considering the work camp had been a munitions factory. Still, it was hard to imagine that these kids had access to so much firepower. As far as I'd known, only the military had access to items like these, not wards of work camps who'd been abandoned and forgotten. Sabara still had so many secrets I had yet to discover.

I jumped up from my seat, as fascinated by the firearm as Brook was. "Wow," I breathed, rubbing my fingertips over the smooth metal surface.

"You wanna hold it?" Brook handed the crossbow to me,

and I took it deftly, weighing and appraising its quality, and wishing we were out in the open so I could try it out. I lifted it so I could peer through the high-powered scope. "Maybe when we stop, I'll teach you to shoot," Brook told me, and my head jerked back in alarm.

I was suddenly aware that Brook had no idea what I could do with this thing. For all her portentous talk about there being no secrets in the palace, she had no idea I'd been training with Zafir all this time. All at once I couldn't wait for a "lesson" with Brooklynn. I wanted to show her what a quick learner I could be.

I grinned back at her. "That's the best idea I've heard all day," I answered, handing the crossbow back to her and trying to look a little clumsier as I did so.

She didn't seem to notice my sudden ineptitude as she turned her attention to Eden. "How'd you talk 'em into letting us take all this? It's like an arsenal back here."

Eden's reflection shot Brook an exasperated look from the mirror that hung above her. "You think my brother was going to send us out in the VAN unarmed? He's young. He's not stupid," she explained, as if Brook were both—young *and* stupid.

Brook shrugged. "Okay, so how is it that these kids still have all this stuff? And why hasn't anyone noticed and come to take it from them? These are military-grade weapons. None of this stuff is easy to come by. What if Queen Elena or some-one else discovers their little operation? Do you think she'll just leave them alone because they're a bunch of kids? They have no adult supervision. No protection."

"They don't need protecting—" Eden started to answer, but Brook stopped her, her eyes narrowing as if she'd just thought of something more.

"Come to think of it, how *are* they able to take care of themselves?" She held up her hand, interrupting Eden once again. "And don't say hunting. I saw how many of them there are. There's got to be more to it than catching some squirrels and fish." Her eyes went wide, as if a thought had come to her. "They're not . . . They wouldn't . . ." She pursed her lips then. "If you ask me, they haven't shut down entirely. I bet they're still doing some manufacturing over there. Maybe not on the same scale, of course, but I bet they're using whatever materials they have left to make weapons." Brook straightened her shoulders as she waited for Eden to meet her eyes in the mirror. "Eden, if those kids are selling weapons and you knew about it . . ." The implication in her words was clear.

Eden didn't respond to Brook's allegations, whether because she had no knowledge of what Brook was accusing Caspar and the others of, or because she was protecting her brother's secrets, I didn't know. Eden looked away from Brook, and her stare became transfixed, as did all of ours, out the window in front of us. The VAN became silent except for the rumble of the engine, as we all watched the land flatten and lengthen, the ground leveling out until it looked like something that might never end. We could see forever from where we sat, but the scenery never seemed to change. It felt as if we were stuck in one place. As if the ground beneath us were moving but we remained in one place.

Only when the tires on Eden's side fell into a rut, and she

had to swerve to maneuver out of it, were we reminded that we were still forging ahead.

"Fine," Brook relented, as if the VAN's sudden lurch were Eden's response. "No questions about the supplies. So what about Caspar, then? Can I ask about him?"

Eden's black expression eased a little as she scowled less from the mirror, which Brooklynn took as permission to go ahead.

"What happened? I mean, to your parents? How did the two of you end up in that place?"

It wasn't what Eden had expected, and her scowl returned, as sour as ever. "They died."

"And you didn't have relatives?"

"Nope."

"No family friends who would take you in?"

The muscle in the side of Eden's jaw jumped, the only visible sign she was even bothered. "Not both of us," she answered.

"How old were you?"

I found myself straining forward on my seat as Brook's questions became my own. The only difference was that she was brave enough to voice them aloud.

"Twelve," Eden replied.

Brook was relentless, undeterred by Eden's abrupt responses. "So Caspar was . . ."

I saw Eden's eyes flick back once in the reflection, but only once. "Was what?" she asked, being intentionally obtuse.

"You know exactly what I'm asking. How old was *he*?"

"Five."

I flinched as if Eden had shot me with the crossbow, the

arrow finding my heart. I thought of Angelina. I couldn't help myself. At five years old she was so little, so innocent. The idea of her in a place like that, especially the way it had been when the chief had been in charge . . . I couldn't fathom it.

"Ouch," Brook stated flatly, her thoughts likely similar to my own.

"We were fine. We had each other." Eden sounded so convinced, so sure of herself, that I almost believed her.

Then Brook said the words that skewered that belief, deflating my confidence in Eden's avowals. "But you left him. Why'd you do that?"

That was when my entire world started to spin. Not literally, but very nearly. The VAN tilted one way, and then the other, and even though I wasn't sure what was happening, I knew enough to hang on for dear life. I clutched the seat back in front of me, just before my chin clipped it as I was tossed forward.

Brook wasn't as lucky. She didn't find anything she could grip fast enough. She fell, and landed like lead against the floorboards, slamming into them face-first.

It all happened so quickly—the unexpected careening, the rocking back and forth. I found myself fighting with gravity, which sucked and pulled at my body, trying to move me all at once to the front of the VAN. While behind and all around me I heard items falling off the shelves and rattling along the floor.

And then just as quickly everything moved in the opposite direction, and I was abruptly pinned against the back of my seat. My head flew back and smacked the bench behind me.

When it all stopped—when the VAN had finally come to a full and complete stop—and everything was still and silent at last, I lifted my head to assess our situation.

Supplies littered the aisle, and dust hung in the air.

Brook didn't seem nearly as confused as I felt, and she shot up from the floor, looking like a hornet, ready to sting. "Why'd you do that?" she accused, and still I had trouble discerning why she was so angry. "Why on earth would you do that?" she demanded as she strode furiously toward Eden.

Eden sprang up too.

My mind was as cluttered as the VAN now, and the dawning that Eden had done this on purpose, by slamming on the brakes, came entirely too slowly.

But Eden didn't back down when Brooklynn confronted her. She approached Brook with just as much will, and I could feel my hackles rising as the situation escalated.

"You have no business questioning my motives," Eden barked in Brooklynn's face. "You know nothing of our lives before Xander. Nothing about what I had to give up to join his rebellion. Or even why I did it."

"I know I wouldn't have left that little boy—"

Without warning Eden swung at Brook. I reacted too, jumping out of my seat and hurtling toward them, not sure what my plan was but knowing that nothing good could come from the two of them coming to blows.

"Stop!" I shouted, but I was too late. Eden's fist found its target, crashing hard into Brook's jaw.

Brook staggered backward, momentarily dazed by the blow. But it lasted only a moment, and Brook came back up almost as fast as she'd gone down. Before I could shout again, she was launching herself at Eden.

I'd seen Brook fight one other time, the day she and Xander's troops had stormed the palace. The day Sabara's Essence had fused into me.

But that day I'd been too weak, and too concerned with other matters, to realize how capable Brook was. My parents and Aron had both been taken hostage and tortured by Sabara. And I'd been concerned about my sister, whom Sabara would just as willingly have taken if I hadn't said the words first, sparing Angelina.

I knew Brook could wield weapons and strategize with the best of them. Otherwise I'd never have made her the commander of my armed forces. But with her unarmed, I half-expected Eden to lay Brook flat after a couple of well-placed blows. Turns out, I'd underestimated Brook's ability to defend herself hand to hand.

They were well matched, these two women. Too well matched for my liking, and I watched as Brook landed a solid punch to the lower right side of Eden's back, making her double over and wince in agony. And just when I thought Brook had the upper hand and Eden might back down, Eden turned, still huddled over, and launched a kick straight at Brook's chest, sending her staggering back once more.

I turned on my heel and rushed toward the rear of the VAN, deciding I couldn't let this go on or someone would end up buried in the rocky soil before we reached the border. I was irritated enough by their childish behavior that when my finger stroked the trigger, I barely had to swallow back a sliver of guilt over what I had to do.

When I released the safety, both of their heads snapped up,

as if they'd been conditioned to identify the sound of deadly arms and react to it.

"You wouldn't." Eden's eyes narrowed as they focused on the crossbow I held, directed at the two of them.

But Brooklynn didn't look nearly as certain, and she backed away, disentangling herself from Eden, her hands slowly lifting. "Charlie," she intoned warningly. "That's not a toy."

"I know exactly what it is and how to use it," I told her, and I watched as recognition registered in her expression. I wondered if it was something in my eye, or the fact that I'd armed it myself and I held it straight and true. "Looks like I won't be needing that lesson after all." I took in the scratches on her cheek, and the swelling that was already starting along her jaw.

I glanced at Eden, too. The skin around her left eye was inflamed and pink, and would probably be a deep shade of purple by morning. My fear now was that it would swell, making it hard for her to see while she drove us, and that worry pricked my ire toward the both of them.

"Get up!" I insisted, waving the point of the arrow from one to the other irritably. "You've had your fun. Now get up and clean this mess. I'm tired and we don't have time to waste on your childishness. The two of you *will* get along, or so help me . . ." If stomping my foot would have punctuated my words, I would have done so. But I worried that I would sound childish, so I stopped myself in time.

"Or what? You'll . . . shoot us?" Brook finished, daring to mock me. "Fine. You're right. We shouldn't be fighting. But let's be honest. You're not shooting anyone, Charlie . . . or Layla . . . or whoever you are. Put that thing away. We'll be good." She glanced at her cohort in this fiasco and held out her hand in truce. "Won't we, Eden?"

Eden glared back at her but then turned to me. I must've looked serious, because she sighed when she took Brooklynn's hand. From where I stood she seemed to squeeze a little too hard, but I was past caring now. All that mattered to me was that the fight was over.

I uncocked the string and lowered the crossbow, feeling moderately satisfied that they wouldn't attack each other again. At least not now.

It took them nearly an hour to undo the mess they'd caused in less than five minutes, and another two hours of driving in terse silence before anyone bothered to speak again.

Brook had settled down in back, on one of the mats where we'd be sleeping. She sullenly stayed as far from Eden as she could, despite the "truce" she'd called for my benefit. I suspected they were both nursing some pretty tender injuries that neither of them would ever admit to, both too stubborn to confess that the other might have bested them.

When I thought Brooklynn had finally dozed off, I dared to ask the one question I couldn't stop thinking about, despite knowing that asking it would probably reopen painful wounds. "Do you ever miss him?" I asked as quietly as I could, and hoped Eden could hear me above the engine.

She was quiet too for a moment, but then she glanced at me in the rearview mirror. "Don't you miss Angelina?" she asked, before turning her attention back to the ramshackle road.

It was all the answer I needed.

And suddenly I understood why Eden had hit Brook. She wasn't mad at Brooklynn for asking all those questions. She was mad at herself . . .

For leaving her little brother all those years ago.

I wasn't sure when I'd actually fallen asleep, or even when I'd lain down on one of the sleeping mats, but the confusion I felt upon waking lasted only a few moments before I rolled over and found myself staring directly into Brooklynn's face. Her mouth was wide, and her breaths were long and deep. She was snoring, which was likely what had awakened me in the first place.

When I turned away from her, I realized that I'd somehow managed to sandwich myself between her and one of the VAN walls. The space I was lying in, like the bedroll wrapped around me, was narrow and cramped. And the floor beneath the lightweight mat was firm, making my back throb.

Trying not to disturb Brook, who continued to snore in complete ignorance of the less-than-comfortable sleeping arrangements, I wriggled out of the makeshift bed and went in search of Eden. Like the morning before, she appeared to have abandoned us. Something she seemed to be skilled at, I was learning.

But I knew she hadn't gone far. The VAN door was ajar, and even from inside the vehicle, I could smell the smoky scent of a campfire.

"Coffee?" I heard her ask as I saw her reaching for the pot before I'd descended the steps across from the driver's seat.

I nodded and grabbed one of the tin mugs she'd already set out for each of us. "Should we be worried about the fire? That someone might notice us here?" I asked as she filled my mug all the way to the top, and when I took my first sip, I recognized the flavor. It was the same caustic blend Caspar had shared with us the day before, only this time my taste buds rejoiced.

Eden just shook her head before setting the pot near the edge of the flames. "Not anyone we should be concerned about. I veered far enough from the main thoroughfare to give us a chance to rest."

"Did you? Rest, I mean?" I looked her over, noting the fact that I hadn't seen a mat for her in the back of the VAN, where Brook and I had slept.

I hadn't been wrong, either, when I'd guessed that her eye would be swollen this morning, but it wasn't as bad as I'd thought it might be. It was bruised and engorged, but she could still open it, which meant she could still see through it. A favorable attribute in someone operating your vehicle, I thought wryly.

"I slept out here," she answered. "Nice to listen to the waves."

"Waves . . ." I started to ask but then glanced around. I didn't know what Eden meant at first, but then I heard it.

It was far-off, the whooshing sound that came and went, first long and insistent, then fading away, only to return again . . . unrelenting.

Something from Sabara's memory—not mine—pricked at me, something I hadn't noticed before. It was the air. It was crisp, which wasn't such a strange thing for the time of year, but the breeze carried a tang that stung my nose.

The sea, Sabara whispered, waking within me. There was something hopeful in her spirit.

"The sea," I whispered aloud, tasting the words, and the salt in the air, on my tongue.

Eden had no idea it was a dead queen with whom I conversed, and she answered my musing. "Just beyond the bluff. We've reached the southwest tip of Ludania, and will start moving east toward Astonia. We took only a slight detour—couple of hours at the most. If we're lucky, we'll be able to slip over the border without being noticed."

I looked where Eden had indicated, but for as far as I could see, all I could make out was pale sand and reedy grass that stretched all the way to the rocky walls ahead of us. Yet, still I heard it.

Whoosh . . . whoosh . . . whoosh . . .

Never-ending.

"Do we have time? Can I go see it?"

Eden's brow lowered, the purple streaks of her hair caught in the morning sun and making her look more severe than ever. "The sea?" she probed. "Have you never . . ." I had once, but she didn't finish her sentence, just nodded resolutely and set her mug on one of the flat-sided rocks that surrounded the fire. "I'll come with you. To be certain you're safe."

"Should we wake Brook?" I asked, suddenly eager to see what had managed to incite Sabara. She was anticipating some wondrous thing that I now anticipated too.

Waving off the suggestion of waking Brooklynn, Eden

started walking in the direction of the whooshing sound, her boots cutting a path through the sticklike grass. The sound grew louder and more insistent, and seemed to be coming from all around us as we climbed higher rather than lower.

When we reached the edge of the plain, where we had to mount several rocky steps onto the bluff, the view before me took on a dramatic transformation.

Suddenly it wasn't just grass and sand, or even rocky outcroppings, in our line of sight. It was water. For as far as I could see, there was water. Not stagnant like that of a pond or a lake. And not meandering, cutting a path through the land, the way a river did. Not even like the sliver of a sea I'd seen once before, an ice-crusted inlet we'd had to cross by ferry on our way to the summit in Vannova.

No, this water was undulating. It rolled and swelled and rippled like a living, breathing entity that kissed the horizon and disappeared into eternity.

Birds with feathers that ranged from the color of downy snow to the deep sooty gray of smoke screeched overhead, circling and dipping as they rode the wind that seemed as ceaseless as the surging waves. My hair whipped and stung my cheeks, making them tingle almost us much as my impatience.

"This way," Eden insisted, leading me away from where we stood overlooking the water from too high up at the cliff's edge. If we miscalculated our steps from here, the drop to the jagged rocks awaiting us below would be perilous. Farther along the bluff Eden had spotted a way down where the water met the sand. "Watch your step," she cautioned again and again, the way I would if I were leading Angelina.

The route we took was not nearly as hazardous as I'd first thought, and as we moved, I realized the grass that had tried to grow here had been trampled, as if the route had been used recurrently. A path to the sea.

The smell grew harsher, and Sabara's memories told me that this was the flavor of sea salt, permeating everything, not just the water but the wind and sand as well. Even my lips when I licked them tasted of salt.

I was breathless when we reached the bottom, and my feet dropped from the firm rocks of the path into the soft sand, sinking almost to my ankles. Above us the jagged cliffs loomed, watching us with their rigid intensity.

I shot Eden a questioning glance, begging for permission to chase after the shifting waves. I was mesmerized by them. I watched with enthusiastic eyes as they rolled in, tumbling over themselves and lapping the shore. They smoothed the sand, compacting it and making it glisten. And then they were sucked away once more, waning into the next one that approached.

Inside me I overheard Sabara's musings. *You'll never know anything as powerful as the sea, Charlaina. Not even I have that kind of strength. It is truly undying.*

I knew she was right. The sea—this great and captivating sea—had been here long before Sabara had taken her first breath, and it would be here still, long after her Essence had sputtered out, dying at long, long last.

And me, I wanted to feel it beneath my feet, between my toes. I wanted it lapping at my shins and splashing at my knees.

Eden showed me a wry smile, an affirmation of my greatest desires, and I set loose, shucking my shoes from my feet as I raced toward the water. The sand slowed my steps, but I persisted, my gales of laughter getting lost on the chilly wind that slapped at my cheeks.

I stepped gingerly onto the wet sand, pulling the hems of my pants up so they passed my knees as I hesitantly approached the surf. The froth-tipped waves swept toward me, and I jumped back, afraid of what they might do. How they might feel.

Go. Go, Charlaina, go, Sabara urged, a siren's chant.

And I went, doing as she decreed.

My toes slipped beneath first, the frigid waters making me gasp. And then delight sang through my veins as I answered the summons of the sea. When I felt the pulsating ocean around my ankles, I turned back to see Eden, her arms crossed in front of her. She was the eternal sentinel.

I waved, hoping to crack her stoic expression. But she remained straight-faced and unflinching, until the water lured my attention once more by crashing against my knees.

I giggled with delight. Then I splashed the ocean whenever it splashed me. I dashed toward the retreating waves as they withdrew back into the sea, and ran again when they came racing toward me. They were faster, always faster than I was, and invariably I was caught by them, until it didn't matter that I'd tried to protect my clothing, to keep it dry. I was wet, from my hair to my toes.

When I heard Brooklynn's voice calling to us from above the constant wind and the ceaseless whooshing of the waves,

I ran across the sand to where she navigated down the path to the shore, where Eden stood watch.

"Brook! Come on," I cried, not glancing at Eden now, knowing she wouldn't give up her post even if I invited her. "It's magnificent, the sea. You have to try it!"

Brook looked at me dubiously, and then at the surf beyond. I used the tips of my fingers to pry salty strands of hair from my mouth, and used the backs of my hands to wipe sand from both my cheeks.

"I don't know," she said mistrustfully as I dragged her toward the awaiting water. "It doesn't look safe. In fact, it looks positively unsafe, if you ask me."

"Well, it isn't," I assured her. "Now, take your boots off. Trust me."

It wasn't my speech that convinced her. I knew because I'd never been capable of such a feat. It was her curiosity that won in the end, and by the time I'd let go of her hand and was jumping into the next incoming wave, Brooklynn had shed her boots and was right behind me.

She didn't jump at first, but she met the challenge of the oncoming surf with as much zeal as I did. And after just a few experimental minutes of wading and retreating, Brook was chasing me into the breaking waves, splashing me the way I'd splashed her.

When at last we emerged, we were both shrieking and laughing, and soaked in water that made our clothing itch and stick to us like a second layer of salt-laced skin. Sand clung to our legs, which were bare to our knees, as we trudged back to Eden with our shoes in hand.

"Finished?" was all Eden asked as she surveyed each of us in turn.

Even wet, Brook managed to look alluring, her damp curls framing her perfectly flushed face, while I was sure my hair looked like damp sea grass and only highlighted the fact that my lips had turned a glacial shade of blue. I shivered as another gust of wind blasted along the coastline.

"Y-y-yes." I bit my lip to keep my teeth from chattering, and tasted the salt that clung to it.

As we trailed Eden up the path, Brook nudged me. "You killed my father," she said, her voice low so there was no way Eden could hear us above the sound of the waves.

I stopped where I was, stunned by her statement, and by the lack of rancor or accusation hidden behind her words. She wasn't sullen, and she wasn't avoiding the topic any longer.

I wrapped my arms around myself, bracing myself against the chill of the wind that beat at us. "I know, and I'm so sorry." I bit out each word slowly, almost cautiously, as if I might scare her away again, and I was so terribly afraid we might never get back to where we'd once been if I did.

Eden was no longer climbing, and stood watching us impatiently. I held up a finger, letting her know we'd be right there.

"I know you are," she admitted, the hint of a smile pricking her lips. "You've said so at least a hundred times." She shrugged, and then sighed a deep and liberating sigh. "I suppose I just wasn't ready to hear it back then." The smile fell away, becoming something less playful and more reflective. She reached out to me, this time holding her hand out like when we were little girls and we held hands everywhere we went, running and skipping and hopping through rain-filled puddles. "I am now, though."

I clasped her hand, squeezing it as tight as I could manage. And then I whispered, "I really am, you know. I'm so very, very sorry, Brooklynn. I never meant to hurt you."

She squeezed back until my knuckles ached and my eyes burned. "I know. And the truth is, I'm glad he's dead. It just took me a while to figure it out."

She pulled me toward her, so our shoulders bumped together, and we started walking again. Hand in hand.

Just like when we were children.

As grateful as I was that Brook and I had mended the rift between us, all I could think about on our way back was the campfire we'd burn when we returned to the VAN. I was chilled all the way through, and even though we couldn't afford to waste any of our drinking water to bathe away the brininess from my skin, I'd at least be able to change into dry clothing.

But when we reached the top of the cliff, it wasn't the VAN or the smoke still drifting up from the smoldering remnants of our fire that caught my attention. It was the people gathered there.

They converged around our vehicle, and I stopped walking, trying to make sense of their presence. To discern what they were doing there exactly.

I watched as a woman came out of the VAN, picking her way down the steps carrying a crate in her arms. I recognized the box as one that was filled with jars of pickled vegetables, and realized that these people were helping themselves to our provisions.

They were stealing our food—our supplies.

My first thought was to stop them, and before I could tell myself otherwise, I was lifting my hand. Already I could feel the tingling in the tips of my fingers. I knew why, of course. I meant to put an end to their looting.

I hadn't considered using Sabara's ability since the night I'd used it to keep Brooklynn's father and his men from taking Angelina, when I'd feared for what they might do to her. I had used it then, killing them all by squeezing their throats closed from the inside out.

The second I summoned her power, I knew I'd made a mistake. Sabara slipped out of the shadows and began taking control of me. Darkness cloaked me, like a heavy curtain, blotting out all reason. Blotting me out.

No, I insisted, *you can't do this*. But already my vision grew black.

"Charl—*Layla!*" Brooklynn smacked my arm down and shoved me aside. "We've got this! You stay put."

I blinked several times, dazed by Brook's actions and her warning. Slowly, however, my judgment returned and Sabara slunk away once more. I wondered how much longer I could keep her at bay. How long I could pretend she wasn't wearing me down.

I stared at my hands, unable to believe I'd been willing to do something so horrific, hardly able to believe I'd been capable of drawing the ability forth in the first place. I'd always believed Sabara had lent me her power when I'd needed it.

Now I wondered if I couldn't summon it at will, a thought that revolted me, convincing me further that the two of us were far too enmeshed.

I turned to see Eden drawing a weapon from the back of her waistband—a small-caliber handgun I hadn't been aware she'd had with her. And when I glanced to Brook, her hand had disappeared into one of the boots she carried, and reemerged wrapped around the handle of a curved knife with sharp, serrated teeth.

Eden called out to the foragers, "Put it back—all of it—and no one gets hurt!"

The woman with the crate froze, her eyes finding us, and then searching out the others who were rummaging around our campsite. I wondered if she were calculating their odds.

I tried to imagine what we must look like, three women out here on our own in the middle of nowhere, with a vehicle chock-full of supplies. Then I really considered who I was traveling with, and how we appeared.

Eden, with her shorn purple hair and muscled arms, was menacing on a good day. But today, after her skirmish with Brooklynn, she was donning a shiner of a black eye that only served to make her more intimidating than ever. And Brooklynn might be pretty, but she wore an air of confidence about her, especially when, like now, her shoulders were squared and her jaw was set. Her own bruises and bedraggled hair only served to emphasize the fact that she wasn't afraid to get her hands dirty.

Me? I had no idea how I appeared. Certainly less daunting than the other two, but looks could be deceiving. I was determined to make it across the border. To get to Elena, to discover the meaning of her message, and to attempt to keep my country at peace. I'd do anything to make that happen.

Besides, I told myself, *I'd survived Sabara. I could certainly survive some local scavengers.*

If I'd had to lay odds right then, my money would have been on the three of us.

"*We don't want no trouble,*" the woman said in strangely punctuated Parshon, her southern Ludanian accent giving it a lilting sound. She bent slowly at the waist to set the crate on the ground at her feet. When she rose again, she kept her hands in front of her. "*Din't know there was someone laid claim to this stuff already.*"

I shot a meaningful glance at the embers of the barely dead fire and doubted the veracity of her statement.

"We don't want trouble either," Brook chimed in, speaking in Englaise. She didn't bother to hide her blade as she approached the strangers. Her feet were bare, but her confidence was in full force. Both Eden and I were right at her back. "But this 'stuff,'" she added bitingly, "is most definitely ours."

As we neared, it became clearer who we were up against, and suddenly my belief that we would come out of this unscathed spiked.

They were kids, mostly. But not like the ones we'd just left behind with Caspar at the abandoned work camp. These kids seemed scrawnier and less organized. The longer I studied them, the more certain I was that the woman who'd spoken was their mother. They all bore hair that was the same honeyed shade of auburn, and their eyes were all varying shades of green—moss, jade, emerald, and even one pair that reminded me of the sea I had just been in.

Two of them, a girl and a boy, both of whom had freckles peppered across their noses, wore clothing fashioned from identical fabric, with perfectly sewn stitches. Since the mother had spoken in Parshon—the vendor's tongue—I wondered if she was a seamstress by trade.

The boy, who'd been poking a stick into the remnants of the fire, dropped it when his jade eyes settled on Brook's knife. He raised his hands in the air, so high it was nearly comical.

The mother whacked him on the backside. *"Drop your hands,"* she muttered, speaking again in Parshon. And then to us, in Englaise, she tossed back, "Honestly, we want no trouble at all. We'll be on our way now." As if reading the knowing look she cast their way, the children—four of them in all, ranging in age from about five or six years to somewhere around ten or eleven—gathered around her, making her look very much like a mother duck gathering her brood of ducklings.

The idea of mistaking them as dangerous thieves now seemed absurd.

Brook sheathed her knife and replaced it in her boot.

The girl who was the smallest of the children and part of the matched set with her brother tugged at the woman's skirt. "But, Mama, I'm hungry. And it's so far."

I hadn't even had the chance to respond when Eden turned to scowl at me, already shaking her head as if she'd read my thoughts. "No, Your Maje—" She lowered her voice. "No way," she amended from between gritted teeth. "They're thieves," she insisted. "We can't. We won't."

But I was already shoving my way past her, my mind made up. "They're children, Eden." And then I told the woman, "We have more than enough. Stay and eat with us before you go." I couldn't imagine casting them off without at least feeding them first. I smiled at the little girl, who peeked at me from behind her mother's back.

Eden sighed, her exasperation as loud as the wind.

"No, no. We couldn't," the woman said, but the little boy, his eyes still wide and transfixed on Brooklynn, despite the fact that she no longer held her knife, quietly pleaded, "Please. Just a little . . ."

That was it for Brook, and she too came over to my side of the argument, proving she indeed had a heart. "Really," she asserted, although a little less adamantly than I had. "It's okay. We have plenty."

The woman's shoulders sagged as she looked around at her ginger-haired brood, all of them watching her eagerly for a sign of consent. Then she nodded, turning to meet my eyes as she reached out to pat the boy's head. "Thank you," she told me.

The children ate voraciously, finishing a first round of salted squirrel and sliced cheese, and then asking for more. We sliced fresh fruit, which they devoured just as ravenously, letting the juices run down their chins and slurping it from their fingers. But even after that they weren't satisfied, so I pulled out a loaf of bread and we warmed it in front of the fire before drizzling it with honey.

While they ate, I quizzed their mother. Her name was Deirdre, and I learned as much as I could about the fishing village they'd come from. She told us how she used to make the finest fishing nets for miles around, and that their village had prospered. Trade had kept them all fed and full and clothed and housed.

Now, however, Deirdre and her younger children were forced to fend for themselves while her husband and her oldest daughter—like most of the other capable men and women from their village—had gone off to volunteer in the militia.

"Militia?" I asked, not sure I fully understood.

Deirdre just nodded. "Locals willing to fight for our country but not wanting—or able—to join the military. Either too old or too young, or not fit enough to be in the armies. Most of our villagers decided to join the militia so they could stay together, rather than being divided and sent to the far reaches of the country. Last we heard, the queen's army was gathering every militia to meet near the Astonian border. Talk is, war isn't so far off."

Guilt knotted my stomach, so I only listened while everyone else ate.

I wondered how many other families were in similar situations. How many other mothers were off scavenging for food, trying to make ends meet for their children while they awaited word of the war. Waited to find out if their loved ones would even return home alive.

"I feel sick." The little girl called Meg rubbed her hand over her protruding belly to emphasize her point.

Brook grinned back at her. "Well, you should. You just ate an entire week's worth of rations. At that rate you'll grow up to be a big, strong soldier like your sister." She tousled the girl's hair. "Too bad we've got to get going, or I'd teach you a few moves myself."

Meg's eyes brightened. "You think I could be like you someday?"

Eden scoffed at the notion. "You don't want to be like her. Look at her. She's not so tough." Her lips curled in wry amusement as she indicated the bruises on Brook's face.

The littlest boy wrinkled his nose. "Then you must not be tough either," he said, ogling Eden's black and swollen eye.

Eden directed her gaze at the boy, glaring as sternly as she could until the boy blinked and glanced away. Then she nodded, as if satisfied in her ability to intimidate.

I made a clucking sound in her direction, letting her know I didn't think she was very impressive, terrifying a little boy and all.

"How far is your village?" I asked, turning my attention back to Deirdre when I didn't get the appropriately contrite response I'd hoped for from Eden.

"Not so far." I caught her shooting one of the older two boys a warning look when it seemed as if he might dispute her statement. "Just past the next harbor." She pointed vaguely along the coastline.

Perplexed by her explanation, I frowned and turned for clarification to the boy she'd prematurely silenced. "And how far would that be?"

The boy looked sheepish and avoided his mother's eyes

when he answered, "Almost a day's walk." He admitted, before she had the chance to stop him, "It's hard on the little ones."

Concurring, Meg nodded vigorously. "It's true. It's awful far."

Again Eden sighed, reading my thoughts before I could even give voice to them.

I tried to reason with her. "It's on our way, Eden," I said under my breath. Deirdre had been pointing southward. Eden could hardly argue. According to Caspar's maps, we had to go south before heading east toward the Astonian border. "Besides, we have more than enough room."

In the end I won and we piled Deirdre and her four children into the VAN. Eden drove sullenly, while I felt downright pious about the decision, especially as the wind died down and the fog churned up from the sea, making the ground difficult to see, and nearly impossible to navigate. Because of the poor visibility, it took us more time than it should have to locate the highway so we could follow it.

To the children the VAN was an adventure. They bounced exaggeratedly up and down in their seats, and traded places every few minutes and pointed out the windows. They chattered among themselves, while Deirdre showed us landmarks along the way. She gave names to the cliffs and the plains, and even the road we traveled, which was in such a state of disrepair that for the most part we drove alongside it, using it only as a guide to mark our route.

The Coastal Highway, she called it, and I had a hard time imagining it had ever been anything but the pitiful mass of crumbling concrete it was now.

Her village, she told us, was formerly 116Southeast but now was called Graylond, and they'd held a huge party to christen it as such.

"That was the day before my husband and my Erin left," she explained. "So we stayed up all night, drinking and dancing around the bonfire, and I pretended it was because our city had a new name. But really it was so I could be with them as long as possible." She looked down at her hands, which were folded and motionless on her lap. "I hope they come home soon. I hope the new queen knows what she's doing, and that all this talk of war is just that. Talk."

I nodded. I hoped everything she did, and more. I couldn't tell her I was doing my best. That I was willing to sacrifice everything—including myself—to bring her family home, so I merely nodded.

"That's it," she said, pointing through the thick layer of fog to a knot of homes that seemed to be built right over the water's edge.

It was almost too silent to be called a village, with none of the bustle or activity I would have expected.

"Where is everyone?"

"Most families were forced to leave after the militia came through looking for recruits. No way to support themselves. The few fishermen we have left—those too old or too young to fight—are probably still out trying to fill their nets. Sometimes they don't come home for days."

The VAN's headlamps barely penetrated the dense mist that grew heavier, clinging to everything like the salt from the sea. As we approached, the few villagers who remained came out from their homes to get a look at our unusual vehicle. They followed us through the narrow streets until we stopped in front of the home Deirdre pointed out to us. I understood the curious expressions on the villagers' faces. It was the same mixture of fascination and awe I'd felt when Caspar had first showed the VAN to us. The vehicle was rare and impressive and atrocious, all at once.

"Come inside," Deirdre told us. "Let me repay your kindness. I don't have much, but we do have fish and a warm fire." She smiled, ushering her children through the doorway. "Glen," she said to one of the older boys with sparkling moss-colored eyes, "start a fire for our guests."

Eden didn't bother arguing this time, and I didn't bother listing the reasons we should accept their hospitality, particularly since I was neither hungry nor cold. My reasons for wanting to stay had more to do with the roiling in my stomach that seemed to grow stronger the closer we drew to the border. To Elena.

To my fate.

SAGE

Sage dragged Xander from his mount and smacked the animal on its hindquarters, sending it loping toward the hills, in the same direction her horse had just gone. She doubted they'd ever see the beasts again. But for now all that mattered was that there was no chance the horses could draw unwanted attention to where she and Xander were hiding.

She crouched low in the bushes, helping Xander settle back against a boulder. When he winced, a soft groan escaping his lips, she dropped so her face was level with his. "You have to be quiet now," she coaxed. "No sound. Do you understand?"

Xander's skin was an unhealthy pallor, pasty and gray, and slick with sweat. His eyes were glazed with fever, but he nodded nonetheless. He understood.

"Good. Now let me take a look at that."

She needed a distraction, something to preoccupy her restless thoughts, and Xander's wounds were as good a diversion as any. She didn't want to spend too much time thinking about the other thing, the reason they'd just had to cut their horses loose.

Or what their next step would be if they somehow managed to get through this unnoticed.

She reached for his bandage and unwrapped layer after layer of the dirty gauze that she'd already replaced once. She tried not to breathe the foul odor that made her eyes water and her nose burn. The fact that the dressing was soaked through with infection and had to be peeled from the rotting wound was a bad sign.

The fever was a worse one.

Yet, even one-handed and febrile, Xander had managed to ride his horse once they'd discarded their vehicle to cross into Ludania. She'd hardly heard a complaint from him, except for the occasional moan or involuntary whimper.

No wonder Elena had been so afraid to release him.

Xander had the heart of a champion. And he had no intention of letting Elena stop him.

"Where are they?" He grimaced, and she wondered if he was talking only to take his mind off the antiseptic she poured over his wound. The shoddy row of uneven sutures where the prison doctor had attempted to stitch him up was raw and inflamed, and still oozing.

Her eyes shot up to his, wide and filled with concern for his welfare. She would have asked if it hurt, or if her ministrations were too clumsy, but she knew his answers. He'd lie even if the answers were yes. "When I was at the top of the hill, I could see them approaching." Her expression was grave as she repeated what she'd seen. "There were thousands of them. I'd say the first wave of troops to cross. But there are probably thousands more behind them, spreading into your country like a plague. I imagine they're crossing at every point—from east to west, and will move north, burning everything in their path." She glanced back down at his arm, going back to work on it. She began wrapping the fresh strip of gauze around the stump where his hand used to be.

"And what about us?"

She stopped. "We're not far ahead of them, Xander. We have less than an hour till the entire battalion could be upon us. Our best hope is that they don't come this far into the hills. That they stay on flatter ground and continue marching north. There's not much up here, and as long as they don't suspect we're here . . ." She trailed off.

"There's no reason they would," he finished, and she nodded, putting the finishing touches on his dressing.

"There," she said, and sat back on her heels.

He watched her for several long moments. His glassy eyes were anything but fatigued. Finally he asked what was really on his mind. "Can you tell where she is now?"

Sage understood the question well enough. He was asking her to use her ability, something she'd been doing since they'd crossed into Ludania.

He was asking her to use her tracking skills.

She closed her eyes, concentrating . . .

Concentrating . . .

Trying to pull an image of the Queen of Ludania from her mind, to find her—and only her—in a country filled with millions of people.

When she opened her eyes again, eyes that were completely

and totally white, and completely and totally sightless, she declared, "She's close. She's very, very close."

And then she blinked, her vision swimming back into focus while she saw Xander leaning forward, watching her intently. She frowned as she realized what exactly she'd just seen in her vision, and where Charlaina was.

"The army," she said ominously, reaching for Xander's only hand. "They're almost upon her."

X

It was well after midnight when we finally departed Graylond. The feeling that we were safer traveling under the cover of darkness was likely an illusion, but it was an illusion I clung to. It made me feel better to think that we were as invisible as the world around us.

I'd wrapped myself tightly in my shawl as we'd prepared to leave Deirdre's home, long after the last of her children had gone to bed and the plates had been cleared from her table. We'd given her the crate she'd tried to steal from us earlier in the day—filled with jars that would likely last them until summer.

I hesitated at the door, letting Eden and Brook go ahead of me to the VAN.

"Here," I told Deirdre as I held my hand out to hers. "I've no idea of its value, but you can likely get a good price for it."

She opened her palm and looked at the sapphire pendant I'd dropped there, still warm from my skin.

She shook her head, her green eyes somber. "I couldn't. It's yours."

But I pushed her hand away. "I insist. You need it more than I do. For your children." And it was true. Where I was going, I had no need for jewelry or sentimental keepsakes. I needed nothing at all, save my name and my blood.

Deirdre could make the money for a necklace like this last for months, years maybe. It could support her even if her husband and daughter never returned. I knew guilt was making my decision, but it didn't matter to me.

I pushed again, until she finally acquiesced, closing her fingers around the jewel. "Thank you," she whispered. "Thank you, and safe travels."

It was Brook who first noticed it, the sound—or rather the feel—of thunder. It seemed to come from nowhere, and yet everywhere, all at once.

We hadn't gone far when she told Eden to kill the engine, and then the lights. And we all sat, awash in the darkness, letting the rumbling sensation fill our lungs, our veins, and find rhythm with our heartbeats.

"What is it?" I managed, when my voice finally found its way free from the drumming in my chest.

"I don't know," Eden admitted. "But we have to go. Now." Neither Brook nor I argued as we followed Eden from the VAN, evacuating it and leaving it where it stood, on the open expanse of ground that had once been a thoroughfare.

We took nothing, saving only ourselves. We followed silently as she climbed the slopes of the stony precipices that dominated the southern coastline. To lose our footing here, now on these rocky cliffs that overlooked the even rockier shores, would mean certain and swift death. All the while, the ground shook and the gravel beneath our toes shuddered and shifted.

But Eden climbed without pause, higher and higher, somehow finding traction where I doubted there was any. She pointed here and there, so we could follow suit. She was patient but demanding, and insisted that we climb higher and keep up with her.

"Where are we going?" Brook hissed, but Eden shushed her.

"Silence" was all the explanation she offered.

The sharp-toothed rocks ripped my pants, and my fingers and knees were raw by the time Eden finally allowed us to rest, leading us inside the mouth of a cave that was carved into the hillside.

She prodded us farther in, until the cavern narrowed and we couldn't go any deeper. As I glanced down at myself, I knew why she wanted us so far inside. Even in the intense blackness of the cave, my skin was notably visible.

"Here," she told us. "We'll wait here."

I looked to Brooklynn, who gave me a slight shake of her head. "Wait for what?" I asked Eden.

"I don't know," she said. "But when the ground stops moving, we'll know it's over."

PART III

MAX

The bird-faced warriors appeared like the scourge of death.

They didn't send a scouting party, the way Max had. Instead they came all at once, a vicious flock, arriving on horses and in tanks and on foot. In the fire from their torches, and from the headlamps of their vehicles, he could see their iron masks, elongated and conical, curving and coming to a spiked point at the tip, like they wore deadly black beaks. Their hobnailed boots and the hooves of their horses ate up the earth beneath their feet as they marched en masse—a deadly wall. Their tanks and armored assault vehicles flanked Max and his men on both sides.

Harbingers, Max thought, *of things to come.*

He started to go down there, to warn the villagers who stood in the warriors' path, so they would at least stand a chance, but Claude held him back.

"There's nothing you can do for them," he whispered into Max's ear as he dragged him back into the darkness of their hiding spot. He kept his hand clamped warningly over Max's mouth. "Not if you expect to save Queen Charlaina."

The mention of Charlie caused Max to stop struggling. Claude was right, of course. He had to find Charlie before the Astonian troops did. But that didn't stop the bile from rising in his throat as he watched the first homes being burned. Or as he listened to women and children and men screaming from within—and without—those walls as they tried to escape. To save themselves.

Fire and gunshots filled the sky, and Max flinched again and again, but never once did he close his eyes. He needed to remember this. To memorize every last reason he despised Queen Elena, and the troops from Astonia, and the terror they rained down on Ludania's citizens.

He never wanted to forget what the Astonians were capable of.

He witnessed the occasional body fleeing from the burning village, someone fortunate enough to make it out of the wreckage.

Some made it all the way, unnoticed by the enemy forces. And others, not so fortunate, were caught before they could make their escape into the blackness.

Those were the ones he could hear the most clearly, because they came the closest to where he and Claude were hidden. He listened to their pleas for mercy, their unremitting sobs and promises to retract their loyalty from Queen Charlaina. And ultimately their final cries as they realized they would die this night, no matter what they promised. No matter where their allegiance lay.

Those were the ones that made Max sick. They were the ones who made him cover his mouth as he gagged and retched, until his nose burned with his own stomach acid and the smell of charred flesh.

XI

When morning came, my eyes were slow to open. They were sticky and raw, and I had to peel the lids apart. My neck ached from being crooked sideways against the rock wall where I'd fallen asleep. Everything about me, all the way to my bones, was cold and damp, and I was shivering long before I'd reached the point of awareness. The fog that had coated the land the night before had found its way inside our cavern, bringing with it a dank chill that saturated every nook and cleft and fissure.

As my eyes adjusted to the daylight coming in through the mouth of the cave, I could now make out the slick layer of moss I'd been able to only feel the night before. It covered every part of the walls and floors and ceiling. Much like the moss stuck to the rocks, my clothing stuck to my skin, damp where I'd been leaning against the slippery surface, and damp where I hadn't been.

Brooklynn had fallen asleep leaning against my leg, and I shook her now to wake her. She was snoring once more, and the sound echoed inside the cavern we'd huddled in for the remainder of the night.

I didn't remember the roar from outside coming to an end; I'd simply grown too weary to outlast it and had closed my eyes.

Now it was gone. The ground was still. The air was heavy and cold.

Rubbing my arms, I searched for Eden, who seemed to never sleep.

I found her outline against the mists, standing just beyond the entrance to the cave. She faced me, and when she saw me watching her, she nodded. Even from where I sat, her black eyes pierced the fog, telling me, without words, that something terrible had transpired.

"What was it? Did you discover the source of the sound?" I asked, climbing to my feet just as Brook lifted her head.

She knew; I could see it in her face as she frowned at me.

"Tell me," I insisted, crossing the cave floor.

She breathed heavily before answering. "Elena's army. They've crossed into Ludania. That was what we heard last night. Her forces."

Behind me I heard Brook scrambling to her feet. "What about us? Do you think they know we're here? Did they find the VAN?"

I saw Eden shake her head, and heard her response, which sounded muffled and faraway in my ears. "I don't think so. Far as I can tell, they passed right by us."

But I didn't care about any of that. All I could concentrate on was the meaning of what she'd said before that.

Elena's army . . .

Here . . .

In my country.

I staggered backward, trying to find my breath and my balance. This was it, then. War, plain and simple. There was no other explanation.

And now, any hope I'd had of bargaining with the Astonian queen for peace had been all for nothing. I had no reason to try to convince her not to attack us, because she'd already done it. My worst fears had come true.

I dropped to my knees. *What am I going to do now? What have I already done?*

I'd made a terrible mistake, coming here. Leaving the palace in the first place on a selfish mission over a vague missive from a cruel and vengeful queen. I'd taken Brook—the commander of my armed forces—away when my armies needed her most. I'd taken Eden from my sister when she was at risk.

And I'd taken Ludania's queen off her throne.

How could I have been so selfish? How could I have risked my country's welfare for the chance to rid myself of Sabara?

It was too much—much too much to process.

"Get up," Brook's voice boomed from behind me. "You don't have the luxury of falling apart now. So get up!" She hauled me up with hands that were demanding and not at all gentle. She was acting like a general, barking orders at one of her subordinates.

"Shut up," I cried, the words falling pitifully from my lips. "Just shut up."

Brooklynn shook me, forcing me to look at her. "I mean

it, Charlie. You don't get to pretend to be someone else anymore. You can't be *Layla*. You're the queen, and these are your people under attack now. *So what* that your plan didn't work. We'll come up with another. But we can't just stay here in this cave. This is your country. This is *our* country," she added, reminding me that I wasn't alone.

I nodded, slowly at first, and then along with her as she released her grip on my arms. She was right. This was no time to fall apart.

I couldn't stay here and let my people down. Not now, not when they needed me most. There had to be something I could do.

"Okay." I nodded again, my chin lifting. "Let's do this." I turned to see if Eden felt the same way, and saw that she was nodding too.

Brooklynn grinned. "That's better. So, what's the plan? Where are we headed, Your Majesty?"

MAX

Max waited till dawn before sending Claude back to the ridge where he'd left the troops they'd been traveling with. He hoped that the bare-branched copse of Swamp Maples had provided enough shelter for them.

Now that the violence was over, he was grateful he'd ordered the soldiers to remain out of sight and to not attack any rival forces, no matter how close the other battalion came to them. He understood the hearts of soldiers. That their instincts and training would make it difficult for them to sit back and watch while Elena's army invaded their land. But he needed them alive, now more than ever. He needed to find Charlie.

He stayed behind while Claude went to collect the others, wanting to assess the destruction left behind by the enemy army. He wasn't sure what he expected to gain from the inspection of the decimated village—he could see from his vantage point on the hillside that the Astonian soldiers had left no witnesses to their rampage—but his curiosity called to him all the same.

The black smoke that coiled and twisted through the air

stood out against the pale morning fog, like an obscene reminder of the night's events. His lungs felt leaden. The sickening crunch of newly charred wood and paper and textiles shadowed him with each and every step he took. The scent of destruction was cloying.

But worse than the burned homes, and the shattered glass that spilled onto the streets, was the blood that splattered stone and dirt and everything. Everywhere.

There were bodies, both those that were whole and those not whole. Burned and unburned.

Max walked through the streets, avoiding as best he could the stares of so many vacant eyes. The corpses of children were piled against the still smoking rubble, their expressionless faces dirty from soot and ash.

Spikes had been speared into the ground at irregular intervals, and there were several with heads mounted on them: an elderly man's, his eyes and mouth open; a woman's, her hair tangled with blood, her eyes mercifully closed; a boy's, not yet to adolescence, with red hair and green eyes that were now hazed over with death.

There were nooses, too, and several victims had been hanged. Max glanced over them quickly, trying not to notice the way their feet still swayed, ever so slightly, as the sea's breath rocked them.

But it was one woman in particular who caught his eye. Her hair was the same as the boy's whose head had been impaled. His mother, if Max were to guess. But it wasn't her hair that drew his attention; it was her neck. Something that glinted in the morning light.

He moved closer, feeling sick as he noted the way her hands were crudely bound behind her back, and seeing the blackened ligature marks that feathered out from the cord beneath her chin.

He tried not to look at her pale face as he reached for the chain that disappeared beneath the front of her bloodied blouse.

"Damn it," he muttered as he ripped the necklace from her body and clutched it in his fist.

He barely registered the sound of hoofbeats behind him as he tried to imagine how this woman had come into possession of the pendant, although he wasn't sure the *how* was the problem.

Fear lanced him, freezing the blood in his veins and making him incapable of moving for several long moments while he considered the implications of finding the necklace here, in this place. Now.

When he turned around, he was facing the division of men and women he'd brought with him to find their queen.

"We need to scour every inch of this village, check every body to make sure Queen Charlaina's not among them. And when we're certain she's not, one of you has to go back to the palace with word of this attack. We need to be certain they know we're at war with Astonia." When Claude approached, his eyebrow raised, Max opened his hand and showed the guard Charlie's necklace. "She's been here," he announced. "And we're going to find her if it's the last thing we do."

XII

Brook frowned as she patted her waistband. She stopped in front of me then and bent down, dropping low and patting her ankle, too.

"Damn," she cursed. "I think I left my blade back in the cave." She raised her hand to her forehead and glanced back up the hillside, her frown deepening. "You two go on ahead. I'll be right behind you."

I watched for a minute as she jogged back up the way we'd just come. Rocks skittered down behind her as her boots found their way more easily in the daylight. The fog was clearing now too, and what remained was only what clung to the ground, wisps that hadn't been whisked away yet by the crisp gusts coming over the cliffs from the water below.

I turned and followed Eden, focusing on making my way back down the rocky terrain.

We couldn't see the VAN yet, but it wouldn't be long. It would have been better if we'd been able to go farther the night before. Unfortunately, we hadn't had enough time to plan, and it had been too dark to see where we'd been going, both of which had limited our escape route.

As the VAN came into view, I sighed out loud, and the tension in my chest loosened. "It's still there," I breathed.

Eden turned to face me, a slow grin spreading over her face, and I could see she was relieved as well. "It'll be good to get out of here." And then her expression changed as her focus shifted. I couldn't tell what it was she was looking at, but I knew it wasn't me. It wasn't Brooklynn either, because Brooklynn had gone in the other direction.

Her attention was fixed on something in the hills, but not toward the cave where we'd spent the night.

Instead she scowled at something just past my shoulder, and then the confusion on her face cleared and she pulled me as hard as she could. She shoved me behind her, and beneath her breath she ordered, "Run, Your Majesty. Run!"

She hadn't even finished her sentence when I saw her pull her gun from the holster and release the safety.

Before she had the chance to fire her weapon, I was doing as she'd instructed, no longer taking caution about where I stepped, just knowing that if Eden had told me to run, I needed to run.

There could be only one reason: Elena's forces *had* found us after all.

The sound of gunfire was earsplitting, and it rang into and around the rock walls of the rugged hills. It echoed inside my head and matched the pattern of my footfalls.

She fired again and again and again and again, until I didn't think she could fire any more, until I was certain she was out of ammunition.

My side ached, and yet, still I ran.

I could hear the sounds of a struggle behind me. And then I heard footsteps, heavy and crashing and rushing right toward me. I prayed they were Eden's, but I never slowed. I didn't dare look behind me.

I was almost to the VAN now, and a part of me wondered what I planned to do once I reached it.

I might be able to drive it, I told myself. I'd spent hours studying Eden while she'd piloted the beast of a machine, and surely I could manage to start the thing myself. Surely I could steer it long enough to get it moving in the right direction.

After that, I didn't know.

I'd figure it out.

But I couldn't leave Eden and Brooklynn behind.

Then I remembered . . . the weapons. There were weapons inside the VAN.

If I could reach them, we still had a chance.

That was when I felt my head jerk backward. I lost my footing entirely, which had nothing to do with me at all. It came from somewhere behind me, as my hair had been yanked—so hard that my scalp felt as if it were on fire.

A strangled half gasp, half scream choked me, rising like vitriol in my throat. I fell, landing on my back, and before I could even blink, I was staring up into the face of a bird.

The mask was melded from black iron, making my attacker look something akin to a steel raven. Metal rivets ran the length of his beaklike protrusion, and round goggles gave his eyes a hawkish appearance that made me feel as if he were peering into my soul.

I imagined him bringing that razor-sharp bill down into my face. Pecking at me. Eating me alive. Goring me, and shredding my skin . . . swallowing it up like worms.

"*Your Majesty*, is it?" Like his beak, his grating voice hovered above my face like an ill-concealed taunt. I could see his mouth beneath the metal mask he wore.

I couldn't afford to wait to find out what he had planned for me, or what he'd done to Eden. Searching for an inner calm I wasn't sure I possessed, I tried to recall Zafir's lessons on defense. I searched for the one that would best help me escape my predicament.

When the man revealed his teeth in a gruesome grin, I breathed deeply and formulated my plan of attack. I reached behind my head to where his gloved fingers were still tangled in my hair, and I grabbed hold of his little finger, making certain my grip was secure. When I was certain I had him, and that he had no idea what I was about to do, I flipped onto my stomach. I moved swiftly, the way Zafir had told me, and when I did, his finger rolled with me.

I felt it—the crunching sensation the moment it separated from his hand.

His surprised screech followed suit, a bellow that filled the skies. Involuntarily he released my hair, and before he could stop me, I was already jumping to my feet, ready for his next attack. And I knew he'd attack again. He wasn't finished with me.

It took only a moment for his shock to subside and for him to collect his wits. I could see the determined set of his shoulders and the way he clenched his jaw. He was coming for me.

I was ready, though. I'd been preparing for this moment for months.

Zafir had made certain I could handle myself.

When he came at me once more, he was still clumsy and lurching with pain. He'd given no thought as to *how* he would assault me, only that he wanted revenge.

I saw his fist, hefty and leathered and enormous, coming at me. But I knew what to do.

I didn't retreat but instead covered my head with both hands and dropped below the trajectory of his ham-fisted swipe. And then I launched myself right at him. I put all of my weight, everything I had, into my body, so that when I hit him, my head colliding with his gut, I heard him wheeze. His fist missed me completely, flying all the way over the back of my head, and yet I kept coming at him.

I wrapped my arms around his waist and planted one leg firmly while rotating on it. The result was that I spun around him, so that I was at his back, my arms still encircling him.

When I extended my other leg and dropped low, it threw the man, who was at least three heads taller than I was, off balance. He careened backward, his arms flailing as he flew over the top of me and landed on his back. He fell on rocks and gravel, and I heard him exhale loudly. The metal of his mask struck the solid ground like lead.

This time, before he could recover, I straddled him and reached for the weapon at his belt, a knife with two separate but equally deadly blades curving from its hilt. I'd never seen such a weapon, but I didn't hesitate. He never roused as I unsheathed it.

And then I stuck it through the sinewy flesh at the side of his neck.

His entire body stiffened, and he shuddered beneath me. I froze, my eyes going wide, as for the first time I stopped to consider what I'd just done. I felt the blood drain from my own face as I waited. When I sensed the last breath escape his throat on an exaggerated pant, I released the breath I'd been holding.

I looked down at my hand, still clenched tightly around the hilt and now smeared in blood that seemed to cover everything. My mouth went dry. I thought I might be sick right there . . . on his corpse.

You've killed before, Sabara whispered, her taunt as vicious as the acts of the man I stood above. *You'll kill again. It's who you are. It's who we are.*

But she was wrong. I'd killed, yes. But never with my bare hands.

I'd never felt someone take their last breath.

I'd never had blood on my hands.

"No," I said, closing my eyes and releasing the handle of the blood-covered knife. "I'm not you. I'm not you."

When I glanced up, I saw Eden.

I barely registered that she wasn't alone, that she was flanked on either side by soldiers wearing the same raven-faced masks as the man I'd just killed. I hardly saw the other soldiers, those whose bodies littered the hillside behind Eden and our enemies.

I was tempted, so incredibly tempted, to draw from Sabara's powers to save her, but I couldn't take the risk that Sabara would overtake me once more.

I might have blinked, or I might not have, when one of Eden's captors saw me there, my hands covered in the blood of his fallen comrade, and he released his grip on her. I was in his sights.

Me. He was after me now.

Run, I heard Eden's words repeat in my head. *Run, run, run!*

I let go of the knife, which was still stuck in the dead man's neck, and with no other thought than reaching the VAN, I ran as fast as I could. There wasn't much distance between me and the soldier behind me, but there also wasn't much distance between me and the VAN.

Ten steps . . .

Five . . .

Two . . .

I launched myself up the steps and shoved my shoulder against the closed door. It opened inward—the way it did—and I exhaled as I tumbled inside, landing in a heap on the floor.

Without looking over my shoulder, I reached up and punched the button with my fist, the one that would close the door again. I needed to keep him out for only a second. Just long enough to reach the weapons cache in back.

Long enough to arm myself.

I leapt to my feet, hopeful that I'd made it. I was safe at last.

And then a voice stopped me cold. "That was impressive. I had no idea you had that in you." I recognized who was speaking immediately, but even if I hadn't, Sabara had.

My entire body started to tingle, starting in the pit of my belly and spreading outward. It was a reaction that made tears burn my eyes.

They weren't my tears, however. They were hers.

I loathed her. For this and a million other reasons, I loathed her.

But it wasn't his fault. He wasn't the one holding me captive inside my own body.

"Niko," I gasped, confused to find him here, inside the VAN. "What are you doing here?" I tried to think past Sabara's response to him. I shoved past him. It didn't matter *why* he was here. He was here and he could help. "Elena's soldiers are out there, and they have Eden. We have to get to the guns."

I reached the place where the crates of munitions had been carefully packed and stowed.

They were open now, the packing materials strewn everywhere and the weapons missing, as if they'd been pillaged in our absence. I dug through the shredded paper, searching in vain for a gun or a dagger or a bow. Anything.

My heart was racing, this time not at all because of Sabara or Niko.

Outside, I realized the soldier wasn't even trying to gain entrance. He hadn't even tried the door.

I glanced back over my shoulder to where Niko was contemplating me.

"Get up, Charlaina." His voice was quiet, tender even.

"Wh-what are you doing?"

He withdrew a gun from behind his back and sighed. He was still watching me with his familiar golden eyes—eyes I'd dreamed of more than once. And for a moment—just for a moment—I could almost believe he meant it when he said, "I'm sorry I have to do this."

BROOKLYNN

It was the last thing Brook had ever expected.

The attack by the bird-faced warriors.

Eden unleashing her rounds into the knolls as Charlie sprinted across the plain, trying to escape to the VAN.

And then Charlie . . . her defensive skills. Battling a combatant at least twice her size.

Where the hell had she learned moves like those? When had she become someone who could kill in cold blood?

She'd watched it all from her perch near the top of the hill. She hadn't even made it to the cave.

Had she thought she had a chance, she'd have joined the fray. Helped Charlie and Eden defend against their attackers.

But they were outnumbered, plain and simple. The strategist in her warned her to wait it out. To stay where she was and observe. To let this battle play out so she could plan her countermeasure.

Battles weren't won by responding rashly. They were won

by outmaneuvering your opponent. By staying one step ahead. Keeping a clear head.

That was what Brook needed now, a clear head.

If only she hadn't witnessed that other part, that last thing, where she'd seen Niko walking Charlie out of the VAN, a gun aimed directly at the back of her head.

Niko . . . that swine! She rolled his traitorous name around and around in her head, wondering how they'd ever trusted him. How they'd ever allowed him to accompany Xander to Elena's queendom in the first place. They should've known better, especially since Charlie had revealed what he truly was.

Brook didn't know what he was up to—or why he appeared to be working in tandem with Elena's soldiers—but if he was involved in this, it was no good.

And now he had Charlie.

She'd half-expected the other soldiers to come in search of her, and when they didn't, she had to assume that they didn't know about her. That they hadn't realized she'd been traveling with Charlie and Eden.

She'd managed to stay quiet by biting her fist, the only way she'd been able to keep from being discovered while she'd watched as Eden had run out of ammunition and been overpowered and taken prisoner. But she'd nearly choked on her own glee as she'd watched Charlie take down her attacker and ram a blade into his throat.

She remained concealed long after Niko and the others had taken Eden and Charlie and the VAN and had gone. She was a fugitive now, inside the borders of her own country.

Brook knew she had to be careful—stealthy, so as not to be discovered.

Slipping away from her hiding spot, she glanced skyward at the sun. At least an hour had passed since the Astonians had departed, so she was certain it was safe to come out.

She followed the same path she'd negotiated before, only this time she stopped along the way.

At the first body, Brook knelt to examine the metal casing surrounding the soldier's face. The pounded iron was thick, like armor. She ran her finger along the side of the beakish mask and noted it had a knifelike edge. It would slice her flesh were she not cautious.

She reached around it and found where it fastened. She removed it, as well as the goggles, revealing the soft skin of a woman beneath. Her black hair was wild and unkempt, but she was young—barely of legal age by Ludanian standards.

Brook's gaze moved downward, to where Eden's bullet had pierced the girl's heart. She couldn't see the blood; it was lost in the sea of black she wore. Brook relieved the girl of her gun and a small-bladed knife she found concealed in the top of the girl's boot.

At the next body, she didn't inspect the mask or the bullet wound. She simply stripped the soldier of his weapon and the spare ammunition he kept in his inside jacket pocket. She did the same at the third and fourth bodies. Weapons and ammo only, until she'd scrambled all the way down the hillside to where Charlie had single-handedly killed the soldier who'd blitz attacked her.

She didn't want to smile—this was no time for smiling—but

she couldn't stop herself. Charlie, it seemed, was something of a badass.

Charlie, the girl she'd known forever. The one who'd worked hard and barely spoken out of turn her entire life.

Charlie, the girl Brooklynn was willing to die for.

Apparently their queen still had a few secrets of her own.

Brooklynn braced her boot against the dead soldier's unmoving chest and gripped the handle of the knife that protruded from his neck. She counted to three silently in her head, and then pulled.

The knife came free, and Brook marveled at the double-bladed design before wiping both sides of it on her pants. She held her breath then, every muscle in her body going stock-still. Every beat of her heart was a distraction as she tried to concentrate. The skin at the base of her neck tightened. The muscles at her shoulders coiled, readying.

She'd heard the snap of a twig just as clearly as if it had been the shattering of a colossal tree trunk. It had come from behind her, and she knew that if she didn't time her actions carefully, they might easily be her last.

Spinning around, she dropped to the ground, crouching low. In her left hand she had a handgun pointed in front of her. In her right the double-sided blades were concealed close to her hip. She was prepared for anything.

Except for what she saw.

Aron took a step backward, his eyes locked on the gun directed at his face. "A simple 'Nice to see you' would have done."

Brook inhaled sharply and squeezed her eyes shut. She

tried to calm her pounding heart before it cracked a rib or bruised a lung.

When she opened her eyes again, Aron was studying the body at her feet. "D'you do all this?"

She narrowed her gaze on him, resenting the question. "Would it matter if I had?"

Aron looked again, and then at the bodies in the hills beyond her. He shook his head. "You planning to lower that thing anytime soon?"

She hated that she couldn't still her heart. She hated that she had to ask this, even though she should know the answer. "Depends. Tell me about Niko."

Aron frowned, and she searched for any sign that his confusion about her question wasn't genuine. "What are you talking about? What does Niko have to do with anything?" He took a step toward her, and she waved the nose of the gun at him, staving him off. "Brook, what's going on? I find my girl out here, all alone in the middle of a bloodbath, and all you can do is ask me about Niko? Should I be jealous?"

Brooklynn blinked. She thought about shooting him right then and there, and then she glowered at him. "Don't call me that," she growled irritably.

He grinned then, a smug grin that made Brook's stomach flip. And this time he ignored her weapons and marched boldly to her, disregarding the fact that she could pull the trigger at any moment. "Call you what? My girl? What do you expect me to call you, then? Commander? Ma'am?" His arm shot out to her waist, and he hauled her up against him, his eyes sparkling devilishly.

Brook let the gun drop to her side. Her heart stopped beating and lodged in her throat. The way he looked at her, the way his eyes roved over her face—"wolfishly" was the only word she could think of to describe it—made her cheeks burn.

"I missed you, ma'am," he whispered, right before his lips claimed hers.

She wanted to push him away—to shoot or stab him, or step on his foot. But his mouth made a convincing argument, and instead she leaned closer, surrendering completely. Telling him with her impatient lips and the coaxing of her tongue the things she refused to voice out loud.

That she'd missed him, too. That she'd hated being apart from him.

That she wanted him.

And that was how an entire band of her own soldiers came upon the two of them, wrapped in each other's arms, groping clothes and tugging hair, and straining to be closer to each other. She never heard so much as a single hoof strike against the ground.

It wasn't until Max—*Max, of all people!*—shouted her name that she was even aware they were no longer alone.

Her face burned for an entirely different reason as she shoved away from Aron, who seemed to feel none of the shame she did. "Let go," she muttered under her breath when he kept her tangled in his embrace.

"Yes, ma'am," he said, chuckling, but he didn't stop touching her. He slipped his arm around her waist and drew her to him, as if daring her to pull away. It was possessive, and sort of endearing, and she'd missed the feel of him far too much to try to step away.

"Where's Charlie?" Max insisted breathlessly as he dismounted from his horse. He broke any spell Brook had fallen under upon Aron's arrival, the immediacy in his tone reminding Brooklynn that Charlie was still out there . . . with Niko.

"We . . ." She glanced down at the dead soldier on the ground in front of her. "We were attacked." She struggled with how to explain it all. "Niko was here, and he . . . he took Charlie." She could hardly believe it herself, and still didn't understand why Niko would be working with Elena.

Max surveyed the scene—the bodies, the bruises on Brook's face, and the bloodied knife, still in her hand. "Well, you did the best you could. I know you wouldn't have let him take her unless you'd been overpowered."

Brook looked down at the knife she clutched, and then at the soldier lying at her feet. "I didn't do this," she explained. "Charlie did. She fought and killed him. I've never seen anything like it. Not from her."

Max looked as stunned as she'd felt, and then a look of understanding crossed his face. "I guess she wasn't joking when she said Zafir had been teaching her to fight." He scrubbed his hand over his stubbled jaw. "But Niko? Why Niko? What did he say?"

"I don't know. I was hiding. I was planning to follow them—" Max stopped her with a raised brow, and she tried to explain. "That—that was when Aron found me," she stammered. "I didn't have a chance to formulate a plan. I'm not sure where they were going, or what Niko had in mind. They have

Eden, too, though. She'll keep Charlie safe till we find her."

Max was already getting back onto his horse and talking to one of her soldiers—one who would normally be taking orders from Brooklynn herself. "Get the commander a horse," he barked. "She's going to lead us to Queen Charlaina."

XIII

"You're making a mistake," I told Niko, even though I'd already said as much. Even though he'd already ignored this very same threat time and time again. "You'll be executed for taking me prisoner. It's nothing short of treason."

Inside, Sabara wrestled with me, attempting to gain control once and for all. She wanted more than to intimidate Niko. She craved so, *so* much more.

The problem was, I was doing a less than impressive job restraining her, and Niko was the reason. His presence distracted me and made Sabara stronger, giving her the incentive she needed to keep trying, trying, *trying*.

He scooted closer to me in the seat we shared, pinning me against the wall of the VAN. I couldn't help but react instinctively to the scent of him, his masculine odor of sweat and leather that should have made me recoil but instead had me straining to be nearer to him.

"It would be treason only if I were one of your subjects," he protested in a low voice that filled every inch of the cramped space. He was too close to me now, and I told myself to pull away. But my head was spinning and I could feel Sabara's stranglehold on me tightening. "Besides, you're not my prisoner. You're my guest."

"Then untie me," I shot back, my voice, at least, not betraying me.

His lips curved into a delicious smile that coaxed me the barest amount closer. I felt a surge of something charged, something dizzying, course through me, and the last of my control slipped away. His words, when I heard them, seemed to come from far, far away. "It's not that simple, Charlaina."

It was the use of my name—and not hers—that broke the spell I'd very nearly fallen under. I blinked, and blinked again. I shook my head to clear my muddled thoughts at the moment when his lips were almost upon mine.

Our noses banged together, and his eyes widened, as if he were as surprised as I'd been to find us so close to kissing. He wasn't fooling anyone, of course.

"Stop it," I hissed, speaking to both Niko and Sabara now. "Leave me alone."

I glanced over to where Eden sat, her hands and feet tied so tightly, her fingers were turning an uncommon shade of blue. There was a gag stuffed into her mouth. One of the remaining soldiers, his mask still on his face, stood above her with the tip of a rifle pressed lightly to her temple as the VAN leapt unevenly over the terrain. I watched his finger, praying it didn't slip on the trigger.

Niko's touch drew my attention; the back of his hand was caressing my cheek and stroking my jaw. "Charlaina, please. Be reasonable. I have no intention of harming you." He came closer, so that his lips were in the same place his hand had been just seconds before. At my jaw. "It's her I want. Only her." Goose bumps prickled my skin everywhere. "Always her."

Sabara knew. She knew what he meant, and she didn't shy away.

I knew I was bested when I could no longer feel the goose bumps, only the sensation of warmth bleeding into my limbs, all the way to my fingertips. I was intoxicated by her power. Drugged and woozy as her Essence overwhelmed me, her desire to be near him winning out over all else.

"Niko," I breathed, even as I tried to hush my vocal cords.

The need I heard buried in my own voice was heartbreaking, and Niko responded to it. He captured me, and suddenly it wasn't just Sabara who overpowered me. Niko's lips crushed mine, and I let him, unable to do anything else.

My mouth parted to let him in. He conquered, and I yielded.

The taste of him was heady, and his touch was electric.

And not one of those feelings—or reactions—was my own. But that didn't stop me from basking in them. From getting lost in the sheer, unadulterated bliss he'd unleashed within me.

I was still pinned, but no longer trapped. I pressed myself against Niko's chest and let his hands rove over my back, my sides, his thumbs finding their way to my stomach. They moved up . . .

And up . . .

. . . too high . . .

I wasn't sure which of us was more surprised when my teeth

sank into his tongue. Or whether it was me or Sabara who flinched first from the taste of his blood.

But I knew for certain that I was the one who'd had enough and had come to my senses long enough to put an end to Sabara's influence over me. At least long enough to stop whatever had been transpiring between Niko and me.

"Bitch," he cursed, and shoved me back as he swiped the blood that trickled from the corner of his mouth.

Bitch, Sabara echoed, and I banished her once more, my resolve strengthening as my confidence returned. I wished I could bite her, too. I wanted to see her bleed.

I saw Eden fighting to free herself. She wanted blood as well.

"We're here," the driver, another soldier, announced from the front of the VAN, and I lifted my head to see where *here* was, exactly.

What I saw caused cold fingers of dread to seize my spine and rattle me to the core. I wanted to cry or scream, but I did neither. My mouth was open as I stared at the tented city that spread out before me.

There were at least a thousand tents. Not multicolored or jumbled or packed together to take up as little space as possible.

No, this encampment was orderly and single-hued. Black like death, and mottled only by the red Astonian banners that waved overhead. The tents themselves were so numerous that they extended for as far as I could see, disappearing into the valley beyond.

I felt sick, and wondered again and again and again why

exactly Niko had brought me here. Why he had turned to Elena's side.

And then she was there. Elena. Waiting for us.

Her expectant gaze searched the VAN as it drew to a stop.

"Why?" I managed at last, just as Niko was yanking me up from my seat. He was no longer tender, and his fingers bit into my arm as he dragged me to the front of the vehicle.

His eyes alighted on Elena, and he plastered a smile to his lips, not bothering to look down at me when he answered. "For her, of course. Always for her."

As he shoved me down the steps, delivering me at the feet of my fiercest opponent, a woman I abhorred almost as much as the soul residing within me, I had to wonder which of them he'd meant—Elena or Sabara.

SAGE

Sage supported Xander's weight the best she could. It had been that way for miles, as she'd forced him to continue walking, if that's what you even called what he was doing. She felt more like she was hauling him at this point. He could barely stand on his own, let alone manage the work of dragging one foot and then the other to keep moving—the work required to be considered walking.

Her shoulders and her back and her own feet ached. She was sweating, despite the chill in the air. But she couldn't stop until she found a suitable place to camp for the night.

No, not camp. Hide.

She watched as the sun set, moving lower and lower in the sky, and she tried to make conversation with her companion. To keep him alert. To convince herself he was okay.

That she wasn't going to have to dump his body somewhere.

"We'll stop when we reach those trees up ahead," she told him.

"Mm," he grunted, making an attempt to raise his head so he could see what trees she referred to.

"We should be able to take cover in them. You can rest then."

Another grunt.

"Just a few more steps. You can do this." She heard the desperation, the plea in her voice. She didn't want him to know how worried she was for him.

There was no sound, no grunt this time, and she glanced sideways to see if he was still awake. His feet shuffled, as if he were automated, kicking up dirt in his path.

"Xander?" Her voice rose insistently.

Still, there was no response.

She tightened her grip on him, around his waist and on his arm, which was still draped around her shoulder. She squeezed as hard as she could until she knew she was pinching him. "Say something. I mean it."

"That . . . hurts," he slurred, almost incoherently, his only reaction to her fingers digging into his flesh.

A relieved laugh escaped her lips. "Good. My back hurts too," she countered. She didn't tell him how thankful she was that he'd understood her demand, and that he'd reacted to the pain she'd inflicted on him. It meant he was still with her.

They reached the edge of the forest. Tall evergreens with dark green needles smelled pungent and sharp, and the scent filled her nose. There were ferns and broad-leafed shrubs and boulders and fallen logs, all things that made it the perfect place to stay hidden for a night. Maybe two.

Until Xander felt strong enough to move on his own.

She set up camp and used the few supplies she'd managed

to strip from the horses before she'd had to set them free. A blanket and a tarp, some bandages and antiseptic, half a loaf of bread, a special blend of tea she'd had the apothecary mix before she'd kidnapped Xander, and a compact hunting bow that had been easier to carry than the Blaster rifle she would've liked to make room for.

By the time she'd returned with dinner—a rabbit she'd shot on her first attempt—Xander was sitting up in front of the fire she'd started, looking mostly alive.

"Feeling better?" she asked, glancing knowingly at the tea she'd instructed him to drink. It smelled like piss, but the apothecary had insisted it would ease—at least temporarily—the discomfort of whomever consumed it.

Xander shrugged, but Sage noted the way his eyes were glossed over now. The tea was doing its job.

She dropped to the ground and began the work of skinning the animal. "You had me scared," she told him, not looking up to see if he was listening or not. She was glad he was improved, even if it meant he was drugged out of his mind. At least he wasn't delirious.

She was relieved when Xander managed to eat and actually keep it down. He needed to rebuild his strength. When they were finished and she'd cleared away the carcass so as not to attract predators during the night, she took great care changing his dressing.

The wound was septic, she was certain, and she worried how much longer Xander would last on tea and good intentions.

When the infusion of narcotics wore off, and the shivering began, Sage crept closer to where Xander slept.

She stroked his face and wiped away the sheen of sweat. She patted his back and caressed his cheek. She watched his face as it twisted with torment and agony, and she longed to see it lying dormant. To watch him sleep in peace.

She guarded him and prayed the fever would pass.

And when it didn't, she curled up close to him and pressed her body to his, hoping that at least some of her strength— and her heat—would transfer to him.

Would keep him safe throughout the night.

XIV

"You've lost your mind," I whispered, hoping to draw as little attention as possible to the fact that I was still awake. "Was I not clear? I don't want to see you."

The tent I'd been escorted to was lavish. I had a bed that wasn't on the ground, as beds in tents tended to be, and it had real bedding that was clean and soft and smelled of lavender. The food too was hot and fresh, and I'd dined on braised pork smothered in carrots and leeks and some sort of stewed plums. The combination should have been revolting, but somehow, after days of eating from jars, it had been delectable.

I wondered if it was the same fare the soldiers dined on, or if I was simply being treated to the queen's leftovers.

Either way, despite my accommodations and the spread I'd been offered, I'd not once been uncuffed. Even now, with only the soft glow radiating from my skin to illuminate the pitch black of the tent's interior, my wrists ached from being bound.

"Hear me out," Niko said, slipping into the tent and letting the flaps whisper closed behind him. He made it seem as if his actions were covert, but I knew better. There was no way he'd snuck past any of the guards who'd been posted around the entire perimeter of my provisional prison.

I felt as if I were truly seeing him for the first time now, and wondered how I hadn't noticed his duplicitous nature earlier. How I'd fallen under the charm of his golden eyes and his inviting smiles.

But I knew why, of course. Sabara.

When it came to her, there was nothing double-dealing about him. He meant every sugar-coated word he spoke to her, every silver-tongued compliment, every overblown promise.

He would kill for her. He would die for her.

And everything in between.

She was his everything.

I knew because she told me so with every ounce of energy she possessed as she fought to take me over, even now.

My head ached from trying to contain her. It would have been so much easier to just give in.

And so much more deadly.

"Charlaina, please. Hear me out. I have the answer. I've found the perfect solution for all of us." I didn't flinch when he climbed onto the side of my bed, and I somehow managed to keep my breathing steady when his fingers grazed over the exposed flesh of my arm.

In the darkness my skin sparked, the only indication he had any effect whatsoever on me—or rather, on Sabara.

The smile on his lips meant my reaction hadn't gone unnoticed. "You see? You can pretend all you want, but I know she's in there, listening to everything we say." His grin widened, his teeth flashing white. "Or was that you? It's all right if it was, Charlaina. You're allowed to enjoy yourself. You are queen, after all."

I flinched from him. "And is this how you treat a queen?" I cocked an eyebrow at him, hoping Sabara was paying attention now. I wanted to prod her, prod both of them, the way he was prodding me. To make her question him, even just the scantest bit. To make her look at Niko the way he really was, a two-faced scoundrel. "Because that's not how I saw it. It looked to me like you and Queen Elena were pretty chummy. From what I could see, you've *enjoyed* yourselves quite a lot. Am I wrong?"

I waited for the explosion my taunts would cause, but my words didn't have quite the effect I'd hoped on Sabara, who remained silent.

Niko, on the other hand, had plenty to say. "It's all for the greater good, Charlaina," he explained. "Queen Elena is exactly who I'm talking about. She's the solution I mean."

"Solution? What possible solution could you expect me to accept?" I bristled. "Is that the 'cure' Elena wrote to me about?" But I already knew the answer. "That's no *cure*."

Enemy or not, I wasn't sure I could do that. In fact, I was certain I could not. How could I live with myself if I were to force Sabara's Essence onto—*into*—Elena? Besides, even if I were willing to allow it, there was nothing to stop Sabara from killing me the moment she had a new host. She would have control of her powers once more, and she could easily turn them against me.

I wouldn't, she insisted, her words echoing hollowly inside my head.

I didn't believe her, and she knew as much.

"I won't do it. How can you expect me to just . . . to . . ." I lowered my voice, not even able to say these words aloud as my eyes searched Niko's. "To . . . ask her to die?" I finally breathed into the darkness between us.

Niko's hands captured mine, which were still bound in front of me. He lifted them to his lips. "That's what I'm telling you. That's what I'm saying. You don't have to ask her. She *wants* this. She wants to say the words. She wants to become part of the Essence and live forever. *She wants immortality.*" He said the last words in the ancient tongue that only he and Sabara understood, the language they'd spoken when they'd first met, all those many, many years ago. When they'd forged their eternal bond.

If only I hadn't understood it too. Because I knew the truth. Elena wouldn't survive the way I had.

"She won't be immortal," I hissed. "You're lying to her. She'll die just like the rest of them. Fade into . . . nothing. Vanish. Then it'll be just you and Sabara, or Layla, or whatever it is that you call her, together again until people start asking questions about you, wanting to know why you don't age the way she does. The way they all do. And then what, Niko?" I jerked my hands from his, unable to stand the feel of his skin on mine. "Then you'll kill another queen, and another?"

"Or a princess," he answered dispassionately. "Makes no difference to me, as long as she has royal blood in her veins, and as long as she's willing to say the words."

"You're as evil as she is," I asserted, not caring that I was insulting Sabara, the one person I could never escape.

"What did you think you were coming for? Did you really believe Elena would perform some sort of . . . exorcism? That there would be no consequences?"

I couldn't admit the truth, that I had hoped more than anything for that.

The silence was long and raw. I couldn't let them get away with this—their plan to murder Elena to satisfy their own selfish desires. I detested the queen for what she she'd done to Xander and for what she was doing to my country, yes. But I couldn't stand by and let them just . . . eliminate her.

I closed my eyes, refusing to speak of it any longer. Refusing to listen to Niko's assurances that this was the key to all our troubles. Refusing to give in to his promises that once the transfer was complete, he and Sabara would have what they wanted—each other—and would leave me, and Ludania, in peace.

But I couldn't shut out that other voice, the one that continued to haunt me far into my sleep. Sabara, who refused to let it go. Who begged and pleaded and cajoled, trying everything in her arsenal to persuade me to give her Essence over to Elena.

SAGE

The whispers were maddening.

They intruded on her dreams . . . out-of-place and fragmented snippets of a conversation she was never meant to hear. They didn't belong in the hazy depths of her sleep, and seemed to come from somewhere else, somewhere intangible and far away. Like clouds or raindrops, or birds that skittered first in and then out of range again, making them hard to distinguish from one another. Hard to catch and hold on to.

They came from somewhere outside of her.

But the jab—the sharp poke that stabbed her cheek—was real. Tangible enough to wake her.

She came up sputtering, her hand reflexively reaching for the knife she always kept hidden in her boot. She never made it that far. The spear—crude as it was, and fashioned from nothing more than a stick that had been whittled to a fine yet lethal point—stabbed her even harder in the face. Jerking back from it, she reached up to feel the faint prick of blood.

Her eyes focused and traveled the length of the makeshift

spear, following the smooth bark that covered it, all the way to the unusual creature who wielded it.

She'd never seen anyone—or anything—quite like it. Small, like a child. Yet armed and smeared from head to toe in the very earth itself. Beyond her diminutive abductor Sage saw twenty more of them just like him or her, all equally undersize. And all similarly coated in mud.

She glanced sideways to Xander, who still slept.

Dropping a hand to his shoulder, she attempted to rouse him with a quick shake while she asked the stranger holding her hostage, "Who are you?" When there was no response, she tried again, this time in Astonian. She couldn't help wondering if, somehow, she and Xander had wandered back over to the wrong side of the border. If they'd somehow slipped back onto her country's soil. "*What do you want from us?*"

The mud-covered face shattered, crackling into fragments that fell in places and revealed bits of skin beneath. A giggle erupted from the creature's mouth.

It's a girl, Sage thought, hearing the lyrical tones that bubbled forth. Only a little girl.

But she knew well enough that even little girls could be deadly. She'd been used as a weapon to seek out her sister's enemies since she'd hit her twelfth year. She'd killed by the time she was thirteen.

Being young meant only that they were smaller. Not harmless.

Xander stirred. He'd had a restless night. She knew because her sleep had been sporadic, and she'd wakened again and again to his fits of malaise.

"They're not Astonian," he managed, trying to sit before the coughing fit seized him.

The coughing had started last night too. It was new, that symptom, and didn't seem to fit with the fevers.

She had no idea what that meant.

"Where's your leader?" he asked in Englaise. No matter their class of birth, if they were Ludanian, they should understand him.

The girl kept her spear pointed at Sage's cheek, and Sage didn't try to swat it away, despite the fact that she could. There were twenty other spears at the ready, and she worried about how many of these children she'd have to kill before one of them managed to get to Xander.

If only he were strong enough to defend himself.

Beside her he hacked again, and she squeezed her eyes shut as she waited for the paroxysm to pass.

"Please," she intoned as gently as she could. "Let me make him some tea. I promise not to try anything. I just want to . . . to make him better."

The response was the sharpened point of the stick jabbing her already bleeding wound.

She raised her hands in surrender. "Okay, okay. No tea." She shot a questioning glance to Xander again when she saw him still struggling to sit upright.

Not one of the filthy children bothered to raise their harpoons at him. They recognized a wounded animal when they saw one. Xander was no threat to them.

"Your leader?" he repeated, this time managing not to cough.

From the back of the gathering there was a commotion. Sage watched as bodies parted and someone slipped between them. Whoever he was—and it was definitely a he, all caked in mud—was at least a head taller than any of the rest of them. He was lean and tall and older than the others, and he was coming right toward the front of the small gathering.

When he stopped, the girl took a deferential step backward. It was like watching those in the presence of her sister—the queen of Astonia. Like he was a king among his disciples.

A king? Sage wanted to laugh at the notion of a king in a position of power, but with Xander beside her, the situation seemed less than humorous.

"What do you want from us?" she demanded. "We weren't causing any trouble."

The boy's unsettling gaze fell on her, making her feel at once apprehensive. He didn't carry a spear, Sage was quick to note, but he had a weapon. His arms rested effortlessly on an assault rifle slung over his shoulder. It was nothing like the makeshift spikes of his disciples, not homemade or easily broken in two.

It was sleek and polished and shiny and new. And he carried it with an ease that conveyed he was accustomed to such weaponry. That he knew his way around a gun of this caliber.

Imagining him with a crown on his head was not so far-fetched.

"You're on our land," he told her. "You're trespassers, both of you." He barely looked at Xander, his concentration solely directed at Sage. His head tipped down as he studied her from beneath his low brow.

He's trying to intimidate us, she supposed as she considered his posturing. The gun, the black stare, the way he lowered his voice.

"We . . . didn't mean to. We were just trying to find someone," she started, but beside her, Xander's rheumy cough interrupted her. "Please," she tried again, reaching out to Xander. "Let me make him some tea."

The boy turned his attention to Xander then as well. He took a step closer, and then a step to the side, his head cocked as he considered the ailing man still struggling to remain upright in front of him. The boy's black eyes roamed to the rounded butt of newly replaced bandages that covered the place on Xander's left arm, just above his wrist, where his hand should have been.

"The thing is . . ." The boy's voice wasn't as low now when he spoke, and his stance had relaxed. As if he'd forgotten he was trying to intimidate them. "I know you."

Sage couldn't imagine when their paths had ever crossed. Not a boy like this. One who covered himself in mud and carried gleaming new guns like this, and who led a pack of children through the forests like a horde of wild beasts. "You do?" she asked dubiously.

His unnerving eyes snapped back to her. "Not you," he responded, and then turned back to look at Xander as he dropped to a crouch in front of him and did his best to wipe away the crusty layer of mud from his own nose and cheeks and forehead. "Don't you remember me, Xander? I'm Caspar. Eden is my sister."

XV

"Well, well, well. Look who we have here. If it isn't the errant queen of Ludania." Elena spoke to me as if we weren't at odds at all, as if we weren't at war and she weren't holding me captive.

She spoke to me as if she were chastising a naughty child who'd misbehaved on her watch.

"I hear we're having something of a disagreement over what to do. And here I thought things were going to be . . . so simple between you and me," she intoned.

I recalled the first time I'd met Elena, as Queen Neva's guest at the summit in Vannova. I remembered how lovely she'd been with her shiny bronze hair and her matching gown, and how I'd considered her an ally then. How, even though I'd balked at the idea of one queen invading the lands of another—something she'd done in her efforts to support Xander during his revolution against Sabara—I'd been willing to put the past behind us, to chalk it up to old rivalries that had nothing at all to do with me. I'd extended an olive branch to her. Called a truce for the good of our neighboring nations.

And she'd been so gracious about it.

I hadn't realized that the entire time she'd been smiling to my face, and kissing my cheek at parties and gatherings, she'd been planning my assassination behind my back.

Standing before her now, and seeing that same inscrutable expression on her beautiful face, I felt as if I were balancing on the tenuous threads of her spider's web, her greedy eyes inspecting my every move. She was waiting for me to make one misstep, so she could snare me in her sticky trap.

"How could you think things would be simple?" I retorted. "You've declared war on Ludania." Just saying the words aloud made my skin blaze.

"Oh, that." Her dismissive tone was infuriating, fanning the flames of my disgust for her even more. "I tried to warn you, Your Majesty. I tried to send you a message so we could settle this without bloodshed."

My teeth clenched as I recalled the package I'd received, as if Xander's bloodshed hadn't counted. "And I came!" I shrieked, unable to remain calm in the face of her callousness. "I did what you wanted, and you still attacked my country."

"Yes, well, that was an unfortunate turn of events. I'd hoped to wait, so you and Xander might be . . . reunited. But plans changed."

I wasn't sure what that meant, but hearing Xander's name, and hearing the indifference in her voice, made me weak. I tried not to choke when I asked, "So, he's no longer . . . He's not . . . here?"

"I'm afraid not."

"All he wanted," I started, "was accord, and you . . . you . . ."
I couldn't finish, and I had to turn my cheek to keep from falling apart completely.

Niko swam into my line of sight then, where he stood off to my side. He watched me as eagerly as Elena had, and suddenly I felt like I was caught between two equally deadly predators.

Elena sighed. It was exaggerated, and less than sincere. "The incident with Xander was unfortunate, I admit as much. We tried to reason with him, but he was obstinate. He refused to play nice."

Play nice. I tried to imagine how they'd presented the situation to him. Surely they hadn't told him everything. Not about what they'd planned to do once they'd lured me to Astonia.

Or maybe they had. Xander would never have allowed Sabara to sit on another throne. She was the reason he'd turned his back on his family in the first place. Why he'd started a rebellion that had divided his country in two.

She was the reason Max hadn't grown up with his older brother to depend on.

Xander would never forgive Sabara for any of those things, let alone put her back in power.

"What about you, Charlaina?" she asked, using my given name now, as if we were old friends. "Will you play nice?"

I squeezed my eyes shut and tried to still my trembling hands. Beneath my skin I could feel the electric pulse of a thousand flares erupting as I tried to quell my rage.

From deeper within I heard the throaty laughter of Sabara ringing up through my ears.

We're not so different, you and I, she urged, and as much as I hated her for saying it, I wasn't sure she was entirely wrong. *You're exactly like me. I think that's what frightens you most, doesn't it, Charlaina? That you'll become me. I know what you're thinking even before you do. Go ahead and try,* she offered. *It'll only make you weaker.*

I knew she was right, but Elena was dangerous. She had to be stopped. I might not be willing to give Sabara to Elena, but I could certainly use Sabara against her.

It was worth the risk.

I reached down—deep, deep down—digging for that power that I'd employed before.

I felt the surge first in my fingertips—the tingling. That was how I knew it was working. I was drawing Sabara's own ability from her and would use it for myself. Her energy coursed through me, electrifying my entire body. Making me feel strong. Complete.

Exhilarated.

Lifting my hand until it was raised in front of me, I glanced sideways and caught a glimpse of Niko. He recognized the gesture. He knew exactly what I was about to do.

"Sabara," he wailed in that archaic language the two of them shared. *"Layla, don't do it. Don't let her do this!"*

I felt a thrill of satisfaction course through me when I saw that it was working. When I saw Elena, the cords of her neck straining as her airway narrowed. Her eyes flew wide and her hands shot up to her collarbone.

I'd seen this before. I'd watched people suffer and claw at their own throats, trying to find a way to breathe. Trying to save themselves.

It was no use.

But Sabara wasn't to be counted out. She'd heard Niko's pleas, and she reacted to them. I felt her responding to the need she heard in his voice, yet I was ready for her this time.

You can't stop us, she jeered.

Sabara came at me then, with everything she had. White-hot rage erupted within me, scorching everything in its path. She was stronger than I'd ever felt her before, more determined to win this battle. To take me down. I could sense her resolve, and her deepest desire. She intended to regain her power.

But I was determined too.

I fought her just as hard as she fought me. I planted my feet and clenched my fists, focusing solely on her now. In front of me Elena sputtered and gasped as she was momentarily forgotten while I battled another opponent.

I refused to give in. I could do this. I was certain I could.

I felt Sabara's Essence everywhere, all at once. She threatened and taunted me, her words tumbling over one another and coiling together until it sounded as if there were a hundred of her trapped inside my head.

You're too weak.

You can't beat me.

Surrender.

I will kill you. . . .

It was those last words that I recognized as the truth—the most honest thing she'd ever said to me. It was the reason I could never unleash her.

Sabara *would* kill me.

But that instant of clarity also made me hesitate. And in that moment Sabara saw her opportunity and reclaimed her ability.

I never had a chance.

I felt her energy—the power I'd borrowed from her—slipping away as she withdrew it, taking it back from me. My fingers no longer itched and tingled. Electricity no longer coursed in my veins. I wasn't just weak; I was debilitated by the transition.

I could no sooner kill Elena by simply waving my hand at her than she could me.

It took me too long to admit my defeat and lower my hand. The ground beneath me felt unstable, as did my confidence, and my shoulders were suddenly heavy.

When I slid my gaze over to Niko, I saw him wearing his triumph in a sly, knowing grin that I longed to smash from his arrogant face.

Elena staggered to her feet, and I realized I'd never even seen her fall. She inhaled, trying to recoup her composure as she glanced at Niko. "Will I . . . When I . . ." She had a difficult time finding the right words. And then she glared condescendingly in my direction. "Will I be able to do what she just did?"

Niko's grin widened and took on a different quality when he directed it at her. I recognized that look. He'd flashed it at me before too. He was making her feel special—as if he cared about her above all else. "All that and more, my sweet," he crooned. He swept her hand into his and lifted it to his lips. "All that and much, much more."

The ecstasy that flooded her face was almost painful to look upon. Her cheeks flushed, and tears glistened in her eyes. Niko was dealing in vanity.

"He's lying." My voice was shaky as I faced her, wondering

why I bothered. I had no intention of letting her take Sabara from me.

Elena just laughed, a trilling sound that implied she had no cares in the world. "He told me you'd say that," she retorted. "He said you'd try to keep her for yourself, that you wouldn't want to give up your shot at eternity."

"There is no eternity!" I shouted back at her. "You won't survive the transfer. She'll kill you."

Automatically she massaged her throat, and I wondered if she even realized she was doing it. "You survived. You think I'm not as strong as you? Stronger, even?" She said it like the notion was preposterous, and she laughed some more, looking around at the soldiers who surrounded her. They laughed too. And then she closed the distance between us and grabbed my arm. "I'm ten times the queen you are, Vendor."

I raised my eyebrow. "Only ten?" I shot back.

She slapped my face. Hard.

My head snapped to the side, and I saw Niko watching us, an amused expression on his face.

"Let's do this," she told him. "I'm tired of waiting."

My chest constricted as I realized her intent. Elena meant to try to make the transfer now.

What if it wasn't up to me at all? What if she said the words and I wasn't able to stop Sabara from leaving—the way I hadn't been able to stop her from taking her power away from me?

"You can't! You can't, Elena! I wasn't lying. She'll destroy you! Sabara will take you over and you'll disappear." I shouted until my voice was hoarse, but Elena was under Niko's spell now.

He'd said all the right things. He'd convinced her she would live forever.

"Take me," she said boldly, ignoring my cautions. Her voice rang out, practiced and strong and resolute, not a single quiver, or doubt, to be heard. "Take me instead."

My eyes widened as I waited to see what would transpire next. And then it happened.

I felt her, Sabara, uncoiling from the very pit of me. She was preparing to make the move from one body to another. Liberating me as she disentangled her soul—her Essence—from mine.

Darkness and hatred and everything vile about her released me, and I felt the swell of those things that had been staved off in me for so long returning in a rush: virtue and joy and warmth. Things I'd had to fight to feel because Sabara had smothered them at every turn.

But I couldn't have those things. As much as I wanted them, I couldn't let my temptation to be whole again—to be me and only me—sway my decision to keep Sabara caged. I had to hold on to her because I was the only one who could.

And I did. With all my might.

It wasn't nearly as hard as I'd expected it to be, to bottle her back inside me. I simply repeated those very same words silently inside my own head, *Take me instead. Take me instead. Take me instead.*

Eventually Sabara stopped grappling against me. She had no choice. She became too weary to fight the truth. I was winning.

When at last I smiled my own triumphant smile, I watched Elena's face crumple.

"It can't be!" she shrieked into the sky. "It can't be!" I stood back and watched as the queen who was ten times the queen I was threw a tantrum to rival any child's. "I will have my eternity! I will! *I will!*" Her face was mottled with rage as she shouted again. "This is your doing, isn't it? You won't let me have her."

I didn't blink or move, just continued to smile that gloriously victorious smile. I had them right where I wanted them.

Elena's voice circled the rim of madness when she bellowed, "Bring the other one! Bring her now!"

It wasn't hard to decipher who she meant, and I felt the floor, which had felt only unsteady a moment before, drop out from under me.

When Eden was dragged in by two of Elena's henchmen, my jaw tightened, but I managed to keep my face expressionless even as my mind spun in a million different directions.

I thought of Xander's hand, entombed in a cardboard box, and acid rose in my throat, burning the back of my tongue.

"Give me the soul of Sabara," Elena demanded from between gritted teeth. "Give her to me or I'll kill your associate here."

I studied Eden. I could feel the fury coming off her—as I'm sure we all could—thick, like black smoke that burned our lungs and stung our eyes. She was everything I'd ever strived to be—loyal, passionate, tough, and sharp. Her face was still bruised from her fight with Brooklynn, and her jaw was set now in steely resolve. I wondered if she understood precisely what Elena was asking me to do. If she knew that Sabara was looking for a new host.

Either way, she knew enough to level her gaze on me.

"Don't you dare," she commanded, as if she were the queen and I the guard. "This is a war, Your Majesty. You do this, and she wins. They all win."

"Shut up," Elena hissed.

But I knew she meant it. Eden could no more hide the veracity of her conviction than she could the color of her shockingly purple hair.

I also knew she was right. If I gave Elena Sabara's Essence now, we'd lose. Not just here, today, but the war. There'd be nothing to stop Sabara from killing me and then marching Elena's forces all the way to the Capitol and taking her place on the throne once more.

She'd have total control over both domains. She'd undo everything I'd worked for—all the freedoms I'd offered the people of Ludania, all the injustices I'd tried to set right.

All I could hope was that Elena was bluffing. That she was simply trying to fool me into giving up Sabara by threatening Eden's life.

Eden, I could sense, had no such delusions.

If she had been able to sense my feelings, however, she would have felt torment and despair. Elena might as well have asked me to kill Eden with my own two hands.

When I finally found the strength to speak, my voice was small and pitiful. "I'm sorry," I whispered, knowing I might very well be issuing Eden's death sentence by refusing to give up Sabara. I almost couldn't finish, and then I managed, "I can't."

Elena's lips thinned, pulling into a hard line that left no question as to whether she'd meant her threat or not. She directed her unfeeling gaze to me, and I wanted to shrink away from it, to take back my refusal. But I couldn't, because that would mean setting Sabara free.

The queen didn't say anything. She only nodded, but that was enough. That single action was all the order she had to give.

I had to close my eyes when I saw the soldiers push Eden to her knees. She didn't resist them, and she didn't try to beg for her life. Around us the air went still and serene as Eden accepted her fate.

And then I heard her, right before the sound of gunfire split the silence: "You're doing the right thing, Charlie."

I couldn't breathe.

My chest was heavy. Crushed with the weight of what I'd done.

I didn't remember being moved, or when I'd stopped wailing Eden's name, or when the night had come again. But all of these things had happened, and when at last I finally opened my eyes once more, they were swollen and sore from all the tears I'd wept, and all the ones that were still waiting to come.

I vowed never to eat or breathe or love again.

Love was too painful.

Life was too painful.

Air was too painful.

I curled as tightly as I could into a ball in the bed I'd been deposited on, only vaguely noting it wasn't the one I'd been in the night before. That didn't matter either.

The only thing that mattered now was that I hadn't given

Sabara or Niko or Elena what they wanted. I no longer cared if I'd done it for the right reasons, or the wrong ones. All I cared about was that they were being punished too.

My heart was hard and bitter, and I envisioned a thousand ways to hurt them, to kill them and those they loved. To flog, flay, and torture them in every conceivable way.

I wanted revenge. Pure and simple.

And Eden's words continued to replay in my head, over and over and over again, *You're doing the right thing. . . . You're doing the right thing. . . .*

I wanted to take solace from her final declaration, but I couldn't. Not now. Not yet.

She might have been right, but it didn't matter because she was gone.

Forever.

Eden was gone.

BROOKLYNN

She would've liked to have more troops, but this was all she had at her disposal. They were a sad excuse for an army—her band of 178 able-bodied soldiers. Plus Aron. He was fine to look at, she supposed, but he had zero experience when it came to things like killing.

She scoped the fields below and noted the impressive expanse of tents crawling with the ferocious bird-masked warriors from Astonia. She saw tanks and cannons, and even from her vantage point she could make out the imposing mounted grenade launchers that would have made her giddy had they been her own. The enemy's firepower was nearly as impressive as their ranks.

Her troops had weaponry as well, but they had to be cautious in utilizing it. They had Charlie to think of.

Charlie was in there, somewhere in that labyrinth of shelters. They couldn't just roll in, guns blazing, or they'd risk catching her in the cross fire.

No, this would have to be an operation built on tactics. She and Max had been trying to formulate a plan in which they could pinpoint Charlie's location and infiltrate the camp to rescue her.

Which meant taking their time. Studying the comings and goings of the soldiers down there. Figuring out where Charlie might be.

She only hoped they didn't have to wait too long. And she hoped, for all their sakes, that Charlie was still alive.

"Anything yet?" Max eased down beside her where she was crouched in the darkness, his voice soft and low, and filled with that same note of fear she heard every time he spoke.

Brooklynn sighed, giving him the same answer she'd given the last time he'd asked, and the time before that. "Nothing. There was some movement about an hour ago, centered right about there." She passed him the binoculars and pointed to a tent near the middle, near what they suspected was the command tent—the nerve center of Elena's operation. "But it was dark, and it all happened so quickly, I couldn't see what they were moving. Whatever it was, I doubt it was a person, because it didn't move at all." She paused, and then added pensively, "Unless . . ."

Max stiffened. "Don't do that," he insisted, almost as much to himself as to her. "She's fine. I know she is."

Brook nodded, shaking off the thought. "You're right," she agreed.

He handed back the binoculars, his voice heavy. "How much longer do you think we can wait?"

Brook reflected on that as she took the binoculars and surveyed the camp again, stopping here and there. She didn't say anything, and Max didn't press her. It was a good question, one that they'd asked each other too many times already. And one that neither of them had an answer for.

Too soon, and they risked putting Charlie in harm's way.

Too long, and they risked that Elena would kill her.

It was a fine line they walked.

Brook inhaled, and was just about to lower the binoculars, when she saw something at the far end of the encampment. A flicker of something, or a flash. Like an explosion.

Exactly like an explosion.

It was followed almost immediately by another. And then another.

The sounds were muffled, because they were so far away, but they were undeniable.

She lowered the binoculars when she realized she didn't need them. The detonations were clear, briefly banishing the darkness. They continued, one after the other, blasting the outer perimeter of the tents, which caught on fire, one by one, on the opposite side of camp from them. "You're seeing this, right?" she asked Max, who was already getting to his feet.

She stood now too, her eyes wide as she tried to make sense of it.

The entire camp seemed to come awake then, sleeping giants prodded by an invisible attacker in the night. Soldiers emerged from their tents half-dressed and carrying lit torches. Fires ignited and weapons detonated as Elena's soldiers returned fire.

Within a matter of seconds the field before them was ablaze in flames and flashes and flares. There were shouts and shrieks and bellowed commands that managed to reach all the way into the hills.

"Who is that?" Brook asked, knowing that Max didn't have an answer for her. She lifted the binoculars again, straining to see who had beat them to the punch and started a battle against Elena's troops. Another battalion of her own soldiers? Civilian militia?

She had no idea. It was too dark to make out the attackers from here.

But Max was already heading back toward their own, much smaller and much less impressive encampment. "It doesn't really matter, I guess. We need to get down there and save Charlie. Now."

XVI

Somewhere in my well of despair, the vacuum in which I existed—just me and the nothingness that tried to engulf me, sucking and pulling at me until I was raw and hopeless and ravaged—a sound emerged.

It was loud, and it shook the ground beneath me, which was already shaky at best. The sound was crisp and clear, however, and penetrated my misery, reminding me I was still alive. Still breathing. Still whole.

I blinked, but it was dark inside my tent, and despite the fact that I'd been glowing every day for months since Sabara had taken up residence with me, I didn't now. At least not enough to crack the blackness of the night.

But something did.

Something beyond the thick canvas walls of my enclosure.

And one sound became another, became another, as the bangs and blasts grew louder and closer and brighter.

There's fire out there, I thought absently. Fire and bombs. Still, I didn't rouse, because my heart was too heavy with ache.

My hands were no longer bound, I realized in that moment, the first real moment of lucid thought I'd had about my surroundings. Apparently, a queen with no will to live was no threat.

They were right, of course. I hadn't even considered trying to flee.

If there was the slightest chance I could actually reach them—either Niko or Elena—with some sort of weapon. If I could find a way to eviscerate them with my bare hands . . .

Well, that might give me some reason to try, I thought, the sliver of a smile finding my lips. Also, my skin shone just the tiniest bit at the idea of the two of them disemboweled.

But since that idea seemed improbable, what with the constant contingent of guards following them wherever they went, there was no point attempting it.

Besides, I thought, looking at my empty and helpless hands. *Where would I find such a weapon anyway?*

All I was now was a prison for Sabara. She'd tried to use my misery against me, to take control once more, but I had somehow found just enough energy to suppress her. The revulsion I felt for her part in all this fueled my resolve to keep her down.

The earth beneath my feet continued to tremble and quake as boots rumbled past and voices roared in disharmony, shouting over one another—orders and instructions and directions, some at odds with others. And above them all the sounds of explosives continued to pierce the night sky.

It was utter madness.

When my tent flaps were flung wide apart, I didn't so much

as lift my head. It was as heavy as a boulder, and the effort would have been colossal.

Eden would have lifted her head, I told myself. But even that wasn't enough to goad me into action. So I lay there, waiting for something to happen.

I didn't have to wait long. I was hauled abruptly to my feet. My legs refused to cooperate, however, and as soon as I was released, I withered limply to the floor.

I was useless. Helpless.

I was nothing.

"Get up. You're being moved."

I heard the voice, and understood the words, but did not comply.

He repeated them. "I said, get up!" This time his grip was ruthless, and he shook me, making my teeth rattle together.

His efforts were in vain, though, and I collapsed the moment he let me go.

"Worthless," he muttered.

That was when I heard the familiar scrape of metal, and a steel click. That was when something inside me clicked as well.

Lifting only my eyes at first, and then slowly, very slowly, inching my chin up just the scantest amount so I could confirm what my ears had told me, I searched him.

My eyes fell on the gun, the polished black gun he pointed right at my head, and I reawakened.

There was no way I could know if he was the soldier who'd executed Eden—they all looked the same in their raven masks. But I reacted to him as if he were.

I didn't fear the weapon that threatened me, or the man who stood behind it.

"Get up, you stupid bitch," he swore, kicking me. "Queen or no, I'll shoot you right here, and no one'll ever know the difference."

I moved, but I didn't do as he asked. I ignored his orders and instead got to my knees and dropped my chin to my chest.

I invited him to shoot me in the head.

Above me I heard his breathy chuckle, and my entire body prepared for what was about to happen. "Suit yourself, you crazy—"

I lifted my head then, so I could look at his birdlike face. Before he could process what was happening, I grabbed the barrel of the gun with one hand, forcing the nose away from my head so that it was pointing past my shoulder. With my other hand I reached around the back of the gun and secured it so I had a solid hold.

When he finally moved, he pulled on his weapon, which is exactly what I'd counted on. With my grip secure, he pulled me up, giving me the momentum I needed. And before he'd gained his balance all the way, I was already kicking.

My first kick connected with his groin. I was prepared to kick again and again—the way Zafir had taught me, but it wasn't necessary. That first kick was solid. I felt it, the way his body collapsed in on itself the moment my toe landed.

I'd found my mark.

In shock and in pain, the soldier released his hold on the gun and staggered backward, away from me.

His gun was my gun now, and I knew how to use it.

Suddenly *he* became the object of my reprisal. He was the reason Eden was dead. He deserved to die, just as Niko and Elena and Sabara did.

I couldn't see his face right before I pulled the trigger—it was covered by the mask—but I heard his last word, which was only a simpering, "Bitch." And then he was quiet.

The gunshot blended into the sounds of the rest of the battle raging around us. I held my breath and waited, but no one came running to my tent to see what had gone wrong. No one came to the dying soldier's aid, or to recapture the queen who was now free and wearing a stolen bird mask.

I was rolling the dead warrior over to steal his cloak, too, knowing it would be far too large on me, when I noticed the blade stashed in the back of his belt.

It was solid in my hand, and its blade was sawlike. It would be perfect for gutting the Astonian queen and her traitorous paramour.

I tucked it into the back of my trousers and reminded myself one last time of what Eden had said, letting it take on a whole new meaning. *You're doing the right thing,* she'd said.

Well, I *would* do the right thing, I decided. I would make Eden's death mean something by refusing to surrender. Refusing to be their victim again.

And by making them pay.

There were bodies and blasts and clouds of smoke everywhere. It reminded me of the day at the Academy, when it had been attacked during my visit there, and so many children had been murdered simply because they'd been in the wrong place at the wrong time. Simply because they'd been so close to me.

It was like that again today. This was all because of me.

All because Ludania had a new queen.

But I refused to feel blame, especially not for these deaths. The guilt was Elena's to bear, if only she had the capacity to feel guilt. The truth was, this was because of her. Because of her lust, her jealousy, her vanity.

She shouldn't be sitting on any throne, and I certainly wouldn't let her have Ludania's.

I suspected those were my men out there launching the assault against Elena's camp, feeling much the same as I did about Ludania's throne. I suspected that somehow the Ludanian armies had caught up with Elena's forces and were waging war against her.

I doubted, however, that they realized I was in here, and that I could become a casualty should I be in the wrong place when their bombs were launched.

I moved quickly now, my disguise making it easy to maneuver through the throng of other bird-faced warriors. No one seemed to notice that I was half their size, or that I was moving in the opposite direction. They were all too focused on their own tasks. Far too occupied with the trappings of battle to pay attention to a pipsqueak underling who ran away from the uproar of the attacks.

I had no idea where I was headed, though. And the mask made it hard to see. The goggles' lenses were transparent, but they were clouded over by residue from the smoke that seemed to be everywhere, including inside the mask. I choked on the taste of ash and the stink of my own sweat. I could hear every breath I took echoing back at me.

"Damn!" I cursed as I reached what seemed to be yet another dead end—a row of tents and tanks and soldiers packed so tightly together, it would be impossible for me to get through without drawing attention to myself. "Damn, damn, damn."

I turned and raced down another long stretch of tents, past more screaming soldiers who barely noticed me. Torches flew past me in a blur as I refused to slow. And all the while, beneath my cloak, my fingers clutched the handle of the gun I'd pilfered, in case my luck soured and someone tried to stop and question me.

I ran, turning corner after corner, and ran some more. I bumped into soldiers and whipped past horses and over-heard voices and smelled fire. I had no sense of where I was. I thought I was running away from the battlefront, but then it grew louder, and the ground rumbled more intensely, until it seemed I was standing at the very epicenter of it.

My heart sped, and so did my feet, carrying me away, until again I thought I'd put some distance between me and the fighting. Corpses littered the ground in places where the earth had been hollowed out by explosions. There were body parts, dismembered and grisly and charred, strewn about, and I could only imagine that the stench I smelled was that of burned flesh.

I ran from that, too.

There seemed to be no safe place. And no way out.

Stopping, my side aching, I weighed my options. As badly as I wanted to go after Elena and Niko, I knew this was neither the time nor place. Even if I managed to find them in this maze, I'd only be recaptured and used against my own troops as a way to force them to surrender.

I could hide in one of the tents and wait it out, stay out of sight until the fighting subsided, and then try to slip away, unnoticed. But that, too, seemed a poor plan. One that would likely end in my being discovered and recaptured by Elena and her men.

No, I had to take a chance. It was now or never.

My best option was to try to slip through the perimeter at its weakest and least defended point. To make a run for it.

Also not a great plan, but better than waiting there to die.

If only I could reach my troops to let them know I was alive. I'd be safe then.

Urging myself to keep going, I ignored Sabara's whispered rancor, *Surrender, Charlaina. Surrender now while you still can.*

She was still angry over being bested by me—still trapped in a place she longed to escape. Her vitriol spilled into my thoughts, and my blood, as she tried everything in her power to poison me.

I ran, knowing there was nothing I could do to save myself from the danger within.

Unfortunately, I ran smack into a wall of soldiers who were marching in the opposite direction. The impact threw me backward, and I landed flat on my back.

The mask, which had been too loose for my head in the first place, slipped halfway up my face. The goggles got lost in my tangled hair beneath the hood of my stolen cloak.

I was virtually blinded by the metal covering my eyes.

"Who are you?" a voice boomed above me.

My heart pounded as I realized I'd been discovered. My mouth went dry. Too dry to form words, or even to move. I was paralyzed by fear. Even my fingers, still curled around the gun's grip, were frozen.

I wanted to answer, to tell him there'd been some sort of mistake. To surrender, even. But I was incapable of doing anything.

And then a gunshot split the air right above me, and I flinched. And flinched again at the next one. And again, and again.

I waited for the pain. For the searing heat of a bullet's wound. For the warmth of seeping blood. Something to indicate where I'd been shot.

But there was none of that. Just the sounds and smells of the battle continuing around me.

When I dared to reach for my mask, my heart was hammering so hard, my ribs ached. I lifted it, pushing it all the way aside.

In front of me, where there had once been a massive wall of beaked soldiers, there was now a pile of gunshot-riddled bodies slumped on the ground.

I scurried as far back from them as I could get, glancing around to see who had done this . . . and saw the last person—or people—I'd expected.

Caspar—or at least I was almost certain it was Caspar, with his black eyes peering at me from behind his mud-crusted disguise—grinned down at me. "Thought I might find you here."

"How—how did you know it was me?"

"Recognized your glow."

I glanced down at myself and could see he was right. There was a definite luminescence radiating from where I'd removed the mask.

I wasn't sure what to say. This was the strangest turn of events I could ever have imagined. All the fighting—the bombs, the bodies—I had been certain it was Ludanian troops. "Why? Why would you do this? Why are you here?"

Caspar reached down, holding out a hand to help me up. I was still shaking, still half-convinced I'd been shot. The kids behind him were all carrying high-tech, military grade weapons that rivaled any I'd seen Elena's soldiers wielding. I supposed I should've been glad it was his forces who'd found me and not my own. Caspar's seemed to pack a heavier punch.

"We can't talk now. We were told you'd be here. Been tracking you, in fact." He drew me along, his underage militia surrounding us, ready to fight. "I'll explain later. But for now, we gotta get you someplace safe."

A new set of rounds started firing at the other end of the encampment, in the direction I'd been heading when Elena's soldiers had cut me off. I raised my hands to cover my ears as blast after blast tore at the air. The ground quaked beneath our feet.

Caspar looked to the black-haired girl beside him, whom I recognized, even without her crow. "What the— Who was that?" he asked.

I looked to each of their faces as they frowned over this new turn of events, but I already knew the answer.

I was about to tell them that this time it *was* my forces, that *these* were the Ludanian soldiers I'd been waiting for, when the ground right in front of us exploded, splitting apart.

The impact threw me, and everyone else, wide and far.

And then everything went black.

The first thing I was aware of was the taste of dirt and the smell of sulfur. Or maybe I was tasting the sulfur and smelling dirt.

There was the ringing, too. It was high pitched and constant, and muffled every other sound around me, if there even were any.

All I knew was the ringing.

I tried to sit up, but the world tipped crazily. Up felt like down, and the other way around. I was so disoriented, I barely noticed the way my elbow was bent at a strange angle beneath me.

I blinked, and blinked again, but my eyes stung. The sulfur that filled my nose seemed to be burning them as well. Breathing was hard too, although not in the same way it had been immediately after Eden had died. This was more tangible, and I found myself panting just to ease the throbbing in my ribs.

White smoke and tears clouded my vision. Between the columns of burning debris, I could see people rushing here and there, and from behind the ringing, I could make out the muffled, faraway shouts of voices, which were probably not so muffled or faraway at all. But I couldn't distinguish a single face among the throng, or make out a single word amid the buzz.

It was like being both blind and deaf, and entirely helpless.

I shook my head, trying to clear my senses, and then I tried to stand.

The world swayed, tipping first this way and then that. But my legs, by the grace of all that was good, held me in place. I kept my arms outstretched. If I stumbled, I wanted to at least attempt to cushion my fall.

But I didn't. Fall, that is.

I stood. Wobbly and unsure, but somehow I stood.

Slowly, ever so slowly, my hearing returned. The ringing remained, continuous and annoying—much in the way Sabara was—but eventually I could make out other sounds too. More gunfire. More cannon blasts. More voices—shouts and commands.

And, along with my hearing, my vision returned. The smoke eventually subsided as well, until I found myself standing near the edge of a crater so massive, I could hardly imagine what could have done so much damage.

Inside the crater, and all around it, were bodies. Bodies of the raven-faced warriors who belonged to Elena's army. Bodies of Caspar's followers, the mud stripped and peeled from their youthful faces. And bodies that could be identified as neither because they were too mutilated from the blast.

I saw the body of the black-haired girl. I knew even without going closer to inspect her that she was dead, because her sapphire eyes remained wide and unblinking, and her neck was distorted gruesomely.

I felt fortunate that I'd been thrown so far from the blast. That I hadn't been standing in the place where the bomb had struck. And at the same time, my heart ached for all those who had been.

The smell of sulfur made me gag, as did a thousand thoughts of children who no longer needed homes, and children who were newly orphaned, and brothers who'd just lost sisters, and lovers whose beds would now be empty.

War benefited no one. We were all losers on this day.

I vomited until my stomach was emptied, and when I was done, I wiped my mouth on the back of my hand. My chest and my elbow continued to throb, and I wondered if my ribs might have been cracked.

I tried to think, to decide what I should do next. I didn't see Caspar, but that didn't mean he wasn't among the bodies that had been flung about the cavernous basin in the earth. It just meant I couldn't identify his remains.

And it meant I was on my own now.

I still needed to escape, to find a way out, so I started back in the direction I'd been headed when Caspar had saved me.

It was the voice that stopped me, cutting through my regret, and the ringing in my ears.

"Not so fast, Your Majesty."

I would have spun to face him, willing my reflexes to match the beating of my heart. But I was too injured to react so hastily, and I likely would have fallen if I'd tried. Instead I turned sluggishly, deliberately.

Inside, Sabara gloated, *I knew he'd stop you. I knew he wouldn't let you get away, you insolent brat.*

"Niko," was all I said, keeping my bad arm braced to my stomach as I glanced suspiciously at the gun he held, and the three masked soldiers at his back.

He grinned then, and I suddenly wished I still had my gun,

that I hadn't lost it in the chaos of the blast. "You might want to come with me. We have a surprise for you."

I'd barely made it two steps into the tent when I saw her.

"Brooklynn!" I rasped, and struggled to break free from Niko's grip on my bad arm. But he wasn't letting me get away that easily. Apparently, one escape attempt made me a high-risk prisoner.

The jostling aggravated the pain, but I refused to give Niko the satisfaction of seeing me wince, so I bit it back, hiding my discomfort.

Brook was in the same situation I was, except that, even though she looked like she'd been through the wringer—her clothes ripped and covered in ash, her face swollen and bruised and cut—she was being held back by guards on either side of her and iron restraints that shackled both her wrists and her feet.

"I killed twelve of 'em before they got me," she crowed, her chest puffing boastfully. Of course, she said that right before she caught an elbow to the side of her head from one of the masked warriors beside her.

She staggered slightly, looking as off balance as I'd felt right after the blast, but she came up quickly, prepared to fight all over again. She threw her body at the soldier, but he cuffed her, this time with the back of his metal-studded glove. The blow sent her reeling into the waiting arms of the soldier on her other side.

"Stop them. No more!" I shouted, my voice sounding

hoarse as it ripped from my sulfur-scorched throat. And still Niko held me back.

Brook refused to stay down. She was in no condition to keep fighting, and she was in no position to wield any real power over these warriors. She was their prisoner, and they could batter and abuse her all day long if they wished.

Because she had no other recourse, she spat a mouthful of blood at her captors before turning to me. "I'm glad you're alive. We were worried about you," she told me, her voice matter-of-fact, as if we'd just bumped into each other in a park or at the market and were chatting amiably.

I gave her a curious look. "I'm . . . glad you're alive too," I said, sounding like it was a question and not a statement, and feeling nothing short of ridiculous for making small talk with her here. I didn't bother pointing out the truth of our predicament, that we were standing in the queen's tactical command tent. "How did you find me?"

"We," she corrected. "How did we find you?" She grinned then, revealing blood-tinged teeth that made me want to frown back at her. "We have an army out there." She fixed her pointed gaze on each of the soldiers at her sides, and then on Niko, before looking to me once more. "We've got this, Charlie."

"No. You don't, actually." It was Elena now, entering the tent with a dramatic flourish.

It was immediate, the hatred I felt for the other queen, resurfacing as quickly as if it had never faded, practically choking me as I glared at her.

Brook's gaze narrowed, and her lips curled upward. She

looked the way she used to, when we were in the clubs and she'd set her sights on a guy she planned to toy with. "You have no idea what you're up against," she practically purred.

Elena looked equally confident as she approached Brooklynn, appraising her in a way that she hadn't Eden. "I heard you caused quite the brouhaha. Killed a lot of good soldiers." She reached a manicured finger out to Brook, and then pressed it beneath her chin, lifting Brook's face to inspect every bruise, cut, and abrasion. "You're arrogant. I like that."

Brook jerked away from Elena's touch. Her voice when she responded was so deadly low, I could barely hear it above the ringing that continued to resonate in my ears. "You're gonna die today."

Elena leaned closer and seized Brook's chin in her hand, squeezing it hard. Her voice was equally ominous when she answered, "Funny. I was going to say the same thing to you."

I gasped at Elena's words, and Niko's hold on my arm tightened, causing a stab of pain to explode up from my injured elbow.

Elena whirled to face us then, still clutching Brook's face. Her cinnamon-colored eyes sparkled when they fell on Niko. "This is going to work, isn't it, my love?" she begged, and I realized how mad she looked. Utterly insane. "I think this time our little queen here won't have any qualms about what needs to be done."

I felt Sabara's confidence swell into something I could no longer dispute, and it made me hate Elena all the more.

This queen was the reason Eden was dead.

She was the reason I was here, while my best friend was being used to force me to make the toughest decision of my life.

Could I really sacrifice anyone else? I'd already watched Eden die. Could I do it again? Was keeping Sabara inside me worth losing someone else I cared about?

But what choice did I have? Nothing had changed, had it? I couldn't set Sabara free just because it was Brook's life at stake instead of Eden's. One life wasn't more valuable than the others, was it?

Suddenly I wanted to tell Brook everything. I wanted to tell her about Elena and what she'd done to Eden. I wanted to tell her about Caspar and his followers, and the blast that had killed so many of them. I wanted to tell her about what I'd done to the soldier, the one who'd come into my tent to collect me when the fighting had started. How I'd shot him and stolen his weapons.

His weapons.

I'd lost his gun in the blast, but that wasn't the only weapon I'd taken from him.

I squirmed, trying to make it seem as if I were shifting on my feet. But it was enough to confirm what I'd hoped. I still had his knife. Tucked in the back of my waistband.

Sabara read my thoughts just as quickly as I'd formulated them, and I knew hers at the same moment.

Sure, I decided, *I'd let them have Sabara.*

And then she and I were going to try to kill each other.

❦　　　❦　　　❦

"Stop stalling," Elena complained, her impatience reaching a crescendo.

What did I care if she squirmed a little? I needed a few moments to gather myself, to collect my strength and assess the situation. My plan, if it was going to work, depended entirely on timing.

There were four soldiers inside the tent with us, more outside should Elena or Niko or any one of the masked warriors call for them. Brook could occupy at least the two who were holding her. The other two were stationed on either side of the tent's entrance.

Elena and I were standing in the center of the oversize enclosure, Niko at my side. All I needed was one moment. One tiny, insignificant moment, and it would all be over.

Just enough time to put my blade through Elena's heart once the transfer was complete.

The problem was, that was all the time Sabara needed too. And she would be trying to use her powers to stop me—to close my airway—before I could follow through with my intentions.

I had to reach *her* before she had that chance.

Four soldiers against one good arm. *I like my odds*, I thought, grinning inwardly as Sabara tried to quash my confidence with her own.

She felt much the way I did. That her chances were good.

"Charlie, you don't need to do this. You shouldn't do this!" Brook fought and fought, trying to break free, trying to get through to me, trying to stop this from happening. But I wasn't listening at all. I barely noticed her.

I reminded myself of everything Elena had done—to Xander,

executing Eden, the attempts on my life, declaring war on Ludania. And all the people Sabara would kill if she had the chance—Brooklynn, Aron, my parents, Angelina, me. Even her own grandson, Max.

Maybe I'd been too long locked in Sabara's dark grip, maybe I'd been poisoned by her venom, but I could see no viable alternative.

I nodded at Elena, ready.

I *was* ready. I could do this.

Niko released my arm, and I stepped forward, meeting Elena face-to-face, letting my anger toward her seethe. I needed those feelings. I needed to revile her as much as I reviled the soul inside me.

I needed all the hatred and rage to overcome any doubts or fears that might remain. To spur my strength.

I felt the warm steel of the blade pressed against the bare skin of my back.

I can do this, I repeated silently.

A look of bliss broke over Elena's face. "Take me. Take me instead."

The words, this time, hit me like a lightning bolt, piercing my core. I opened myself up to them, hoping against hope that this would work. That the transfer would take place and Sabara would leave my body, and I would remain whole.

I worried about that, too. That with Sabara's evacuation of me she'd take my life force with her—that we were eternally intertwined and would be forced to spend an eternity bound to each other. I worried that I, too, would be trapped in Elena's body.

Or worse, that Sabara would vacate my body for Elena's and I'd fade away to nothing without her. That my body would simply be left empty. A withered shell.

But there was no going back now. Sabara uncoiled from within me, plumes of her Essence releasing me. I hadn't expected to feel every nerve, every neuron, separating like currents of electricity—charged and piercing. It was as if Sabara were wholly being ripped away, torn from me, leaving everything inside me raw and angry and throbbing.

But in the wake of all that agony was another sensation. I could feel my old self resurfacing—all the good returning. I could feel all the memories Sabara had tried to block breaking free like a dam opened wide. But unlike before, when I'd had only a glimpse of my former nature, I was truly letting her go, and I could feel the blackness that *was* her vacating me as she moved from my center and spread to my extremities, searching for a way out.

My heart began to beat its own rhythm as my own Essence awakened once more. Light flooded my veins, and heat surged all the way to my toes. My injured ribs and elbow no longer ached.

"Take me . . . take me . . . take me . . . take me . . ." Elena repeated the words over and over, and I let her.

I kept my eyes closed, until I felt the final surge. It was jarring—the jolt as Sabara left me—and my eyes shot open. I watched Elena, her own eyes wide with shock as the transfer took place.

I couldn't think clearly, but even from the haze I was in, I saw the moment when Elena sensed Sabara slipping into place. When she felt the black soul—Sabara's Essence—taking control.

Elena's expression clouded over, and then her mouth formed an alarmed *O*, as she recognized, at last, what she'd done. What was happening to her. I hadn't witnessed it before, when Sabara's—or rather Layla's—Essence had made its exchange to me, so watching now was . . . fascinating . . . horrifying . . . exhilarating.

Behind me I heard shouts coming from the entrance, and a scuffle, but I didn't turn to see who it was or what was going on. Brook was shouting too, and still struggling to break free, but I ignored them all.

And then, right before the light faded from Elena's eyes, she gasped a single name, "Sage?"

At no point did I turn to gauge Niko's reaction to any of this, because I knew he cared nothing about the dying queen before him. All he cared about was the new one who was coming back to life—Sabara.

Sabara, I thought vaguely, still aware of the fray taking place behind me. *Sabara was coming back to life.*

An explosion rang through the space of the tent, clearing my mind, just enough.

I was here, still alive. Still whole.

Everything clicked into place then, as I realized what I needed to do.

I reached for the knife at my back at the same time that I saw Sabara take full and complete control of her new body. Cinnamon-colored eyes that had once belonged to Elena, queen of Astonia, now blazed with the fire of their new resident as they lit on me.

I had only seconds, if that, to stop her, and I launched

myself at her, my blade ready. My will determined.

But halfway to her, I felt it.

My airway . . . shutting in on itself.

Sabara was strong enough already, and she had every intention of killing me first. Her hand raised, her fist closed, and she unleashed her powers on me.

The result was instantaneous, and debilitating.

My eyes grew huge as I gasped, greedily sucking in as much air as I could. I was ravenous for it. Insatiable. Terror seized me all at once, and I told myself to keep going.

And I tried, willing myself to stab her . . . to stab her . . . *to stab her* . . .

But ultimately I did what everyone did when under Sabara's spell. I panicked while I choked and gagged and gulped for my last few precious breaths. I released the knife, let it fall to the ground as my hands closed around my own throat. I opened my mouth as wide as I could. And when none of that worked, when I could feel Sabara's choke hold growing, intensifying, I dropped to my knees as my vision began to blur around the edges.

I hadn't been fast enough, I admitted.

I'd been bested by a ghost.

SAGE

Caspar had left Xander and Sage outside the encampment, warning them to stay put, to keep away from the fighting. But Xander had been insistent. Despite his injuries, he'd refused to just sit back and watch, knowing Charlie was in there somewhere, being held hostage by Elena.

Sage hadn't disagreed. She knew her sister, and what she was capable of.

So she and Xander had done what anyone in their situation would have: they'd killed every soldier who'd gotten in their way. Or at least Sage had, diverting as much notice as she could away from Xander, who'd moved more slowly than she had, and more tentatively, guarding his bandaged arm to keep it from being jostled and jarred.

Even with only one hand, and a fever that continued to keep him weak on his feet, he'd proven to be deadly. His aim was true, and he'd saved her butt more than once. At least until his gun had jammed and he'd thrown it aside.

Somehow they'd made it to the centrally located tent with

the biggest banners waving from the top of it—the one where she'd known she'd find her sister, cowering from the fighting, the way a good queen did. Elena preferred to let her soldiers die in her stead.

Sage had never understood such nonsense. To her, a good queen belonged on the battlefield with her troops. Taking up arms and leading them into war only when war couldn't be avoided.

Unlike her sister, who preferred to kill by proxy, Sage knew what it was like to wash blood from her hands.

She and Xander had much in common in that regard.

"Stay here," she whisper-shouted above the battle that continued to storm around them.

She didn't expect him to obey, any more than she would have if he had given her the order. And when she slipped through the tent flaps, her knife drawn in the hopes of offing at least one of her sister's guards before she was noticed, she could feel him breathing down the back of her neck.

Her blade moved like hot metal through butter as it slid across the first guard's throat. She might've dropped the bird-masked woman without so much as a single sound, if it hadn't been for the one last sputtering noise that erupted from the bloodied wound. But that was enough, and the second guard saw her, and threw himself at her.

Sage tried to brace herself, but it was no good. She was already hunched over, trying to relieve the first guard of her weapon—a rifle with a strap that had been secured around the woman's shoulder. When the second guard crashed into her, she went down hard, landing on top of the dead woman, the beak of the mask grazing the side of her cheek.

She lifted her head, and that was when she heard her sister calling her name. Her voice was so weak, so distant . . . so pitiable. "Sage?"

She wanted to feel something for Elena, but she couldn't muster anything.

This was the sister who'd used her as a weapon. The sister who'd envied her to the point of suspicion. She'd worried that Sage would someday usurp her position on the throne, that Sage could never be happy being only a princess of the realm.

So Elena had put her in harm's way again and again, always with the purpose of serving her queendom. But Sage had always suspected the truth. That her sister had secretly hoped she would never return.

And now here she was, watching all of her sister's hopes and dreams come true.

Except they weren't, it seemed. Not from the look of abject horror on her sister's face.

Not from the fading expression in her eyes.

Yet Sage felt nothing. Not for her sister.

The soldier on top of Sage punched her in the jaw. Her teeth clattered together, but it wasn't a solid blow, and she didn't see stars the way she had in the past when she'd been clocked in that same spot. She wriggled out from under him and grappled for the rifle of the lifeless soldier lying beside her. At the same time, with the knife in her other hand, she sawed at the strap restraining it.

The rifle came free with a snap, and she scurried away from the dead woman, moving just far enough so she could leverage the gun against her shoulder. She aimed it at the soldier who had attacked her.

He paused. And then she pulled the trigger.

His mask, and everything behind it, exploded.

That was when she saw Queen Charlaina, whom she'd met at the ball in Vannova. Sage couldn't see exactly what was happening, but it looked as if the queen had a weapon—a small sword or a knife of some sort—and that she meant to kill Elena.

Sage clambered to her feet to get a better look, but what she saw made her stand stock-still.

Elena—or whoever she was now, because she was no longer the sister she'd always known; she stood wrong, and her expression was all wrong—lifted her fist and pointed it at Charlaina, stopping the queen of Ludania in her tracks.

The younger queen dropped her knife and fell to her knees. Her eyes bulged as she dug at her neck like there was a noose secured around it.

"Charlie," she heard the dark-haired girl, the one with the huge brown eyes, shout as she was held back by two more soldiers in the tent with them. "Breathe, Charlie! Breathe!"

Charlaina's eyes grew wider for a moment, and then they relaxed, everything about her going limp, and the dark-haired girl screamed, "Kill her! Kill Queen Elena!"

Sage glanced at the rifle in her hand, and hesitated. It was one thing to feel apathetic about a sister who'd shunned her her entire life. It was another thing altogether to actually kill her.

But as it turned out, she wasn't the one the dark-haired girl was shouting at, because Xander was there, moving so fast, he was practically a blur in her vision.

He swooped in like a bird of prey, seeming to come from nowhere as he snatched up Charlaina's discarded knife. And before Elena or either of the remaining two guards could stop him, his blade was buried five inches deep in Elena's chest.

NIKO

Everything he'd ever wanted was within his grasp.

He and Sabara—*his Layla*—were going to be together again, at long last.

He watched her move from one queen to the next, holding his breath, the way he had so many times before. The way she transitioned was so smooth. Effortless. Like watching a dancer.

He heard the commotion behind him, and he turned in time to see Sage cutting the throat of one of the guards who stood watch. The other guard, caught unaware, was unprepared with his weapon, but he tackled the troublesome princess.

It was no matter; she was too late.

And then everything went wrong. And it all happened so fast.

The gunshot booming through the tent and echoing in his head.

Charlaina falling to her knees. Almost finished . . . almost . . .

And then Xander . . . Xander appeared from nowhere, and

before Niko could move, or breathe, Xander had the knife. . . .

And blood. So much blood. Elena's . . . Sabara's . . . Layla's . . . all intertwined now.

The whole thing was all over in a blink.

He heard himself before he heard anything else, his cry a sharp keening sound, louder, surely, than the gunshot or any bomb had been. Dropping to his hands and knees, he hovered above Layla's new form and stared down at her face, wondering at the fragility of her life. "No, no, no, no, no . . ." He couldn't say anything else, and he couldn't find the strength to touch her as he watched her—the real her, the her he'd been waiting for all these years—flicker, and then fade, behind those new soft brown eyes.

He knew the moment she was gone. The moment the body was nothing more than an empty husk, its stare fixed skyward on the tent's canvas ceiling.

He felt as empty as that body he gazed down upon.

"NO!" he screamed. But this time he leveled his rage at Xander, who still held the bloodied weapon in his only hand. "We should've killed you," he screeched.

The two guards who had been restraining Brooklynn released her, and they all stood there watching as Niko jumped to his feet and threw himself at Xander, ramming him with his shoulder. The two of them went sprawling, and he heard the knife land somewhere too far away from them to be of any use.

He didn't care. He planned to beat the life out of Xander with his fists.

When he heard the blast, he knew that definitively it had come from a firearm. That it had without a doubt come from

behind him. But the sensation, the one centered between his shoulder blades, was indescribable.

It was as if he'd been stung . . . or impaled by a fire-tipped arrow.

But he knew neither was true, because he knew exactly what had happened.

He'd been shot.

XVII

I was confused about where I was, but that confusion lasted only a moment.

It was the gunshot that had awakened me—if "awakened" was the right word, since surely I hadn't been asleep. It had been more like I'd been swimming in a black abyss of nothingness, where I'd been alone—truly alone for the first time in so very long.

It felt strange to hear the silence inside my own head. To hear my thoughts, and my thoughts alone.

I blinked as I tried to assess the situation through bleary eyes.

It seemed I'd missed quite a lot while I'd been . . . indisposed.

Beside me Niko's wheezing drew my attention. I turned to see him lying facedown, his cheek resting on the tent floor as his glazed eyes watched but did not see me. He gasped and sputtered while his fingers clawed at the ground halfheartedly, as if he might have been making an effort at one time, but now it was only a reflex. Blood spread wide from a wound in the center of his back, and it was plain to anyone who looked—even someone who'd been out cold for the duration—that it was he who'd been shot.

He made a few more attempts to breathe, and then it was over, his eyes going blank. His fingers going still.

In front of me Elena's body too was prone, and her skin was already turning an ashen shade that meant death had settled over her.

Which meant . . . Sabara . . .

She was gone too.

I wanted to rejoice, but before I had the chance to revel in those feelings, I saw Xander, and a different kind of joy coursed through me. Not one born of an enemy's demise, but one of true, unadulterated relief.

"Xander," I breathed, trying to sit upright.

Brook was still shackled but was no longer being restrained, and she rushed forward, helping me up.

Xander stood above me, grinning. "You're alive."

I took him in. His pale skin, the blood on his hand, the bandage where his other should have been. He'd never looked so good. "You, too." I beamed.

And then he toppled over.

A girl shot forward then, rushing to Xander's side. I tried to place her face—the freckles, the soft brown hair. There was something eerily familiar about her.

And then I knew. She was Elena's sister. I'd met her once before, in Vannova.

"Sage," I accused, glancing nervously to Brook. "She's . . . she—"

"Saved you," Brook finished. "Saved all of us."

Sage eased Xander's head down, gently, carefully. "He's sick," she said over her shoulder, ignoring my misgivings and the fact that we were talking about her. "His fever's back." She glanced to one of the soldiers who'd survived the massacre inside the tent. "Go. Fetch a doctor. And tell no one that my sister is dead. I still need to decide how to handle this."

The soldier did as she instructed, and I wondered at how quickly the tides had turned. Unless I'd miscalculated, this girl was their queen now.

I thought of her sister, and how she'd conspired against me. I thought of Sabara, too, and how she'd only needed royal blood to make the transfer.

Sage had that blood.

I dropped my voice, not really caring if Sage overheard my question. "Are you sure she's not . . . that Sabara didn't . . ." I indicated the princess with a suspicious look, making it clear what I meant.

Brook shook her head, but it was Sage who answered. "Only my sister would be stupid enough to try something so reckless. She couldn't bear the fact that she was—different from all the others. Niko played upon her weakness. He knew exactly which nerves to strike. He knew how to play on her insecurities."

"Different? How?" I asked, getting to my feet now. The inside of my throat was irritated and felt bruised.

A sly smile spread over Sage's lips, and I couldn't help noticing that she wasn't overly saddened by her sister's demise. "You didn't know? Sabara never shared my sister's deep dark secret with you?" She didn't wait for me to answer, but her impish smile grew. "My sister was impotent. She was an anomaly in the royal bloodline. She may as well have been born a male, for all the power she was blessed with."

I frowned, trying to absorb the meaning of her words. "Are you saying . . . that she didn't have any power at all?"

"That's exactly what I'm saying. And it killed her. She tried to hide the fact for years, teaching herself parlor tricks and dabbling in the black arts, hoping to fool people into believing she'd been gifted with sorcery. But after a while, when it became clear she could do nothing useful, she stopped trying. She envied me, and every other royal who had an ability. She felt like a freak." Sage shrugged. "Which I suppose she was. What kind of queen has no power?" She stopped talking then and knelt low, pressing her cheek to Xander's, concern replacing her mischievous air. "He's burning up." She looked to the remaining soldier in the tent, as if he might know something. "Where's that doctor?" she questioned.

When the tent flaps flew open, all eyes shot that way, but it wasn't the doctor coming to nurse Xander back to health.

It was Max.

My heart stopped, and everything inside me strained to be near him.

I didn't hesitate long enough to consider anything else, like whether he hated me for leaving in the middle of the night the way I had. All I knew was how badly I'd missed him, and how much I needed him. And that he was here. Now.

I crossed the space in one breath, and was in his arms in the next, practically throwing him off his feet as I hurled myself against him.

His scent was that of wet earth and pungent sulfur. It enveloped me, as did his arms.

His lips, however, tasted like home.

I got lost in that taste, wrapping myself around him in turn, and curling my fingers through the soft, damp hair at the base of his neck. His armor was rigid, but his body managed to find mine and fit itself against me. My entire body tingled, but in a whole new way. I suddenly wished we were all alone, away from here, so I could show him how badly I'd missed him.

When he drew away, it was just far enough so I could see the dirt and ash that covered his forehead and cheeks, and I was certain I'd been equally smudged by it.

"You look terrible," I breathed, unable to keep a smile from my lips.

"And you," he said, his mouth still so close to mine, "are the most beautiful sight I've ever seen."

My heart hammered once at the sound of his words. And then once more when he lowered his head and kissed me again.

"Ahem," I heard. And then again, but this time with a nudge to my side. "A-hem." It was Brook, of course, waiting for us to notice her.

I sighed into Max's mouth as I reluctantly dragged myself from his embrace.

I hadn't realized that the tent had swelled with bodies, and that we were now standing before a crowd of faces, all watching us expectantly. Behind Max I saw Claude, as well as Aron, and I saw the way Aron looked at Brook, much the same way Max looked at me. But he stayed where he was, and reminded me of one of her soldiers as he stood amid them. Beside them all was Caspar, looking far, far too much like his sister.

I smiled sadly at him, grateful he'd survived the explosion.

Outside, the sounds of battle had died down. They'd not stopped completely but had faded now. I could still hear minor skirmishes coming from beyond the tent walls—shouting mostly. But there was no more gunfire, and there were no more bombs or cannons or grenades.

"What's happened out there?" I asked Max, who was busy surveying the interior of the tent, taking in the bodies that littered the floor—the two masked soldiers, Queen Elena, Niko.

He took a step back when his gaze landed on Xander, lying unconscious. "What's happened in here?" He glanced curiously at Sage, who scowled back at him suspiciously.

"He needs a doctor," she repeated. And as if on cue, a thin woman shoved her way through, wearing what could only be described as an animal pelt—a wolf or a coyote—drawn up over her head, so that her enormous green and yellow eyes peered out from beneath its upper jaw.

She said nothing but went immediately to Sage and dropped down beside her. They whispered between themselves, and I stepped closer, straining to hear what they were saying. The woman shot me a warning look, cautioning me with only those too-big eyes to stay back. And I did as she indicated.

She reached into her pocket then, and pulled out a pouch, dumping a handful of what appeared to be crushed powder into her palm. Then she proceeded to sprinkle it into Xander's mouth.

She uncorked a small flask and chased the powder with a translucent red liquid.

Xander came up choking and coughing and spitting, but alert.

From the look on Max's face, he was as relieved as I was. I slipped my hand into his and let our fingers intertwine. "So, is it over?" I asked. "The war?"

Max looked down at me and sighed. I could read the regret on his face. "Just this battle, Charlie." He looked to Caspar then, and I wondered if Max knew that Caspar was Eden's brother. "With the help of Caspar here, we were able to overtake the camp. But the war's not over yet. Elena's soldiers have done a lot of damage, and have covered a lot of ground. I don't know how long it'll be before we can stop them."

"*My* forces, you mean."

Max looked at Sage again, as if considering her for the first time.

Sage didn't seem to care what Max or anyone else had to say in the matter. She stood up and brushed the ash from her pants. "I guess it's time for me to start spreading the word," she announced, "so I can fix this mess my sister started." She turned to the one soldier from Elena's army who still remained in the tent. "You. Fetch the general." He started to obey, pushing past those who had been his enemies just minutes earlier, but she stopped him. "And for crying out loud, take off that stupid mask."

It took several hours to sort everything out.

And several more before we were ready to leave the encampment.

Sage was as good as her word, and by the time we were saying our farewells, she'd already sent messengers to every general under her command, recalling her forces and withdrawing them from Ludanian soil.

That had been the easy part. It was devastating to make our way back out onto the battle-ravaged land. To see the damage that had been done, and the people who'd lost their lives. All for nothing. For a queen's selfish pride.

My fingers closed around the sapphire pendant in my pocket, hardly blemished after what it had been through. Max had returned it to me, recounting the horrors he'd witnessed when he'd watched Elena's soldiers burn Deirdre's village to the ground.

Brooklynn had lost too many of her soldiers as well, as had Sage. And I watched as Caspar bent down time and again to wipe mud away from the faces of children, making mental notes of those who'd died.

We all lost someone, I thought achingly, and then I was forced to tell Xander and Caspar about Eden. I had to tell them about my decision *not* to release Sabara's Essence, and how Elena had executed Eden for it. It was like reliving the moment all over again.

Caspar sobbed openly, tears cutting a path down his mud- and ash-streaked face.

Xander, on the other hand, remained stoic, almost to the point of appearing heartless. If it weren't for the way he clung to Sage—who seemed never to leave his side—I might have wondered if he'd even heard me.

But I saw the way his fingers sought hers when I told them.

The way he clutched her like a lifeline, as if he might topple over if she weren't there to hold him up.

It made me think her support went deeper than just the fact that she'd saved him from the dungeons of her sister's palace and kept him alive while they'd been on the run.

My suspicions were confirmed when it was time to leave and I had to watch them saying good-bye to each other.

I felt like a voyeur, inadvertently seeing the way she whispered softly to him, privately. And the way he glanced around, making certain they couldn't be overheard, before responding. I turned away and busied myself with other matters. Whatever their relationship was, I had no business prying.

"Are we ready?" I asked Aron when I saw him securing a pack on one of the horses we'd be taking until we reached the train.

It had been so long since I'd seen Aron, since I'd sent him to 11South to set up the new communications hub. That seemed like another lifetime ago, and Aron looked older. Aged by the weeks—and the events—that had passed.

I felt it too.

He gave me a fatigued look and said, "Brook's making sure everything's set with Eden's body . . ." He paused when his voice became thick. He turned his attention back to his work, avoiding my eyes. "As soon as she's done, I think we can go."

I wasn't sure how I felt about that. Part of me couldn't wait to get away from this place, from all the death and the reminders of all we'd sacrificed. Couldn't wait to leave it all behind and try to forget.

But another part of me . . .

A part I was still trying to reconcile felt like this was a place of great closure for me, and for Ludania.

It was the site where a queen had been born, once and truly.

Where I'd finally been freed of Sabara's tyrannical reign at long, long last, allowing me to be myself. To rule without her constant misgivings and disruptions.

"Here," Sage said, coming up behind me and interrupting my thoughts. I looked at her, realizing I'd been wrong. This was the place where two queens had been produced.

She held out her hand, and in it was another vial of the red liquid the doctor had given to Xander. "He'll need this. It won't cure him," she added, forcing me to meet her gaze. "For all the advantages we have over your country because of Sabara, Elena was far too dependent on conjurers and sorcery for herself. She was always looking for someone to fix her, which made her easy prey for tricksters. Her doctor isn't a true apothecary. She dabbles in the dark arts. The best she can do is mix a decent potion to keep him comfortable. He'll need better care when you return home."

I nodded, and only then did she release the vial to me.

"Good." She nodded too, seemingly convinced that she could trust that I would take care of him. "And in return we'll offer you our assistance. I can help you with fuels and communications. We have some of the best minds, and some of the most technologically advanced systems in the world." She smiled. "Even though she didn't have a power of her own, my sister understood what it took for Astonia to be formidable."

I wondered again at what had transpired between her and

Xander in the short time they'd been together. Their bond, whatever it was, was important enough that she was willing to barter valuable resources in exchange for his well-being. "You don't owe me for taking care of him," I said. And then I stopped myself, smiling good-naturedly. "But I won't turn you down either."

"No good queen would," Sage answered with a small smile of her own, and then she turned away, giving me her back as she strode toward Xander.

EPILOGUE

It was as if Eden herself had planned her own funeral.

The black sky had opened up, and it was raining torrents upon us as we assembled in the small cemetery, a place where guards and members of the household staff and family had been buried for as long as the palace had been standing. Huddled together, we converged around the freshly dug grave in the earth, beneath canopies and umbrellas as we tried our best to stay dry despite the gales that continued to push and pull at our makeshift shelters.

I clung to Angelina's small hand, as I had for almost every moment of every day since our return, afraid that she might suddenly change her mind and stop allowing me to do so. That she'd stop letting me touch her and hug her and kiss her. So far, however, she continued to permit such behaviors, and I continued to be grateful that she remembered what we'd been like before Sabara.

Angelina had known I was different the moment I'd crossed

the threshold of the palace entrance. That Sabara was gone, now and forever.

I'd nearly been knocked over by her enthusiastic greeting as she'd come barreling at me like a miniature gale force of her own, her gossamer blond hair tangled and twisted around her face. I'd caught her with equal fervor, throwing my arms around her and whispering promises to never let her go again.

Promises like the one I'd made before I'd left her, that I'd do everything in my power to return home. And like the one I'd broken, about bringing Eden home safely.

Yet, here we stood, sister and sister. Hand in hand.

Angelina had taken the news of Eden's death exactly as I'd expected she would, and her swollen eyes glittered even now, days later. I wondered how long it would be until she slept an entire night without waking from a nightmare, or when she'd be able to do so in her own room.

Until that time, I was more than happy to share my bed with her once more like when we lived in the city.

Despite the weather, everyone had come to say their farewells to Eden, and I stared out at a sea of mourning faces: my parents, Max, Brooklynn and Aron, Claude and Zafir, and two hundred other members of the palace guard and household.

Caspar and Xander were there too, standing side by side, the two men who'd known Eden best.

I was grateful that Xander was here at all, a testimony to my sister's power to heal.

By the time we'd returned home, I'd been convinced he was beyond saving at all. The fevers had ravaged him, becoming so intense, so brutal, that even the apothecary's brews had no longer been able to ease his discomfort. He'd spent the last stretch of the journey thrashing and crying out incoherently, as he'd begged for death.

Max had vigilantly remained at Xander's side the entire trip, refusing to allow anyone else to relieve him, even when Max had become bone-weary from sleep deprivation. He would not abandon his brother.

But Angelina had been able to cure Xander. As simply as if it had been a scrape that needed only the most minor healing. And it had taken just a graze of her hands, so slight, almost unnoticeable as her fingers had deftly feathered the side of his jaw. A brush, really, and over that quickly.

Xander's fever had broken within seconds, and he'd been speaking—clearly, coherently, lucidly—within minutes. He'd known it too. That it had been Angelina.

If only she could have repaired his missing hand. But her abilities extended only so far.

"Thank you," Xander had told Angelina, his silver eyes clear at long last as they'd settled on her blue ones.

She'd nodded then, because it was all she'd been able to manage. Her heart had still been too heavy with the weight of the loss of Eden.

I was still awed by my sister. I sensed that she was growing more powerful with each day, with each breath that she took. I wondered at the things Sage had told me about how Elena had been jealous of her sister's abilities, and how she'd put Sage in harm's way because of that. I couldn't imagine feeling envious of Angelina. I couldn't imagine faulting her, or feeling anything other than what I did—sheer pride.

I wondered too how far Angelina's abilities might one day evolve. Already she could sense people's hearts, and whether they could or couldn't be trusted. Already she could heal. What else would she be capable of?

I thought about what those skills might mean were she to be queen, and how useful it would be to know if someone had a deceptive soul.

Maybe there would come a time when Angelina would be better suited to be queen than I.

But I knew something that Elena hadn't. That the measure of a true queen didn't lie in her magic. It had more to do with *who* she was, and what she was willing to give of herself, than it did with the powers she possessed.

In that, I had no way of knowing which of us—Angelina or me—would make the better queen. But for now none of that mattered. It was I who sat on the throne. And it was I who would continue to do so for as long as Ludania needed me.

Caspar drew my attention then when he cupped his hands to his mouth and blew. It was that same long and mournful whistle that I'd heard on the day Eden had first taken us to the work camp in the forest. When she had signaled to her brother high above in the trees and he'd answered her in kind.

Now, however, it sounded like a dirge. Desolate. A final send-off to Eden.

I blinked, my fingers tightening over Angelina's as I heard her whisper beside me, "I wish I could have saved her."

"I'm leaving," Xander announced when Angelina and I came into the main hall and found him waiting. He had a look about him that told me not to argue, not that I would have. And he didn't have to explain what he meant or where he was planning to go.

I knew. I think I'd known for some time now, ever since Eden's funeral, almost two weeks before.

He'd tried to resume his duties since his return, but it hadn't been enough, and he'd been growing more restless and impatient with each passing day. He did as I asked, of course, helping to relocate Caspar and the children Caspar had been in charge of. Trying to keep them as close together as possible so they could still maintain contact with one another. To find them homes and get them enrolled in schools. There were a lot fewer of them now, after the fighting, but there were still more than a hundred to house.

It had been a time-consuming task, and one that Xander had taken on with the same attention and care he'd given any undertaking I'd ever asked of him.

More so, maybe, because this was Eden's brother he'd been charged with finding a home for.

Caspar had balked at the notion of needing guardians and an education, but ultimately he'd acquiesced, if only to serve as a role model for the others. To lead by example.

Now, as Xander stood before me with that same recognizable restlessness in his eyes that I'd noticed for weeks, I turned to Angelina. "Go with Zafir, will you? If I'm not mistaken, it's past time for his afternoon snack."

Zafir glared at me over Angelina's head, but she nodded eagerly, reaching for his calloused hand. Her fingers were small and pale as they curled around his larger, darker ones, and she tugged him insistently, leading him in the direction of the kitchens.

He'd been a good protector for Angelina while I'd been away, and he would continue to be in his permanent role as her royal guard. He scowled over the duty, and liked to pretend he didn't want to be in charge of a child, but I knew Zafir, much the same way Angelina knew who was loyal and who was not, and Zafir was all bluster in his complaints. He no more wanted to be transferred from his role than I wanted to have Sabara dwelling inside me once more.

Zafir, I was beginning to suspect, enjoyed his *snack breaks*.

When they were out of earshot, I turned my attention back to Xander. His arm had healed—faster, likely, because of Angelina—and the place where his hand had once been now ended in a puckered stump. The skin was pink and was peeling where there had been scabs, but he no longer needed the bandages that had once festered and oozed.

He reached down and lifted a leather satchel, balancing it in the crook of his elbow.

"Are you certain?" I asked, not sure what more I could say, and wishing I could talk him out of going at all.

He met my gaze, and I saw the answer in his eyes, the reason for his restlessness. "I am. I think I decided before we even left the encampment," he replied. "I miss her."

Blinking, even though I understood, I nodded. "Does Max know you're going?"

Xander looked past my shoulder, smiling at someone behind me. "I already told him."

I felt Max's hand on my shoulder then, squeezing it reassuringly. "I told him you'd cry," he accused, but there was no admonishment. His voice was soft and filled with tenderness.

I nudged him with my elbow. "I'm not crying," I lied, blinking harder.

Max's lips grazed the sensitive skin of my ear, sending a shiver everywhere over my body. Now, however, he could no longer see my reaction to his touch. It was mine and mine alone.

The glow had vanished, along with Sabara.

Max kissed my cheek, too, and that was when I felt it. The moisture on my cheek, making it clear that just because I no longer shone didn't mean he couldn't read me. "Of course you're not."

Xander watched us, a wistful smile finding his lips. "I'll miss you. Both of you," he said. "But it'll be easier now. The new communication ports will make it easy to stay in contact." His eyes crinkled. "No more waiting days for envoys to deliver messages. What a strange new world."

I didn't mention that the last time I'd received a message from Astonia, it had been a box that had contained his hand. And I didn't tell him I'd be happy to never see another messenger in my lifetime.

"A wonderful new world," I breathed.

It was Sage who had made it all possible, sending teams of her own engineers and technicians to help us install a complex system and the necessary power sources to keep it running. I couldn't believe how quickly it had been connected, but the tests, up to this point, had far exceeded my wildest dreams.

Of course, I suspected she'd had ulterior motives for outfitting us with such elaborate equipment so soon after our return, and she and Xander had used it far more than anyone else in the palace.

Now, however, they would no longer need such sophisticated technology to converse. Xander would be making a new home for himself in Astonia.

"We'll miss you, too," Max said, and I felt the weight of his arm tightening around my waist as he watched his brother turn to leave.

"Wait!" I called out, stopping Xander before he could go. "You should be here for this."

My heart fluttered, and I was suddenly grateful for the fact that my emotions were no longer visible. If they had been, Max would have seen a million fireworks bursting beneath my skin, revealing my nerves as I slipped my hand into my pocket. My fingers moved over the linked metal of the chain, and my mind raced over the scenario I'd replayed in my head a hundred times already.

And then I glanced up and met Max's steely gaze, and everything inside me went still. Every explosion went silent, every beat of my pulse settled.

I wanted this.

Removing my hand from my pocket once more, I held it out to him, my fingers curled in a ball. "I think it's time you give this to me. Properly."

Max looked at me, his eyebrows knitting together as he studied my fist curiously. "What is it?" he asked, even as his hand moved over to meet mine.

I opened my fingers and dropped the pendant into his waiting palm. The chain bloomed outward, like petals opening around a sapphire eye.

He blinked uncertainly as he looked up at me. "Are you . . ." He hesitated, his voice filled with restrained hope. "Are you absolutely sure, Charlie?"

My heart swelled and my face broke, the grin I could no longer contain spreading wide. "I've never been more sure of anything in my life," I answered. "I'm ready. I want you to be my husband—my king—Max."

I'd imagined so many scenarios, yet in not one of them had I imagined Max dropping to his knee as he took my hand and pledged his fealty to me all over again.

Yet that was what he did, his fingers closing around mine as the pendant was pressed between our palms, warm against my skin.

"I promise," he began, his words unwavering as his eyes reached all the way to mine, "to protect you, Charlie, for as long as I live. I will love you with everything I have. And I will stand by your side for an eternity."

I bit back my own emotion as I watched his gray eyes glisten, and then he stood and unclasped the necklace.

I watched with breathless anticipation as he slid it around my neck and the meaning of the stone settled over my chest. When he clasped it this time, I knew what it meant. It was a promise—a vow.

Max and I were engaged.

And then he kissed me, the way I'd envisioned he would. But so, so much better.

When at last he released me . . . when my head stopped spinning, as did the world beneath my feet . . . and Max's hand slipped around mine to steady me, I heard Xander's voice and remembered he'd been standing there all along.

"Welcome to the family," he said.